**Han grabbed hold of an ankle and she fell back onto the bed in a tangle of blue silk and gauze.**

Li Feng blinked up at him, dark eyes glittering. 'Always you!'

She was dressed like a courtesan, in one of those robes that appeared to be made out of paper-thin cloth and air. The silk had fallen from her shoulders, revealing smooth bare skin from her throat to the topmost swell of her breasts. Han prepared to defend himself as she reached for him.

Instead of gouging his eyes out, her hands slipped past his to bury themselves into his hair. Li Feng dragged his head down, her gaze on him the entire time. Before he knew what was happening his mouth was pressed against soft, inviting lips.

She tasted of cinnamon and the faint tang of cloves. Though he was positioned over her, his weight pinning her legs, he was the one who felt trapped. This was a ploy, he told himself, while his body greedily strained against her.

Han lifted his head forcibly. 'At any moment you're going to slit my throat.'

There was a glint in her eyes that was both predatory and playful. 'Perhaps.'

# AUTHOR NOTE

I've always found it sexy when a hero and heroine cannot only match wits, but also match swords.

A common theme in Chinese adventure stories is the idea of the vigilante hero—a hero guided by honour and chivalry. But how much fun would it be to have the heroine in that role? And the hero, of course, would be the thief-catcher intent on capturing her.

Often people ask me where I get my ideas. For this book the origin was a famous poem by the poet Du Fu of the Tang Dynasty, titled *Observing the Sword Dance Performed by a Disciple of Madam Gongsun*. The poem starts with a description of a mesmerising sword dance, then moves into a nostalgic look at how much has changed in fifty years like 'the turn of a page'. The sword dance ultimately becomes a symbol of the end of a golden age.

A final historical note: Wudang Mountain, which is mentioned in the book, is an actual location. In the Tang Dynasty the mountain was already established as a centre of Taoism. A Taoist master, Lu Dong Bin, known as the Sword Immortal, was also a famous figure of the Tang Dynasty. With these elements in mind, I took the liberty of associating my heroine's sword-training as well as her Taoist upbringing with Wudang.

I hope you enjoy the adventures of my sword dancer and thief-catcher as they chase their way across the cities and rivers of Tang Dynasty China. There's no better place to fight and fall in love, in my humble opinion.

For more information about the stories, or to contact me, visit me online at: www.jeannielin.com. I love receiving mail from readers!

# THE SWORD DANCER

## Jeannie Lin

MILLS BOON

First published in Great Britain 2013
by Mills & Boon, an imprint of Harlequin (UK) Limited.
Large Print edition 2013
Harlequin (UK) Limited, Eton House, 18-24 Paradise Road,
Richmond, Surrey TW9 1SR

© Jeannie Lin 2013

ISBN: 978 0 263 23286 8

Harlequin (UK) policy is to use papers that are natural, renewable and recyclable products and made from wood grown in sustainable forests. The logging and manufacturing process conform to the legal environmental regulations of the country of origin.

Printed and bound in Great Britain
by CPI Antony Rowe, Chippenham, Wiltshire

**Jeannie Lin** grew up fascinated with stories of Western epic fantasy and Eastern martial arts adventures. When her best friend introduced her to romance novels in middle school the stage was set. Jeannie started writing her first romance while working as a high school science teacher in South Central Los Angeles. After four years of trying to break into publishing with an Asian-set historical, her 2009 Golden Heart®–winning manuscript BUTTERFLY SWORDS was sold to Harlequin Mills & Boon.

As a technical consultant, backpacker and vacation junkie, she's travelled all over the United States as well as Europe, South Korea, Japan, China and Vietnam. She's now happily settled in St Louis, with her wonderfully supportive husband, and continues to journey to exotic locations in her stories.

You can visit Jeannie Lin online at: www.jeannielin.com

**Previous novels from this author:**

BUTTERFLY SWORDS
THE DRAGON AND THE PEARL
MY FAIR CONCUBINE

**Available in Mills & Boon® Historical *Undone!* eBooks:**

THE TAMING OF MEI LIN
THE LADY'S SCANDALOUS NIGHT
CAPTURING THE SILKEN THIEF
AN ILLICIT TEMPTATION

**Did you know that these novels are also available as eBooks? Visit www.millsandboon.co.uk**

First of all, to my husband Fritz.
Though a dedication is a small prize after being dubbed 'The Greatest Dad in the World' (with the shirt to prove it), this book would not have been possible without your love, support and laughter.

I must thank my editor Anna Boatman for her patience and guidance in helping me turn scattered ideas into a coherent story. Also a thank-you to Gail Fortune, my agent and avid cheerleader.

THE SWORD DANCER wouldn't have been possible without the tough love and critical eye of authors Bria Quinlan and Inez Kelley, as well as the continued support of my local critique group: Shawntelle Madison, Amanda Freeman, Kristi Lea and Dawn Blankenship.

Thank you to Giovani Dambros and Phillip Puzzo from Team TRICKset for the information and demos on freerunning. For assistance in providing historical insight and extensive research materials I must credit wuxia author John Dishon.

Though this story has many influences, I must give a nod to Jennifer Roberson's fantasy novel *Sword Dancer*—the book that convinced me that there's nothing sexier than a hero and heroine who can cross swords. And finally to Jackie Chan. Enough said.

# Chapter One

*Heaven and earth moved in tune with her rhythm.*
*The sword flashed like Yi's arrows that shot*
*down the nine suns.*
*She moved quickly and spiritedly like the dragon*
*ridden by gods.*

Du Fu from 'Observing the Sword Dance
Performed by a Disciple of Madam Gongsun'

*Tang Dynasty China—AD 848*

A lone reed flute sang the opening melody. It was enough to hush the gathered crowd into silence. A dancer stood, still and patient, at the centre of the circle. The long sword poised in her hand captured the sunlight as an intermittent breeze fluttered through the peach-blossom silk of her tunic. It was as if nature had aligned itself with her for this performance.

There was stillness again before the melody

swelled. The musicians were situated at the edge of the clearing, blending into the crowd. All focus was on the dancer.

The young woman gradually lifted one foot; knee curved outward, toes exquisitely pointed. Her free hand took on a classic lotus shape. Her expression remained tranquil. She held the position effortlessly, the graceful lines of her body belying the strength and discipline in the pose.

Zheng Hao Han eyed the sword in her grasp. Its presence added a hint of tension and drama, and the crowd waited eagerly for the dancer to fulfil the promise. Performance troupes such as this one travelled from city to city and always drew a crowd.

'An unworthy task for the illustrious Thief-catcher Han, eh?' Longxu remarked beside him. 'This should be easy work after Two Dragon Lo.'

Han scowled at the snide remark. His newfound fame was an ill-fitted garment he was forced to wear.

Longxu earned his nickname from the dragon-beard hook that he roped around his quarry with stunning accuracy. They had worked together in the past, splitting the reward for apprehending danger-ous criminals whom the local magistrates and con-stables were ill-equipped to handle. Han wouldn't say that they were partners in this venture. Longxu had the nose of a scavenger, eager to feed off someone else's catch. He had encountered Han on the road and immediately chained himself to his side.

They weren't the only thief-catchers in the crowd. The amount of money offered for this case had lured many fortune-seeking mercenaries. All of them had followed the same lead to this remote village within the rugged hills of Fujian province.

A shipment of jade and gold had been stolen from a security warehouse a few counties over. The magistrate had issued an arrest warrant that singled out a band of travelling performers as the culprits, unlikely as that seemed. Han scanned the musicians and dancers at the centre of the market square. Longxu was right about one thing. These weren't the sort of bandits he usually dealt with.

An explosion of drums shook the street and the audience leaned in close, clamouring for a better view, as the dancer leapt into motion. This was no soft seduction of willowy arms and flowing silk. Her technique was sharp, precise and powerful as she executed sword forms one might see in a fighting drill. She extended her limbs through each movement, exaggerating and accentuating the beauty of the underlying structure.

'She's good,' Han remarked.

'It's all show,' Longxu said dismissively. 'I've yet to meet a woman with any true sword skill.'

Han chose not to answer. He would rather concentrate on the sword dancer than bicker with small-minded vagabonds. There was no doubt that what they were seeing was a performance, yet there was something in the dancer's stance and her grip on the sword that triggered some instinct within him.

With each thrust of the sword, his pulse rose. With each lunge and leap, his heart beat faster. It was the essence of the sword dance, the balance of contrasting elements. The hardness of the warrior techniques served to highlight the sensuality of the dance. He was enchanted by the suppleness of an exposed wrist. Enthralled by the hint of rounded calves and gently curved thighs beneath the flowing costume.

The dancer's eyes met his at the end of a turn and his heart forgot to beat. Han kept his expression blank as he returned her gaze. Her skin was glistening, her cheeks flushed. After the brief pause, she moved on and Han swallowed past a sudden dryness in his throat.

The rival thief-catcher had also stopped talking to stare, the same as every other man in the audience. Han needed to focus, maintain a critical eye. He was here to complete a job, not to be charmed by a dancing girl.

The drummers transitioned to a quicker tempo, beating out a driving rhythm as the dancer took to the air. The sword flowed with her, the flash of the blade highlighting each turn while the audience murmured with excitement.

To everyone else, the sword dancer's movements were nothing more than a performance, but the underlying technique caught Han's attention. There was training there. Years and years of training. Not something one usually found at a dusty street fair in some back-road town.

At last the penetrating rhythm fell away to the soft refrain of the flute. The melody floated through like clouds parting to calm the storm. The sword dance took on a peaceful, almost languid quality before dropping back into stillness.

The crowd erupted into applause and the dancer took a graceful bow, sword tucked carefully along one arm, as the troupe sent their minions through the crowd to collect coins. A commotion erupted among the musicians. A few of the thief-catchers had become over-eager and were moving in, shouting and attempting to make arrests.

'Novices,' Longxu snorted.

Han shook his head in exasperation. A few of the entertainers started shoving through the crowd in an attempt to break free. A sword was drawn from somewhere within the chaos and suddenly everyone was in full motion like ants on a hill.

His first inclination was to back away. There was too much confusion and he wasn't even clear who the suspects were, but a flutter of rose streaked with gold and green caught his eye. The sword dancer.

*Her,* his thief-catching instinct shouted.

Instinct was all it took to set him into motion.

She wove through the crowd and ducked into the tavern across the street, slicing through the beaded curtain. Han followed, but the strings of beads swung and tangled around him. By the time he shoved through, the dancer was flying up the stairs. He pushed past startled customers to bound up the steps after her.

He crashed into a server at the top, sending a tea tray and a stack of cups flying. Before he could recover, a sword came at him. Han side-stepped and tried to lock on to her wrist as the blade slid by, but the sword dancer evaded his grasp, her movements as fluid now as they were during the performance.

A cry came from the customers as they stood and skirted to the edges of the room. The sword was aimed at him again. The dancer wielded a *jian,* its long, thin blade suited for the precision cuts and jabs of the more artful duellists. The weapon itself was fake, the edges dulled, but the skill behind it was very real. Han unsheathed his *dao* and blocked in a single motion. His blade was heavier by comparison, suited for the swift, decisive attack of a battlefield.

The sword dancer avoided the swing of his blade, attacking into the opening it created. Strategy, controlled breathing, eyes sharply focused without a hint of fear. Han struck at the sword rather than the fighter, using force and momentum to twist the blade out of her hands. There was no time to celebrate as the dancer grabbed a plate and flung it at his head. Followed by a wine jug which shattered overhead as he ducked. Followed by a wooden bench.

*Heaven and Earth,* she fought like a demon.

The dancer ran over the tables rather than weaving around them. By the time he shoved the bench away, she had dived out the window. Han raced out on to the exterior balcony to find it empty. He peered down below into a similarly deserted street. She'd somehow landed and disappeared into an alleyway.

A furtive shuffle overhead told him differently. He stilled, head tilted to listen. There it was, the faint pad of footsteps. She'd gone up, not down.

Han shoved the *dao* back into its scabbard and climbed on top of the rail. From there, he grabbed on to the looped carvings that ran along the eaves and used them to hoist himself up on to the roof. The dancer was already at the far end of the rooftop. With a running leap, she sailed across the alley on to the adjacent rooftop, the ribbons of her costume floating behind her like the long feathers of an exotic bird.

The heat of the chase was upon him. He followed her trail, running hard and jumping just before the edge. Grey tile cracked beneath his feet as he landed. He had some experience chasing criminals through winding streets, but this was entirely different. The city below disappeared and the rooftops became a new, uncharted landscape.

The dancer leapt again and again he followed. The rooftop sloped upwards and she disappeared over the rise. The sun was high overhead and as Han began the upward climb, he was momentarily blinded by the glare of it. Suddenly a pink blur whirled towards him, followed by the snap of a well-placed kick at his mid-section. The impact knocked him back. He landed with a thud and started to slide. His hands clawed futilely over the slate tiles.

He hit the edge and his stomach plummeted just as something closed over his wrist, stopping his fall. Han looked up, stunned.

It was the sword dancer. Her feet were braced against the raised edge and the muscles of her arms strained against his weight as he dangled partially over the street below. Their gazes locked. It was only a moment, a blink, a breath. Her eyes were black and luminous beneath the dark lining of make-up. They narrowed on him in challenge.

She let go of him and was again in flight. Han hoisted himself back on to the rooftop and struggled to his feet. The dancer slipped over the edge, but rather than dropping to the street, she hung by the grip of her fingers and swung into an open window that wasn't much larger than she was.

Her training had made her as surefooted and daring as a cat. Han suspected it was more than just acrobatics or dance. He leapt on to a lower rooftop, then searched around, found a wagon below and landed in back among sacks of grain.

This was now familiar territory. In his head, he'd mapped out the area and tracked the dancer's speed and direction. Sure enough, he caught up to her as she darted behind a shop. Earthen walls rose high on either side of them. Longxu appeared at the far end of the alley with his hook and rope in hand.

The dancer paused mid-step. Han seized the opportunity and grabbed her, clamping both arms around her torso. She was strong for her size, long-limbed and wiry, and she fought like a wild animal in his grasp.

'I won't hurt you,' he said through his teeth.

Her knuckles caught the bridge of his nose in a bright flash of pain, but he held on and managed to wrestle her arms down.

She was breathing hard, her body tense. She twisted around to look at him. 'I haven't done anything.'

'You ran,' he pointed out.

'You were chasing me!' she snapped.

She had fled the moment the thief-catchers had

made themselves known. It made her immediately suspicious.

Han had her trapped against his chest and, now that she was turned, their position disturbingly resembled a lovers' embrace except that every muscle in her was coiled and ready to break free at the first opportunity.

'Huh, you should split the reward money with me.' Longxu shoved the hook back into his belt and approached. 'I helped you capture her.'

Han tore his gaze away from the dancer. 'Hardly.'

'What? The great Zheng Hao Han is too exalted to share?'

The dancer stilled. Her gaze moving over his face as if seeing him for the first time. 'Thief-catcher Han?' she asked incredulously.

'That is how I'm known,' he replied.

Apparently he'd made a name for himself, though not any name his family would be proud of. Han shifted his grip, taking a hold of the dancer's wrist and locking it behind her back. This time she didn't resist.

'He can't be Zheng Hao Han,' she said in a biting tone as he marched her back towards the municipal hall. 'Thief-catcher Han goes after notorious murderers and villains.'

Han did feel quite the bully. She was slight of build and deceptively delicate in his grasp, but she was no ordinary dancer. She'd been formally trained in the fighting arts, which meant she deserved some respect...and caution.

The village municipal hall was a single building not much larger than the tavern. A clerk sat at a desk. He unrolled a scroll as Han approached. 'The suspect's name?'

'Wen Li Feng,' the dancer said.

The clerk looked her over with morbid interest. She glared back at him and he shrank back, writing down her name quickly.

'There were several others brought in as well. But we only have two holding cells here.'

The prison was built much like a stable with a separate pen for prisoners and vents cut into the walls for light and air. Infractions were punished swiftly and there was no need to hold prisoners for any length of time. The constable relied on shackles and other heavy restraints to keep prisoners in line.

Han clamoed irons over the dancer's wrists, forgoing the cangue, a heavy board which was locked around the neck to trap a prisoner's head. She was a woman after all. Tomorrow she would be transported to Taining where the crime had occurred.

'You've been trained,' he said, meeting her eyes. 'Who is your *shifu*?'

'I have no master.'

Her reply was spoken without emotion, but something flickered beneath the calm surface of her face.

'I don't believe you,' he said.

'It's all for show, thief-catcher. A dance.'

It wasn't just the skill with which she wielded a sword that had him convinced otherwise. The inner calm and confidence she exuded during their battle and the subsequent chase didn't come without discipline.

'Are you arresting me because of the sword?' she asked. 'It was fake, as you must know.'

'I'm arresting you on suspicion of theft.'

'I'm not a thief,' she stated evenly.

'Then you'll be found innocent and released.'

She arched an eyebrow at him. 'Do you really think that is how the tribunal works?'

Not many realised it, but Han had more knowledge of how the judicial halls operated than he had use for. The dancer wasn't acting guilty, but she wasn't quite acting innocent either. Not that it was his place to determine guilt or innocence. That was for the magistrate in Taining to decide.

The constable had finished transferring the other prisoners into a single cell. The dancer was the lone female who had been captured. Han had a feeling the others were harmless performers, but Wen Li Feng was something very different.

She'd fought ruthlessly, as if her life depended

on it. But when he'd lost his balance on the rooftop, when she could have made her escape, she had reached out to stop his fall instead. That debt hung over him and he didn't quite know what to do with it.

Han wasn't one to be swayed by the pleas or protests of his targets. He caught the criminals and brought them in. Yet the sword dancer was neither pleading nor protesting. His last vision was of her looking around the holding cell, her hands weighted down by thick chains that appeared grotesque and imposing over such a graceful figure.

Li Feng lowered herself to the floor of the prison cell, leaning her back against one wall. The floor was packed dirt and there was a bucket in the corner that she preferred to stay away from.

Her instinct was to get up, to move even if there was nothing to be accomplished by it. Fighting against the urge, she closed her eyes. She tried to breathe in deeply and then out, circulating the energy as *shifu* had taught her. Trying to stay calm. To stay focused.

It wasn't working.

Li Feng raised her knees and laid her head down upon them. By nature, she didn't like small spaces. She had grown up on a mountainside, away from the confines of the city.

She had been right to leave Bao Yang and his band

of rebels. There was a time when she had thought she fit in perfectly among them. That they were the only people who would ever accept someone like her.

*Shifu* had taken care of Li Feng after finding her in hiding and alone in the woods, but he had always treated her like his disciple rather than a daughter. It suited her fine to call him *shifu,* to respectfully refer to him as her master, because she already had a mother and a father. They had been taken from her by force.

Maybe that was why she had been charmed so easily into Bao Yang's cause as well as his bed. Two years ago, she had just left the isolation of Mount Wudang to venture back into civilisation. In her heart, she had always dreamed of one day finding her family, or at least discovering what had happened to them. She had been too young to remember anything but fleeing with her mother's hand clasped around hers. Mother had told her to hide. Li Feng remembered they had been running, but she couldn't remember why. She also remembered the men with the swords who were chasing them.

After an indeterminately long time, she raised her head. It was getting dark inside the cell. She heard the sound of a door opening, followed by footsteps which stopped outside. She stood and peered through the cell door to see a young man holding a tray of food.

'This must be the most generous village in the province to feed prisoners so well,' she remarked.

The boy lacked the grim countenance of a watchman. 'This is from your admirer.'

Admirer? She read the answer from his lopsided grin. 'Thief-catcher Han?' she asked in disbelief.

He nodded. Apparently he found it funny as well. 'The other prisoners in the next stall are eating watery rice porridge. Your dance must have made an impression.'

Zheng Hao Han must have had a strange sense of humour to lock her up yet see that she was fed.

'Should I take this back?' he asked.

Li Feng shook her head and he slid the tray through the opening in the door.

'Tell me,' she said as he turned to go. 'Is the thief-catcher standing guard out there?'

'No, he's at the tavern drinking with his cronies.'

Celebrating, more like. The dog.

She had first noticed him during her performance. The intensity of his eyes had been enough to break her focus. There was a broadness to his nose and chin and he had an overall rough-boned look that was tempered by the subtle curve of his mouth. She'd noticed because he had been smiling at her, or rather smiling to himself while he was watching her. It was a sly sort of smile, with one corner lifted higher than the other, as if he'd figured out all her secrets.

And of all the thief-catchers that came for her, it had to be the famous Thief-catcher Han that captured her. The formidable warrior, the relentless hunter, the this and the that. Though Han was tall, he certainly wasn't the giant ox of a man she'd expected, yet he was still strong enough and fast enough to catch her.

Zheng Hao Han had stood out from the surrounding crowd, dressed in a sombre dark robe, with the hilt of a weapon protruding from his belt. She should have known to flee then.

Her *shifu* had trained her to fight so she wouldn't have to be afraid, yet seeing those men brought back not only that old fear, but also all of the untold anger she had kept inside her. All her life, she had hated those nameless, faceless strangers who had taken her mother away.

Her anger was without focus until she had met Bao Yang. He had provided the perfect target. General Wang was a tyrant, he'd told her. All of the local authorities were afraid to challenge him and he was intent on seizing more power.

So Li Feng had joined Bao Yang's group of dissidents. They had disrupted the General's supply lines, stolen back the grain and livestock he would commandeer to feed his garrison, and worked to cut away at General Wang's stranglehold over the district in any way they could. But the moment she had seen that extravagant cache of jade and gold, Li Feng knew it was not the typical tribute demanded by General Wang of the local aristocrats and merchants. She had become involved in something more dangerous than she had realised.

Something else in that shipment had finally pulled her away from her alliance with Bao Yang and his rebels. Something that reminded her of why she had originally returned to Fujian province. For the first time in nearly twenty years, she had seen something that was possibly connected to her mother. It was a sign from heaven.

Li Feng knelt before the tray. There was a bowl of rice with a mix of bamboo shoots and mushrooms. It was a simple meal. The real extravagance was the small lamp set beside it. The flame danced within the saucer, providing a tiny orb of light so she wouldn't have to eat in the dark. Li Feng finished every last grain of rice. When adrift on endless roads, one never knew when the next meal would be.

It was late into the evening now and the sounds of the village outside the prison house had quieted to a murmur. The constable would be off to his bed. The night watch, if there was one, would be settling in for their vigil. She could hear the sound of muted voices through the wall. The poor members of the dance troupe who'd had the misfortune of being in her company.

Li Feng waited a little longer. It was difficult to exercise such patience when trapped as she was. Once she was certain the sky was dark outside, she stood and wrapped one hand around the other. She pushed at her knuckles and shifted the joints beneath the ring of iron. After some twisting, she tugged her hand free. The other manacle quickly followed. She dropped the heavy chain at her feet and blew out the lamp, leaving the cell in complete darkness.

## Chapter Two

After escaping from the prison house, Li Feng was forced to leave her companions behind. The thief-catchers and constables would be searching for a dancer so she thought it best to stay away from the performance troupes she typically travelled with. Besides, her quest was now a personal one.

Li Feng approached the jade shop as she did all the others—with a sense of hope. An artisan in the last village had directed her to this mid-sized town, indicating that the shop here was a successful one that would know more about the type of piece she was interested in.

It was only a few hours until the closing of the market. Soon after that, evening would be upon her and she needed to be in a safe location for the night. A woman on her own had to be careful of these things.

There were two worlds beyond the solitude of Wudang Mountain. There was the realm of the cities, an orderly and structured place separated by walls and governed by law. A gong dictated what time merchants were to bring their wares to market and when to close up shop and go home. Then there was another world alongside it. A place of roads and dust and dark city corners that didn't adhere to the same boundaries. The inhabitants here were dancers and musicians, monks and beggars. This was also the world where smugglers and bandits operated.

An unspoken fellowship existed among those that travelled the roads for the sake of both companionship and protection. When Li Feng left her *shifu,* she had met up with a dance troupe that travelled from village to village. Sword dancing had become popular with the crowds, and with some practice she had executed one that was entertaining enough that the performers welcomed her into the fold.

With the dance, a part of her had reawakened. Mother had been a dancer, she was certain of it. Li Feng had a memory of her in colourful costumes: a princess in mourning, a flying goddess, a flower bearer. Li Feng could almost hear a firm, but gentle voice from long ago, telling her to hold her head high and keep her back straight, her toes pointed.

She also remembered travelling with her family as a child. They would sleep under a different roof every night or sometimes beneath the stars with Mother curled up beside her. She had had a father, too, but his face was blurred and faded like all the others in her memory. She was afraid that if she didn't come back and reclaim her own past, one day her mother's face would fade as well.

When she had joined Bao Yang in his campaign against the warlord, that struggle had momentarily taken the place of her determination to find her family. She had nothing tangible to connect her to the past except for a few vague descriptions of hills and rivers from Wen *shifu* and a jade carving that her mother had pressed into her hands.

A carving that had been a complete mystery to her until now.

The inside of the jade shop was undecorated other than the figurines and trinkets gleaming on the counter. The shopkeeper who greeted her was also dressed in a plain brown robe. No one trusted a shopkeeper who looked like he made too much of a profit.

'Miss.' His respectful tone tapered off as he eyed her up and down. He was likely accustomed to wealthier customers and her plain tunic failed to impress.

Li Feng glanced over the array of bracelets and finery. She had been in so many of these shops in the last days that she was nearly an expert herself.

She pulled out the carved pendant from her sash. 'Sir, can you tell me more about this?'

It was an oblong tablet that fit easily in the palm of her hand. A magnificent bird was carved on to it, with wings spread in flight. A red tassel adorned one end. Years of being kept close to her body had changed the creamy jade to a deeper, richer colour.

The shopkeeper held the pendant up and his eyes lit momentarily, just long enough for her to catch the interest in them, before his expression became hooded.

'Not very high quality,' he said, affecting a tone of ennui. 'I can give you twenty cash and that's generous.'

Did he think she was a child of three? 'It wasn't my intention to sell. There is an inscription on the back of the jade that I was told someone here might recognise—'

He shook his head and pushed the jade back to her. 'That is my final offer, young miss.'

This sort only cared about the number of coins in his drawer at the end of the day. Perplexed, Li Feng picked up the pendant and wove around the counter. She ignored his squawk of protest as she pushed through a beaded curtain.

An elderly craftsman sat at a table in the workroom in back. He was busy polishing a statuette of a dragon with a pearl in its mouth. He paused to look up at her with mild interest while his hands remained poised over the pale-green stone.

'Honourable sir,' she began. 'If you would kindly look on the back of this pendant. I was told by the jade carver in Quantou village that you might be of assistance.'

He looked her over just as the shopkeeper had, but the craftsman took the jade and turned it over in his hands with care.

'Nanyang jade,' he proclaimed. 'The carving depicts the Vermilion Bird. Most likely part of a set of four.'

Her heart thudded with excitement. She had indeed seen three others in the same style and with the same inscription on the back, an inscription she didn't recognise. Bao Yang had noticed her strange look when they had sifted through the stolen treasure. He had offered the set of three to her as a gift as they had been at odds at the time. It always seemed that they were in disagreement about one thing or another during their brief liaison.

Li Feng had no interest in any of the riches from the heist. Bao Yang's rebellion against General Wang had started to appear more and more like a personal feud. Coming across that set of jade had been fate, if one believed in such things.

The old man held the pendant up, squinting at the corner. 'The artist inscribed it with his name.'

Li Feng leaned in close, waiting as patiently as

she could to hear more, but instead of continuing, the craftsman glanced up at her.

'I know who you are.'

'You do?' Her pulse skipped and her deepest dreams beckoned from the shadows. Maybe this man had known her family. She was about to find the answer to a riddle. To *her* riddle. Where she came from. Who she was.

'You stole this,' he accused.

Her hope shrivelled to dust. 'I didn't steal it. It's mine.'

The craftsman ignored her protest and started shouting for the shopkeeper. Li Feng darted forwards to snatch the jade from his fingers before hurrying out the front door.

The street outside was thick with activity. Painted signboards marked each shop and wares were displayed out in the street to entice customers. She slipped into the crowd, matching the shuffling pace of those around her though her heart pounded insistently, telling her to run. At any moment, she expected to hear the merchant from the jade shop shouting after her. 'Thief! You stole it!'

But he was wrong. This jade pendant was the one thing that belonged to her. Her mother had put it into her hands with her final parting words. 'Don't cry, *Xiao Feng*. Don't cry.'

*Little phoenix, don't cry.* Those hadn't been words

of comfort. Her mother was giving her a desperate plea and a warning. Li Feng remembered that she and her mother were running from someone, but she couldn't remember why.

Her current hideout was a hovel a short distance from the main road. The roof was missing shingles and the wooden structure was overgrown with moss. Such a place had once provided shade, drink and a convenient place to rest one's horse on the journey between cities. Now it provided her temporary shelter from the wind and rain.

Li Feng took care before returning. She held back and led her horse on a meandering path through the woods outside the city until she was confident that no one followed her. The sun was setting as she ventured back to the abandoned tavern. This stretch of road had become a hunting ground for bandits, according to local gossip, and was treacherous for travellers day or night.

Ever since her arrest, Li Feng had sought out shelter in deserted areas or in not-so-legitimate establishments where she could avoid the scrutiny of law enforcers. She had borrowed, or rather liberated, the horse from a courier station. A woman travelling alone was vulnerable to all manner of danger. She needed to be able to move swiftly.

Her master had wandered through the province

before settling in the foothills of Wudang Mountain to meditate and dedicate his life to seeking the Tao. He had learned how to fight to survive against bandits and had passed on those skills to Li Feng as well. A sword was difficult to conceal, so she carried knives for protection. Li Feng slipped one into her hand as soon as she dismounted in front of the tavern. She needed to be inside with the door barricaded before nightfall.

Li Feng brought her horse to the hitching post and removed the saddle before tying him down. She entered through the back door to find the main room dark and still. There were a few benches and tables left behind, mostly broken. She shut the doors behind her and fitted the wooden bar into the latch.

The scant daylight that remained filtered in through the empty panes of the windows. The paper that had once covered them had long crumbled. She would sleep here for the night and tomorrow she would find shelter somewhere else. Maybe there was another jade artisan nearby who would be willing to help her.

Li Feng felt through the darkness to find where she'd set her oil lamp. She used her tinder pouch to light the wick. As her eyes adjusted to the glow, a shuffle of movement sent her heart racing.

She reached for her knife just as an immense

weight slammed into her, tackling her to the ground. The knife clattered out of her reach.

She knew what, or who, it was, even before she saw him. She knew from instinct and reflexes and the tension in her muscles as they encountered an unmovable barrier. That bastard thief-catcher's weight was on top of her.

Struggling for breath, she jabbed him in the side, aiming a pinpoint strike against his floating rib. His body jerked at the impact, but he recovered quickly to grab at her wrists.

Her back was against the ground. Blood pumped through her muscles, feeding the fighting instinct within her, but she had no leverage. There was no power behind her strikes. Still Li Feng fought with everything she had. She needed to try to break his hold somehow. She wrenched her hand free to claw at the soft part of his belly—except it wasn't soft on him.

'She-demon,' Han cursed with a grunt.

She had some good names for him too, but she wouldn't waste her energy. He threw his forearm across her chest while he groped for something just out of reach with his other hand. The rattle of chains made her blood run cold. She renewed her efforts, twisting beneath him, but it was no use. The cold snap of metal over her wrists took the fire out of her.

For now.

He didn't get off her immediately. Fear choked her as his hand curved over her waist. Instead of tearing her clothes open, he felt around her sash, her sleeves, then checked her boots where he finally found her other knife. She didn't know whether to feel relief or anger as he threw the weapon into the corner. She felt both.

'Surrendering already?' he gritted out.

She had gone still beneath him, first from the fear of being violated, but now because she needed to conserve her strength and think. There was little she could do while he pinned her. Han was too strong, but if he let down his guard now that she was chained—

The thief-catcher ended that thought by grabbing a rope and coiling it around her wrists. He secured her arms to her sides for good measure, wrapping the length around her torso. She thought he might cocoon her like a silkworm, but he knotted off the rope just below her elbows and finally released her.

Panic stabbed at her once again when Han reached for her sash, but it was only to remove the jade pendant. He released her abruptly and sat back, as if in a hurry to put some distance between them. He was breathing hard and his dark hair was askew over his face. Strands of it had been dragged from his topknot during their struggle.

'Wen Li Feng.' His expression was far from smug

as he looked her over. 'You look like you're plotting my death.'

He was right.

She rolled on to her side and tried to sit up, which was difficult tied the way she was. She glared at him.

'I hate you.'

He barked out a laugh.

She did hate him. There was no reason, no rational reason for him to go chasing after her. Why wouldn't he give up like any other lowlife thief-catcher?

She finally managed to prop herself up against the wall, flopping like a fish to do so. Han leaned back to watch her. Bastard.

'You have sharp elbows,' he complained, running a hand over his ribs.

'Sweet talker,' she retorted.

The lantern cast the thief-catcher's face in deep shadows. He regarded her with an expression that was both curious and assessing. It made her nervous.

She finally calmed down her breathing enough to sound rational. 'Why did you come all this way, thief-catcher? Surely the reward money isn't worth the trouble.'

'You're not going to claim innocence?' he asked.

'I'm innocent.'

He grinned. His eyes danced with light when he smiled.

'There is a matter of a stolen horse,' he remarked.

'Which you can take back. He's outside.'

'That hardly negates the crime.'

She narrowed her eyes at him. Her crimes were insignificant compared to those of the corrupt bureaucrats that governed over the province. Bureaucrats that this thief-catcher obediently served.

'Then there's also the matter of a stolen shipment of jade and gold.' He held up her carving. The lamplight flickered over the jade.

'This is not stolen.'

He raised his eyebrows at her.

She felt a twinge of loss at seeing her sole possession in his hands. 'It's mine.'

Han gave the jade a passing glance before tucking it into the fold of his robe. 'What about all the other missing treasures?'

'I don't know what treasures you're speaking of,' she said blandly, her face showing nothing.

More raised eyebrows and a disconcerting touch of amusement at the corners of his mouth. That sort of smile in the right sort of light could disarm a woman, but Li Feng only gave him a hard look in return. She was already disarmed and this was definitely the wrong sort of light.

They loved telling stories about Thief-catcher Han in Fujian province ever since he'd defeated the bandit chief known as Two Dragon Lo. Zheng Hao Han had become somewhat of a romantic figure, yet her thoughts were anything but romantic while she was trussed and helpless before him. Especially when he seemed to be enjoying it.

'Miss Wen.' He suddenly appeared serious. 'I've been wondering about your sword skill. You say you have no master, but if I had to guess your style, I would say its foundation is from Wudang Mountain?'

She tried not to let her surprise show. They'd had a brief exchange at the tavern, hardly enough for him to discern any particular technique.

He kept his gaze levelled on her, scrubbing a hand over the hard cut of his jaw. 'From your silence, I think I must be correct. The Wudang forms are known for their fluidity and are often likened to dance.'

Whether or not she hated him, Li Feng had to admit that Han had captured her. *Again.* He was more than a dim-witted sword-for-hire. He had been carefully tracking her and assessing her abilities. All while she hadn't given him a single thought. She deserved her defeat.

Li Feng looked at him now with new eyes—as the enemy. His fighting experience, like so many thief-catchers, probably came from serving in the military. His choice of weapon, the straight-bladed *dao,* confirmed that.

'The shopkeeper in town told you about me,' she ventured.

'You seem to have a fondness for jade shops across the county. Yet you never have anything to sell. I would expect a thief to try to profit from her bounty as soon as possible.' He was watching for her reaction. 'I considered that you might be gathering information for more underhanded activities, but that doesn't seem to be the case.'

'I told you, I didn't take any of the jade.'

He wagged a finger at her. 'So you had accomplices. Don't try to be clever with your words, Miss Wen. I'm wondering why, after such a grand take, you are not enjoying newfound riches? A falling out with your comrades, perhaps?'

'If I told you, would you release me?'

'No.'

'I don't suppose begging for mercy would do any good either,' she remarked drily.

He paused at that. 'No,' he said finally, his expression inscrutable. After a tense silence, he spoke again. 'If you are indeed guilty of the theft, you must accept the consequences. You might be sentenced to time in the cangue for theft. At worst, you may suffer a public beating. Most likely you'll be sentenced to servitude to make up for your crimes.' Han listed off the punishments as if reading from a code book.

'Are you certain?' she challenged. 'There was quite an expensive amount of jade stolen...as I hear.'

'The magistrate will be lenient seeing as you're a woman.'

'I'll be shown mercy after I confess under torture.'

A frown creased his brow. It was clear he was disturbed by her directness, but said nothing to refute her claims. She may have lived for most of her life away from the affairs of the world, but she'd learned very quickly about how justice truly worked. Some magistrates were crueller than others, but none, by the very nature of their position, was particularly kind.

'I will do my best to see that you are treated fairly,' he said, though it was a faint promise. He apparently thought having her head and arms locked in the cangue or publicly beaten was 'fair'.

'Why would Thief-catcher Han want to help a suspected criminal like me?'

'Because you rescued me.' He wasn't pleased to admit it.

She sat up straight, confused. 'I did no such thing.'

'On the rooftop, you could have let me fall.'

Li Feng recalled reaching out for him, her hand closing around his wrist. She hadn't even remembered the incident until he brought it up. 'I acted on instinct.'

'Most criminals only have the instinct to save themselves.'

They regarded one another across the tavern. There was an undeniable connection between them. Like Han, she didn't particularly like it. Li Feng didn't believe in fate, but if she hadn't caught him, he would have fallen. Perhaps he would have broken an arm or a leg. It would have been very difficult to pursue her while restricted to the use of one leg.

'What are you smiling about?' he asked warily.

She thinned out her lips. 'Let me go and you can consider your debt repaid.'

'No.'

'But I'm a helpless woman.'

'Justice is justice, for man or woman.'

She exhaled in exasperation. He spoke the words with such conviction, but she found it hard to believe him. A mercenary didn't care about justice or injustice. He only cared about his reward.

'Did you promise leniency to Two Dragon Lo?' she asked.

His expression darkened and his light, casual demeanour disappeared. Everyone knew the story. Two Dragon Lo had murdered every other thief-catcher who had gone after him. His gang had even defeated a constable and his entire squad of hired swordsmen. Yet Zheng Hao Han had ventured alone into the forest that was Lo's stronghold and had killed the notorious bandit with his own hands.

'Two Dragon Lo was a different matter.'

Tension gathered in his shoulders as Han came forwards and wrapped a hand around her ankle. His touch was firm, but oddly gentle. She considered kicking him out of spite, but their gazes locked and he gave her a sharp and pointed look that was full of warning. In brusque, efficient movements, he coiled another length of rope around her ankles before extinguishing the lamp. She heard the sound of him settling on to the ground not too far away.

She didn't know if Han deserved his reputation for being the god of thief-catchers, lowly god that it was, but he had thwarted her on her one advantage. Her joints, which had always been flexible, were made more so by rigorous discipline and practice. Irons were easy to slip out of. Coils and coils of rope, less so.

After some time passed, his breathing grew deep and steady. Quietly, she tried to wriggle her hands free beneath the ropes. Perhaps one of his knots could be worked loose.

'Go to sleep.' Han's voice sliced through the darkness. 'The sound of you struggling is keeping me awake.'

With that, he settled down again. She scowled at him, even though there was no light for him to see it.

# Chapter Three

When Han had originally decided to go after Wen Li Feng, his primary reason was that she was an oddity. She was too skilled with the sword to be just a dancer and she had demonstrated the ability to bypass heavy chains and locked doors.

Now, he was certain she was hiding something. Her behaviour was suspect, with her numerous visits to jade merchants. The same instinct that told him Li Feng was more than a dancer also told him that she wasn't motivated by greed and that there was more at hand than theft.

His father had always told him to find the one detail that was out of place and start his search from there. Father always seemed more concerned with how things fit neatly together rather than any specific moral code. Right and wrong were values that were subject to interpretation. Order was the natural intended state of heaven and earth and to commit a crime was to violate that state. Their household had once been kept with that same philosophy in mind.

Father also believed that every time a crime went unpunished, society was one step closer to ruin and decay. It had been several years since Han had spoken to the man, but he was sure Father's ideals hadn't shifted one bit.

If Han didn't hunt the sword dancer down, he was certain no one else would or could. So now that his prisoner was trussed up before him, society was safe from ruin.

'This is absurd,' Li Feng muttered.

She was face down and draped over the saddle in front of him with her wrists and ankles tied

'It will take at least a week to reach Taining.' She tried to lift her head, but failed. 'Are you going to keep me like this the entire time?'

'Yes.'

'I won't try to run away. You'd just capture me again.'

'Liar.'

Han looked down to where she lay practically in his lap, squirming. He was trying very hard not to notice the squirming or the flush of warmth it brought to his lower half. She was his *prisoner*. Not a dancer. Not a woman. Definitely not a somewhat pretty woman with exceptional skills.

He still had an ache in his side. His ribs were

likely bruised after their wrestling match. Li Feng might be slight, but she struck with purpose. If he untied her, if he even allowed her to have a single finger free, he had no doubt she'd somehow get her hands on a knife and leave it protruding from his heart.

'I should thank you for providing the horse,' he added jovially.

She called him something impolite under her breath. He'd been called worse, but not much worse.

'You're no hero, picking on the small and weak.'

'You're far from weak, Miss Wen.'

'Aren't there more evil and loathsome villains for you to chase after?'

Li Feng looked neither evil nor loathsome at the moment. More troubling than the fact that he found her not unpleasant to look at—and that she had a very well-formed backside—was that he found her interesting. How did a young woman acquire such an extraordinary set of skills? Why would she be involved with thieves and vagabonds?

At the next rest stop, he slipped her from the horse like a sack of grain and propped her against a tree. After tending to the horse, he poured water into a cup and brought it to her.

She closed her eyes and let her head fall back against the trunk with a sigh. 'The indignity.'

Han waited. Without its cynical expression, her face was delicately shaped, tapering only slightly towards her chin. Wen Li Feng was much easier to deal with when she was coming at him with a sword or spitting venom. This show of helplessness made him as uncomfortable as it did her. After a moment, she opened her eyes and tilted her head to accept the water. He had to kneel beside her to place the cup to her mouth. Her lips parted and she looked away as she drank. Han watched the lines of her neck as she swallowed, his own throat going dry.

'Thank you.' Her eyes were closed again.

The first time he'd seen her, her face had been heavily accented with make-up for the performance. Without it, her features were softer. A dancer's true beauty was in the lines of her body and the way she moved. Her face was one that Han might never have noticed if he hadn't seen her dance. Like the rest of her, its beauty was in movement. It was an expressive face, quick to show anger or amusement. Granted he'd seen more anger than any other emotion during their short acquaintance, but even that was beautiful in its intensity and fire. No one had ever schooled her to hide her emotions, to not let her face display her thoughts. It made one vulnerable to reveal so much, so easily.

When Li Feng performed, her expressions were coy and full of fire, but there was no such artifice now in stillness. Since he'd observed her so closely, the features which he might have considered plain or pleasant before took on a mysterious quality. Her eyelashes were long against her cheeks. Her skin was smooth, the tone of it warm with a natural flush. The shape and curves of her face were so subtle one might need to touch her to truly experience them.

He moved back, further away than he needed to, and seated himself on the grass opposite her. She opened her eyes, perhaps after sensing he had moved away, and had to lift both her arms to wipe her mouth with her sleeve. Then they just sat there, both watching each other warily.

'Tell me how you caught Two Dragon Lo,' she said after a pause.

His back stiffened. 'Why would you want to know that?'

'I want to hear your account.'

'You mean whether I indeed walked on water or flew through the trees?'

She gave him a reluctant smile that was really just a twitch of her mouth.

Everyone asked him about the bandit lately and it seemed the stories were getting more fanciful no matter how much he denied them. Han settled his arm across his knees. 'There isn't much to say. I went into the woods to find him. We fought. I won.'

'You don't know how to tell a story, thief-catcher,' she complained.

'I think a more interesting story—' he fixed his gaze on her '—would be why a girl who seems to like jade so much would steal it, yet not take any for herself. Save for one small trinket.'

She stared at him blankly, or at least she tried to. There was much, much more lurking there beneath the surface. If he could just feel along her smooth exterior, turn her this way and that to look for imperfections.

'You were betrayed and cut out of the stake,' he suggested.

Li Feng looked away, seemingly absorbed by the play of sunlight on the grass.

'Your mother is aged and sick and you were stealing to save her,' he threw out lightly.

Her gaze snapped back to him with a tinge of annoyance that told him he was wrong, but had hit upon something. 'Is this effective, asking so many questions with no direction?'

His laugh was directed at himself. 'I've actually been told by a very wise man that it is always best to say as little as possible.'

Criminals tended to reveal themselves. It was in their nature to want to confess, the crime staining their soul as it did.

'I was only curious,' he admitted. 'And it's a long way to Taining.'

Han usually wasn't so interested in knowing the reasons behind the crime. That was for the tribunal to sort out, if the motivations of the accused were even pertinent. Han found that in most cases, the reasons were quite clear. Only in a few instances did the accused ever confound him. The bandit Lo was one. Wen Li Feng was another.

There was another reason Han wanted information. Once he handed the dancer over to the authorities in Taining, she would inevitably be questioned about her accomplices. If she was more forthcoming to him, she might avoid a more ruthless interrogation at the hands of the magistrate.

Li Feng shifted her weight from one shoulder to another against the tree, her bonds constricting her movement. The dancer was not one for remaining still.

'Were you so cordial to Two Dragon Lo?' she asked.

His stomach knotted. It was back to Lo again. He couldn't escape the man. Han conjured the remote tavern in the hills and a long night of trading drinks and stories with a fellow traveller. The wine jug was nearly empty when they had raised their cups in a salute. Lo's sleeve had fallen just enough to reveal the tail of a dragon.

'You killed him,' she remarked.

So the tale goes. 'That wasn't my intention. He was to be brought to trial like any other criminal.'

'An outlaw like Lo would fight to the death rather than be taken alive.'

Her fascination with the bandit disturbed him. She spoke of killing and death too casually, with a worldly air that was unexpected in a young woman.

'Lo was more than a common thief. He had been enlisted in the provincial army and trained to fight with sword and spear,' Han explained. 'He didn't stop at attacking merchants on the open road. The bandit formed a gang of outlaws and started threatening local officials as well.'

'You say that Two Dragon Lo needed to be stopped,' she said. 'He was growing in power and greedy for more.'

He didn't quite understand Li Feng's cynical expression. 'Many of the local armies have been disbanded in recent years. The situation has left too many dangerous men wandering with no direction, no discipline.'

She snorted. 'Do you know who truly controls Taining? Not the magistrate or his constables. The county is controlled by a man named Wang Shizhen, who regularly extorts bribes of jade and silver and gold.'

'General Wang Shizhen is the appointed commander of the southern garrison,' Han pointed out.

'You say there are too many soldiers without wars to fight and no commanders to keep them in line.' Her gaze was unflinching on him. 'Some of them turn into bandits like Lo while others forcibly take control with their armies. Is there any difference between them?'

'This is dangerous talk,' he warned.

She shrugged, too easily. 'Just talk.'

Theft was punishable by beating or servitude, depending on the circumstances, but rebellion was unpardonable. The province had been plagued by famine and flood over the last ten years, pushing desperate men to banditry or insurrection. His own family had suffered in the aftermath of a rebellion in Fuzhou province to the east.

The singular punishment for rebelling against the state was both harsh and swift: public execution by beheading.

'Time to go,' Han muttered, his stomach knotted tight.

'Are you going to carry me?' she taunted.

It was awkward between them with her bound as she was. He was reduced to behaving like a servant, seeing to her needs.

Li Feng shrank back as he went to kneel beside her. Han paused with his hand at her foot, a pose that with any other woman would have only been possible in a moment of intimacy. He heard the quickening of her breath and tension built along her very well-formed calf.

She was his *prisoner,* he reminded himself.

The conversation had revealed more about Wen Li Feng than he'd intended, though it shouldn't have mattered. If she was a criminal, she deserved to be punished according to the law.

'Don't try to run,' he warned through his teeth. Han cut away the rope at her ankles and dragged her up. 'If you do, I'll catch you and beat you myself.'

The town was a fledgling one that had sprouted up at a convenient distance between two larger cities. The main road cut between two rows of buildings: an inn, a few shops and a stable. There was little else to the place aside from a few huts built of wood and thatched with hay.

They stopped beside a road stand serving food and drink. Han had to once again assist as Li Feng dismounted with her wrists still tied in front of her. His hands rounded her waist before settling her on to the ground. She shot him a look, though he hardly deserved it. The touch was purely innocent. There was just no getting around the fact that he was a man and she a woman.

'I need to use the privy,' she said.

He expected as much. The grey-haired woman standing behind the cooking pot pointed to the back area. Han followed closely behind as Li Feng started towards the outhouse.

She cast him a slanted look. 'You're going to follow me there?'

'This is when every prisoner attempts to escape.'

'I need my hands at least.'

'Absolutely not.'

She huffed at him, blowing a strand of hair away from her face in the process. With a gesture, he beckoned the serving woman over and gave her a coin.

'Please assist this young lady,' he directed.

The old woman nodded. As they disappeared inside the hut, Han circled around to make sure there was no way to escape out the back. Then he returned to the benches where he had a full view of the door. By the time the old woman and Li Feng returned, the table had been set with a pot of tea and two bowls of mixed rice. She settled down quietly on to the bench beside him.

'I asked for a serving spoon,' he said, feeling quite generous. 'So you can feed yourself with your wrists tied.'

It wouldn't be the most elegant of meals, but he was sure she could manage.

'Thank you,' Li Feng murmured, head down.

She sniffled. He bent to see her face which was suddenly hidden behind a veil of hair.

'Have you been crying?' he asked incredulously.

Her nose and eyes looked red and she ducked away even further from him. Her shoulders were slumped and defeated. Her sniffling grew more pronounced. This was quickly becoming embarrassing.

'Li Fe— Miss Wen?' It was awkward having to be so polite to a prisoner, but there was no other way to address a woman. 'What is this?'

She pushed at him, flinging his hands away. 'No. Don't touch me!'

*Heaven and Earth.* 'Stop this nonsense,' he demanded.

She scrambled off the bench and cowered away. 'Please don't beat me again.'

Too late, Han realised a crowd had gathered by the stand. A crowd of rather concerned, rather angry-looking townspeople and some of them quite large. There was no chance to explain. Rough hands grabbed at him. He shoved them away, took a punch in the jaw, threw a couple of strikes of his own.

He drew his *dao* and a few of the men backed off, but not all of them. They were in a fervour. He was grappled from behind while two other men clawed for his weapon while swearing and calling him a kidnapper and a slaver.

'She's a thief!' he growled, throwing another would-be hero off his back.

Out of the corner of his eye, he saw the serving woman cutting away Li Feng's bonds with a kitchen knife. Li Feng wrestled the iron rings past her knuckles with no more effort than a couple of twists and turns. The chain was left behind in the grass like a lifeless black snake.

Damn his stupidity. With her training, he should have guessed she had that ability.

Han freed himself in time to see his former prisoner galloping into the distance, leaving a cloud of dust behind.

# Chapter Four

Li Feng walked through the front door of the public bath house, slipped the host a quick coin to assuage any protests about impropriety, and entered the dark and tepid interior.

Business was slow early in the morning. The day labourers and tradesmen who served as regular customers were hard at work, leaving the communal bath and lounging areas nearly empty. Steam hovered over a wide pool where several bathers, all male, lay soaking. No one gave her more than a cursory glance.

She slipped through the adjacent chambers, finally finding what she was looking for behind a bamboo screen.

Thief-catcher Han was reclined in a wooden tub behind the screen. His legs were bent, pulling his knees above the water line. His eyes were closed, head rested back against the rim, and his hair was untied and loose about his face. The effect, combined with the fullness of his lips, was disturbingly sensual.

It had been two days since her escape and she'd managed to evade him while still remaining close. She had been tied up and tossed about too many times by this scoundrel. This time, she had him at her mercy.

Han didn't open his eyes even as she stood over him. His breathing remained deep and relaxed. It must be wonderful to feel so confident in one's skin. To feel so safe without fear perpetually hanging overhead.

A light mist hung in the air. Through it, Li Feng let her eyes roam over the bared contours of his chest and shoulders, confirming what she'd known from the few times they'd battled. Zheng Hao Han was made of hard, unyielding muscle. The dark line of a scar curved from below his collar bone to disappear over his shoulder. It was the remnant of a blow that had just missed his throat. She found herself wondering who had made the wound and with what weapon?

She had practiced fighting stances for thousands upon thousands of days, had been forced to defend herself many times with the knife and the sword, yet she'd never suffered serious injury. It reminded her that Han had knowledge that she didn't—knowledge of fierce battles survived—and that she should never overlook that or underestimate him.

'A private bath, thief-catcher?' she remarked lightly.

His eyes snapped open and he started, sending a cascade of water splashing on to the floorboards.

'Wen Li Feng,' he choked out. His hand gripped the edge of the tub and his muscles tensed all up his arm and throughout his body.

There was something both vulnerable yet undeniably virile about the sight of Han naked. Her tongue cleaved to the roof of her mouth. She attributed the warmth creeping up the back of her neck to the steam that surrounded her, dampening her skin. Needless to say, she was no longer thinking about battle scars.

She worked to keep her gaze on his face. 'Your work must be quite profitable.'

His breathing had quickened and he fought to regain his composure. 'You should be careful of your reputation, Miss Wen. Everyone will assume you are here to provide me an intimate service.'

Men's bodies weren't unknown to her. Li Feng had lived in close quarters with other performers. She might have lost her first kiss along with her virginity recently, but even before that she'd simply never learned to be shy. Despite having had a lover in the past, it was still a shock to see Thief-catcher Han's naked form.

The two of them had wrestled, fought and had so much physical contact that now the sight of him unclothed completed the picture. Her knowledge of his body was nearly as intimate as a lover's.

She moved to stand over him. All that shielded him from her view was a layer of bath water and the haze of steam. Neither the water nor the steam was clouded enough.

An unwelcome heat flooded her cheeks. She hoped it wasn't accompanied by a blush that Han could see. Li Feng had chosen this particular location to confront him so she could finally have the thief-catcher at a disadvantage and she hated the thought of losing it.

'You should know that I can track you as easily as you can track me.'

Han made no effort to curl up his knees to hide that part of himself. 'You are relying on my sense of modesty to prevent me from capturing you right now,' he said as he started to rise.

With a flick of her hand, she unsheathed the short sword hidden beneath her sleeve and pressed the tip to his chest. 'I'm relying on this blade.'

His gaze remained on her, unflinching, but he did sink back into the tub. 'Have you ever killed anyone, Miss Wen?'

She cocked her head. 'You can be my first,' she said with a smile.

His eyes darkened at that and the air thickened between them. She suddenly wished she had brought a longer blade. The length of the sleeve sword kept her too close to him. The point of it remained over his heart, pressing firmly against flesh without breaking skin. He seemed unafraid. She, by contrast, was suddenly very afraid. Not of him, but rather the skip of her pulse.

'It is customary for disciples to take on the name of their *shifu*,' he continued, as if they were conversing over tea. 'Wen Zhong is the name of a renowned master of the Wudang sword style and rumoured to be a disciple of the Sword Immortal. I wondered if he was the one who trained you.'

'I told you, I have no master. Why won't you be done with it?'

'I'm—' He appeared troubled. 'I'm curious about you.'

She didn't quite know how to take that, but her stomach fluttered as his dark eyes moved over her. 'For someone with the sword skills of a butcher, you seem to have much interest in the martial world.'

'Even a butcher can appreciate an artist. I have respect for the old sword masters.'

Her master had chosen a solitary life of study and meditation which had been interrupted when he found her abandoned in the wilderness. When Li Feng had left him to seek out her past, she had vowed to herself not to drag him back into the affairs of the world. With so many rebellions, any form of training was looked upon with suspicion. Many of the ancient sects continued to teach in secret, becoming protective of their techniques and passing them on to a few select pupils.

'Stay away from me,' she warned. 'And you should be careful when out in the open. There are many of the rivers and lakes who would consider it a great triumph to kill you.'

'I'll lose face if I let you go,' he said. 'My reputation is at stake.'

'You have a reputation for being a mercenary and a scoundrel!'

He shrugged. Smiled. It was said that Thief-catcher Han had friends in every town and connections in high and low places. He was relentless, a touch arrogant and charming through it all.

'You came here only to deliver that warning?' he asked.

'I don't care what happens to you, thief-catcher. You took something from me and I want it back.'

His clothes were stacked on the stool beside the tub. He reached out and searched through the folds with one hand until he found her jade pendant.

'A phoenix,' he remarked. 'Like your name.'

She kept her expression flat. 'Give it to me.'

He caressed his thumb idly over the surface, the gesture unmistakably sensual, before tossing it to her. She caught it with her left hand, still keeping her sword trained on him.

'Till next we meet,' he said softly.

'This will be the last time,' she declared.

With the jade back in her possession, Li Feng had the link she needed to search for her past. This time she wouldn't let anyone deter her, not a smooth-tongued rebel nor a relentless thief-catcher. She grabbed his clothes and threw them out the window before turning to leave.

The sword dancer disappeared after the incident at the bath house. None of his informants could locate her. A young woman travelling alone would have been easily noticed, but Li Feng didn't appear at any more jade shops or inns or any of the common hideouts for those who made their home on the road. The worst of it was she could be anywhere. The rugged terrain of the province provided a landscape of mountains and valleys where outlaws could hide away from civil authorities. It was one of the reasons his profession was so lucrative in this region.

Li Feng had spoken of the world of rivers and lakes. It was a phrase common among outlaws that referred to the forests and open land outside the government-controlled cities as well as the unspoken code this community of dissidents abided by. The rivers-and-lakes world was a place of disorder and a dangerous world for a woman. It was a dangerous world for anyone.

As a thief-catcher, Han existed at the border between civility and lawlessness. It could even be said that he had thrived in it. To track down the most notorious of criminals, he needed to venture into their domain. Yet for this case, even his underworld confidants knew nothing.

According to the official account, the heist had been carefully organised and it was suspected that there were many hands involved. Han had assumed that he would find Li Feng and, through her, he'd track down the rest of them. But Li Feng had escaped and there was no sign of any accomplices.

The odd collection of musicians and dancers that had been imprisoned along with Li Feng proved to be harmless, just as he'd originally suspected. They had told him that she was a new addition to their troupe. She was a drifter and seemed to have moved among several different sets of performers. But she was trustworthy, they insisted. When their wagon had needed repairs, Li Feng had volunteered the funds without hesitation. She had paid in silver from her own stash.

Silver. If that sort of money wasn't suspect enough,

her pointed remarks about General Wang couldn't
be ignored.

Han had no choice but to return to the place where
the theft had occurred and renew his investigation
there.

When he reached the capital city of Taining, his
search for the jade thieves proved much easier than
anticipated.

One was being readied for execution in the public square.

The prisoner was kneeling, head bowed. His face
had all but disappeared beneath a dark mask of
bruised flesh. What was left was swollen beyond
recognition. He wore a torn, stained tunic and leggings. A sizeable crowd had gathered around him.
Depending on the nature of the crime, one could
expect to hear taunts or insults from the onlookers,
but in this case, the crowd remained quiet with no
more sound than a tense murmur.

Han was surprised to see a broadsword in the executioner's hands. Beheading was a particularly cruel
punishment. It not only took the life of the accused,
but defiled his body for the afterlife.

The executioner went to stand behind the condemned man and Han moved away, leaving the
crowd behind to gawk as they would. He had witnessed one execution in his life and felt little need

to witness another. He was far enough to avoid the thud of the blade, but not far enough to miss the collective gasp of the crowd, their voices united to expel the single breath they'd held since the executioner had raised his weapon.

It wasn't the violence of death that disturbed him as much as the severity of the sentence given the crime. The code of law outlined specific punishments depending on the crime as well as the circumstances surrounding it, but sentencing was left to the discretion of the magistrate. Perhaps it was necessary to be harsh in these remote parts where lawlessness was more rampant.

Han sought out the magistrate's yamen, hoping to gain access to the case report, but he wasn't admitted much further than the front gates. He wasn't all that surprised. A thief-catcher was slightly above a peasant or a day labourer in society and his presence was tolerated by the bureaucracy as an unpleasant necessity. He did manage to locate the constable who was on duty.

'Zheng Hao Han?' the constable echoed upon introductions.

The stout, middle-aged man looked over Han's plain robe and the *dao* at his side, but gave no indication that he recognised the name.

'I am looking into the matter regarding the jade thieves,' Han began.

'Ah! One of those scoundrels was executed just today.'

'None of the others have been caught?'

'Not one. They've probably run far away by now, if they have any sense.'

'Then it was fortunate you were able to catch this one.'

The constable shook his head. 'Not I. I have enough responsibility watching over the streets of this city.'

Surprisingly, the man seemed unconcerned about what was likely the most serious crime in his jurisdiction. The constable had a duty to pursue the culprits in a timely manner. Han stepped carefully as he tried to glean more information.

The crime had actually occurred one town over, a day's travel from here. The shipment was accompanied by an armed security escort, which meant the thieves were bold enough to face trained fighters to get to the riches.

'But no sword was ever drawn,' the constable recounted. 'They crept in, overpowered the night watch, and carried away enough jade to buy a palace. No one saw anything.'

'No one was harmed? There were no injuries?' Han questioned.

'None.'

That was fortunate, for the sword dancer's sake.

'I had heard that the main suspects were a group of performers.'

'Dancers and musicians!' The constable sniffed sceptically. 'They were drifters who were passing through. Easy to lay the blame on them.'

'You had mentioned that you were not involved in the arrest.'

'It was General Wang's men that caught him.' The constable shook his head. 'Unfortunate fellow.'

Han bowed and thanked the constable. He was a stranger to this city, with no prior established contacts. So his next step was to visit the local tavern to make a few friends. There he learned a few details not in the report. Wang had a bounty for any man who recovered the jade or reported the thieves. The general had also sent several squadrons through the city as well as to adjacent towns to search for the stolen goods.

On the third cup of wine, two soldiers entered the tavern and came directly to his table. 'General Wang looks forward to meeting the famous thief-catcher in person.'

Apparently the constable *had* recognised him. Han glanced up at the soldiers, who stood grim-faced and fully equipped with armour and weapons.

'When?' he asked.

'Now.'

Han downed his drink in one swallow and stood.

He was brought to a pleasure house, a two-storey establishment lit with red lanterns and filled with music. The sound of female laughter rang from inside, like the chiming of bells. There were soldiers at the front entrance and more flanking the door to the banquet room. The entire building appeared to have been cleared out except for the general's men.

Wang Shizhen was seated at a low table speaking with a handful of his lieutenants. He was dressed in a sumptuously embroidered robe. His shoulders were as broad as an ox's and the lower half of his face was covered with a thick beard. He looked up and grinned as Han entered.

'The famous thief-catcher!'

Wang was, on first glance, a much livelier and cheerful man than Han had expected. It immediately put him on guard.

'General Wang.' Han set palm to fist and bowed in proper deference.

'Sit.' The warlord spoke louder than he needed to be heard. He was a large man with gestures equally large. He rapped the spot at the table beside him and his lieutenants immediately shifted aside and took their leave.

A courtesan with painted lips bent to pour Han a cup of wine. Another moved to refill the general's cup. Then they similarly receded to the edge of the room. Everything and everyone seemed to recede in the general's presence.

'I hear you've been trying to catch these jade thieves,' Wang said.

'I haven't met any success, unfortunately. Not as successful as the general.'

He laughed at that. 'You are one person. I have all the men under my command to seek out these scoundrels.'

'It seems such a trivial task for a man of your stature.' It took some effort for Han to navigate the web of flattery and humility that defined official discourse. If things had been different, he would have been educated in poetry and rhetoric and become versed in such slippery conversation. As it was, he knew enough to keep from being immediately dismissed by his betters.

'It's my responsibility to maintain order in the province. Otherwise such outlaws would run rampant.'

'The accused didn't reveal any of his accomplices?'

'Not a one. Surprisingly strong-willed, for a common criminal.' He drank, obviously displeased to have to report failure.

Han recalled the bruises on the face of the accused. The man had been beaten and broken before he was executed. The thought of Li Feng ending up in the general's custody left Han cold.

'If I may be so bold—' Han had to be careful here. Men like Wang Shizhen didn't tolerate their authority being questioned. 'I was surprised that the magistrate would decide on a sentence of death for theft.'

'Well, it was an extraordinary amount of treasure that was stolen. And there was no need for a tribunal when the outcome was obvious. The thief had the stolen jade on him.'

Han nodded slowly. He even lifted his cup to mirror Wang's gesture and drank in accordance.

'If you ever need a position, you come to me,' Wang offered, happy with drink. 'I can use a warrior like you. These bandits are getting out of control, attacking boats and raiding our supplies.'

'That is very generous of the general,' Han replied, keeping his tone neutral.

He waited with fists clenched until he could finally disengage himself. Han exited the drinking house into the cool evening. The streets were quiet with Wang's men scattered here and there as they patrolled the corners. As far as he'd seen, the soldiers far outnumbered the civilians in the city.

Justice was meant to be dispensed with a balance of forcefulness and restraint. The proper procedure required careful inquiry and evidence. Han knew that there were repercussions for officials who neglected their duties just as there were punishments prescribed for criminals who disobeyed the laws. It was clear that the local magistrate had lost control of the district—or had had control wrested from him.

The conversation with Li Feng came back to him. Was there any difference between Two Dragon Lo and a man like Wang Shizhen?

There was no denying that Wang was a power-hungry warlord. He ruled over the county without any adherence to the codes of government. His garrison, who was supposed to protect the citizens, was instead used to intimidate them. And General Wang continued to recruit more men to its ranks. His power had grown to the point that the civil government had no control over him.

Han might be a thief-catcher by profession, but his father had held an appointed office at one time. There was no crime worse than the abuse of power. A common bandit might steal a sack of grain or a string of coins from an individual, but a dishonest bureaucrat stole from the entire population.

The authorities here would be no further help. If Han wanted the truth, he would have to seek it elsewhere and he had the urge to leave this place before the taint of corruption reached its infected and withered hand out to him.

It was impossible for Han to gain access to the official report, if any report was ever taken. Instead he relied on the unofficial account from the locals.

The man that Wang Shizhen had executed had been a labourer who had been found with a jade bracelet hidden in his room. Despite rigorous interrogation, he had neither revealed the location of the other missing pieces, nor the names of his accomplices. The other labourers in the man's tenement said he kept to himself.

Han recalled that the constable had mentioned that a *biaoju,* an armed-escort service, had been hired to guard the shipment. Apparently, the outfit had been hired out of Nanping. He joined up with a merchant who was headed there and arrived at the headquarters three days later.

The signboard over the doorway read 'Zhao Yen Security' and the walls in the main room were conspicuously decorated with an array of swords, crossbows and other weapons.

'Thief-catcher Han,' the head man acknowledged after introductions.

'Sharpshooter Zhao.'

Zhao laughed. They fell into the easy camaraderie of weaponkind, but Zhao's expression darkened when the jade heist was mentioned.

'We were en route. The shipment was secured in one of our storehouses—we use them for very important cargo. The thieves bypassed the outer guard patrol and broke in.'

'They took the shipment without a fight?'

Zhao took some offence at that. 'We had two guards stationed inside. Wu and Lin are strong fellows. Both trained fighters. They claimed the thieves materialised like ghosts, black as night as they dropped from the rafters. Now my fellows wouldn't admit this easily, but they were disarmed and overpowered before they could sound any alert.'

The thieves would have had the element of surprise as well as the advantage of launching an attack from higher ground.

'This was why acrobats were suspected,' Han remarked.

'There was a troupe passing through town. The authorities figured with their skills, they might have been able to scale the walls and enter through the roof.' Zhao rubbed at his neck, embarrassed. 'I told the constable he was mistaken. No bunch of performers could defeat my men. These thieves were highly skilled and quite deadly.'

Han excused the man's flair for the dramatic. Of course Zhao would have to insist that the band of thieves that overpowered his security force possessed extraordinary powers. He was at risk of losing face.

'Do you have a record of everything in the shipment?' Han asked.

'It's in the manifest.' Zhao went behind the counter and rifled through a drawer, finally producing a scroll which he handed over.

Han scanned the list of valuables. Jade and gold, assessed at a value equalling a hundred bolts of silk. Among the items was a set of three carved pendants. Three was an odd number for such a set. The classic grouping was usually four. Han read through the descriptions: dragon, tiger, tortoise.

Also notable was the lack of any jade bracelets.

'Your record keeper does good work,' Han commented.

Zhao nodded with a grunt. 'This is a serious business. We're more than just another band of rabble carrying clubs.'

With the rise of bandits and outlaws, the armed-escort business was flourishing along with the thief-catching business. Too many undisciplined warriors about with no wars to fight.

The scroll contained additional information. The names of the sender and the recipient. Both go-betweens.

'I suspect the final recipient was likely Wang Shizhen,' Zhao said.

Han concurred. The general certainly had a great interest in recovering the stolen goods. The person who had enlisted Zhao's services was a man by the name of Cai Yun. Why would an individual from another prefecture send so much wealth to General Wang?

There was definitely something more than a simple theft at work here and somehow Li Feng was entangled in it. He sincerely wished that she wasn't. Han had come across some of the worst outlaws and Li Feng didn't belong among them. Despite her talk of rebellion, she was motivated by honour and self-sacrifice. Why else would she give up her own silver to assist others? Or reach out to rescue a thief-catcher who would turn around and make life difficult for her?

'Do you know anything more about this Cai Yun?' Han asked.

'He paid in advance and appeared well off. He's petitioning for us to forfeit our fee as well as incur an additional dishonour penalty for failure to deliver.'

Zhao cursed a little. Han gave his sympathies.

'It's unusual to see a thief-catcher so dedicated,' Zhao said. 'They say you've never let a criminal get away.'

That was a new addition to his ever-growing story. 'I do what I can,' he replied humbly.

'Hmmph. Find these thieves and I'll add to your capture money. The penalty on such a shipment would bleed us dry.'

Han left the headquarters with the name of the man who had hired the security escort, but few answers otherwise. Li Feng was more than capable of the feat Zhao had described. He'd seen her leaping on to rooftops and if she could deftly slip out of locked buildings, she could just as easily sneak into them. That information by itself wasn't enough to condemn her.

There was only one piece of evidence that connected her to the crime—though it appeared she had been telling the truth about it. The four celestial animals were a popular motif in artwork: the Green Dragon, the White Tiger, and the Black Tortoise. The final animal in the quartet was the Vermilion Bird. It looked very much like a phoenix.

# Chapter Five

The lanterns of the Pavilion of the Singing Nightingale were always lit, night or day. The doors were always open and no matter when a visitor walked through, they were always greeted by the most elegantly dressed and graceful of ladies. The Singing Nightingale was located in a busy river port located along the Min and served as a crossroads for merchants and travelling officials.

The journey from Taining had taken a week, during which he pondered the possibilities. The thieves could have masqueraded as a dance troupe to get close to the warehouse without raising suspicion. Li Feng was certainly connected to the shipment in some way, but her pendant wasn't stolen. Han was all the more determined to pursue her just to unravel the mystery she presented.

Finally, the shipment itself was suspicious. It certainly appeared to be a bribe or payment, but for what? Hopefully his contacts in town would be able to provide more insight. Han was nearly out of leads.

According to Zhao, the head of the security escort, the jade shipment had been transported by riverboat from its origin and had changed hands at this port from the mysterious Cai Yun over to the armed guards. Fortunately, Han was familiar with the area and immediately identified the Singing Nightingale as the sort of establishment a wealthy man would visit while in town. It was a brothel with aspirations and attempted to recreate the atmosphere of refinement found in the pleasure houses of the larger cities.

Han had the honour of being greeted by the lovely and talented Lotus. In age, she was perhaps just past the height of spring, but not yet in her autumn years. She would never admit to a number in regard to her age and Han had politely never asked.

Lotus still remained one of the leading beauties of the pavilion and served as hostess for the wealthiest and most distinguished of patrons. In Han's case, neither applied. Lotus liked hearing dramatic tales of adventures and villains and heroes. Han always thought she enjoyed his company for that reason—though Lotus had made a lifelong profession out of convincing men she sincerely enjoyed their company.

'Zheng Hao Han.' Her fine silk robe brushed

against him as she took his arm. A light cloud of perfume encircled him. She was all that was soft and feminine and elegant as she led him into a sitting area. 'It's been so long, I was certain you had forgotten about me.'

Her tone was mildly reproachful, but it was all part of the game. He apologised and professed that he could never forget her while the attendants brought wine and small dishes of boiled peanuts, scallion cakes and other refreshments.

'What can you tell me about a man named Cai Yun? I already know he's been here,' he prompted as he detected the slight flicker in her expression as she considered his request.

Lotus pursed her lips prettily. 'Will you say nice things about me?' she bargained.

'Of course.'

'A man by that name has visited on occasion. Well dressed, well mannered. He seems to have money, but doesn't brag too much about it.' The courtesan paused and shot him a sly look. 'Very nice things?' she insisted.

Newfound fame had its benefits. 'You'll be notorious.'

She leaned in close, most likely so he could be ensnared by the sight of her graceful neck and the low cut of her bodice. 'He seems to always be meeting with rather important-looking men. Merchants and the local official of this or that.'

'Is this Cai Yun an aristocrat of some sort?' That would explain the wealth and Lotus had an instinct for pouncing on such patrons.

She shook her head. A pearl ornament in her hair danced as she did so. 'He has no name that I know of,' she said coyly. 'But one of his guests last month was someone noteworthy.'

He gave her an equally coy look. 'Who could that be?'

'The agent overseeing the district branch of the Salt Commission.'

That bit of information sparked his thief-catcher instinct immediately. The Salt Commission controlled the buying and selling of salt throughout the empire, managing the prices and taxes on it through countless offices. Agents travelled into even the most remote locations of the empire to enforce the commission's policies. The salt trade and its taxes were a significant source of revenue for the government, and consequently spawned an entire underworld of illegal activity. Han had apprehended his share of salt smugglers.

Lotus draped an arm casually around his neck. 'Now tell me what evil deed he committed to warrant your attention.'

She was so close that she was nearly in his lap,

all because she *genuinely* liked him, of course. Despite the flirtation, Han knew he was unlikely to be invited into Lotus's bedchamber. She was very selective about her lovers, enjoying the attentions of notable scholars and officials. They were friendly enough, however, that he was able to take hold of her chin to direct her eyes to his. He wanted a clear view of her expression for his next enquiry.

'When I first mentioned Cai Yun, you looked surprised. As if you'd encountered some coincidence.'

She tried to look innocent now. 'What do you mean?'

A silhouette passed by the outside of the curtain that divided the sitting room from the main hall. He wasn't able to discern much more than a shadow. Definitely not a face or distinct form. But the quality of the movement sparked something in him.

'Who was that?' he asked.

Lotus laughed lightly. 'You're trying to make me jealous, Han.'

*'Lotus.'* The one word served as admonishment and enquiry.

'The new girl.' She shrugged, handing him a cup of wine. 'There's not much to say about her.'

Lotus wasn't jealous. Han would have to be an imperial minister of the first rank to make it worthwhile for Lotus to be jealous.

'Does she dance?' he asked, his tone casual.

The courtesan smiled at him slyly. 'You are single-minded when something catches your eye, aren't you?'

'I'd like to talk to her.'

At that, Lotus tilted her head obligingly and stood. She glided from the room without any further attempt to deflect. She was as smooth as silk and cunningly accommodating. Han took his time finishing the wine before setting his cup down and following her through the curtain.

Lotus was already coming back down the main staircase. 'She isn't feeling well—'

'How caring of you.'

Heedlessly, Han moved past the courtesan and continued up towards the private chambers on the second floor. He had a certain instinct when it came to this sort of thing. The first door he opened revealed a group of scholars listening to a pipa player. He opened the second door to the sight of the 'new girl' trying to climb out the window.

Han grabbed hold of an ankle and she fell back on to the bed in a tangle of blue silk and gauze. She squirmed and struggled as he brushed aside the sleeve that had fallen over her face. He only caught a flash of dark, glittering eyes before Li Feng twisted beneath him.

She rolled on to her side and the unexpected shift in momentum threw him off of her. He'd forgotten how agile she was. With a rustle of silk, Li Feng was on top of him, her forearm shoved against his chest.

'Always you!' she seethed.

She was dressed like a courtesan, in one of those robes that appeared to be made out of paper-thin cloth and air. The silk had fallen from her shoulders, revealing smooth bare skin from her throat to the topmost swell of her breasts. It was too long of a pause before he could drag his gaze upwards. Her eyes narrowed at him, fully aware that he'd been staring at her.

He grabbed hold of her wrist and yanked, causing her to collapse over his chest. Li Feng recovered quickly and clawed at his face. From there, it became a brawl, more cat and dog than tiger and dragon. Finally, he took hold of a handful of silk and flipped her on to her back.

'I don't—' he lifted his head to avoid a swipe '—want to hurt you.'

Li Feng was breathing hard and her cheeks were flushed with colour. Her hands shot up before he could trap them. Instead of gouging his eyes out, Li Feng slipped past his guard to bury her fingers into his hair. She kept her gaze on him as she ruthlessly dragged his head down. Before Han knew what was happening, his mouth was pressed against soft, inviting lips.

His hands fell to the bed on either side of her,

his fingers curling reflexively into the bedding. She tasted of cinnamon and the faint tang of cloves. Though he was positioned over her, his weight pinning her legs, he was the one that felt trapped. This was a ploy, he told himself, while his body greedily strained against her.

Han lifted his head forcibly. 'At any moment, you're going to slit my throat,' he muttered, his voice deep with desire.

There was a glint in her eyes that was both predatory and playful. 'Perhaps.'

Her hands cradled either side of his face. She stroked his cheek and senselessly their lips were joined once again, breath against heated breath. Her body arched into him. He knew how strong Li Feng was, but right now she was perfectly pliant, moulding herself to him. All of the blood in his body rushed to his lower half. What little remained in his head told him that if he was about to die, he completely deserved it for being so stupid.

He ran his hand along her arm and another down her calf. Beneath the slide of silk, he could make out both the sword in her sleeve and a dagger beneath her skirt. As expected. Already, he knew her so well.

'You have a strange way of making love,' she said.

'We are not—' It took some effort to breathe. 'Making love.'

'But, Hao Han—'

The breathless way she spoke his name stroked like fingers down his spine. He took hold of her wrists as she started to embrace him.

He pinned her arms on either side of her head. 'Stop this.'

He was painfully hard and trying to fight it. Li Feng chuckled, pleased with herself and mocking him. She'd only been teasing apparently, which was—

'Damned stupid,' he growled. 'Any other thief-catcher would have taken advantage.'

'But you aren't any other thief-catcher. What do you think of it, Zheng Hao Han? If I seduce you, will you let me go?'

She no longer looked playful. She looked serious and it made him even angrier.

'I may find you pretty. I may even desire you, but that only strengthens my conviction that I must bring you in.'

She rolled her eyes, lips pouted. 'So honourable.'

Not so honourable. Despite his lofty speech, his body was fully aroused. Her lips were red and she was wearing that ridiculous robe that clung to her breasts and waist and made her look like a goddess floating in water. The thin layers of silk revealed too much skin and at the same time not enough. It was hardly fair.

'Justice is justice,' he gritted out.

'Well, then,' she murmured against his ear before nipping at it. Those long, strong, exquisitely shaped legs were curving around him, urging him into oblivion. 'Bed me anyway.'

Every muscle in Han's body tensed above her.

'Li Feng.' He was hoarse, his tone a warning.

'This bed is so much more comfortable than a prison cell.'

She wasn't sure why she said it. Maybe it was just an attempt to torment him further. Thief-catcher Han was so difficult to take off balance. But the jest was her own undoing because suddenly she was considering it.

Would it be so very bad? A sweet ache took hold of her. She moved her hips in a restless little circle.

Han's pupils darkened and suddenly she was crushed beneath him. He dragged her hands over her head and kissed her. Really kissed her, with his tongue stroking deep until her body heated and her limbs turned to liquid beneath him.

It wouldn't be bad at all. It would be so very good.

She knew the dangers of rushing headlong into an affair, but it was hard to heed her own warnings with Han on top of her, anchoring her so perfectly with his mouth caressing hers. For once, she didn't want to run. She wanted very much to stay.

What was his relentless pursuit of her, if not some

strange courtship? They'd fought, but he had never hurt her. And she had a sense he never would, not willingly. She admired him as a worthy foe. And after seeing him naked in the bath house, so beautifully masculine with his skin gleaming, she might have had a few dreams about how he would kiss.

He was better than the dreams.

She wanted to slip her fingers beneath his robe and stroke every line and contour she'd seen exposed in the bath house, but her hands were still trapped. She moved restlessly within his iron grip.

'Let go,' she urged softly.

'If I release you, you're going to do something to me and it's going to hurt.'

She wanted to laugh. She wanted to devour him. 'What if I promise not to?'

*'Li Feng.'* His voice was rough, with an urgency that made her shiver.

He kept her trapped as he kissed her nose, her chin, the hollow of her throat. His mouth sank to the line of her bodice. His lips closed on the area just over her nipple and the scrape of his teeth through the cloth made her arch up desperately against him.

Maybe this was worth prison. She could just escape again…later.

Han went still and she realised she'd spoken aloud. He laid his forehead against her breast and gradually lowered his hands from her wrists. It was a silent and momentary truce and she wasn't quite certain what to do with it.

After many heartbeats, Han spoke. 'We must have known each other in a former life. Fate keeps on bringing us together.'

'We keep on meeting because you keep hunting me down,' she said with a scowl.

He lifted his head and gave her a look that bordered on fondness. The grin transformed his rough features into something delightfully compelling, almost wicked. Her skin flushed and heat pooled in her belly. His smile did more to disarm her than the kiss.

'What are you looking for, Wen Li Feng?' he asked, completely serious.

For just a moment between them, all pretence was gone. 'There is something I need to find out. Something that happened a long time ago.'

She was no longer trying to torment or seduce him, though his weight did feel unforgivably wonderful over her. She hated being trapped or confined, but she felt none of that fear as he held her now. There was almost a familiarity to it. A strange comfort in Han's strength and his control over it.

'I went to Taining,' he said. 'What you said about Wang Shizhen being a tyrant might be true, but that doesn't absolve you of guilt.'

A thief-catcher to the bone. She wriggled out of his

grasp and Han let her go without a struggle. Once again, she had been fooled by the natural pull of yin and yang. They weren't friends. They weren't anything, though she was disturbed to find she missed the feel of his arms around her. Just a little.

'What do *you* want, Hao Han? No thief-catcher works this hard to chase a warrant.'

'To know the truth. I know your pendant wasn't part of the heist.'

'It was given to me.'

'By whom?'

'It doesn't matter,' she insisted.

But it did. *Don't cry,* her mother had pleaded. Li Feng wouldn't surrender the memory of their last moments together over to him. He was nothing but a man whom she had found intriguing two seconds ago.

Her irrational attraction to danger had got the best of her again. No matter how much she liked the look of him, she had to remember that Han was still a bastard thief-catcher and she couldn't trust him. The momentary feeling of being close to someone, of feeling secure, was an illusion. She should know that after her disastrous affair with Bao Yang.

She straightened. Her sword was in quick reach if he made any movement towards her. 'It seems our truce is over.'

'One of the jade thieves was caught last week,' he told her. 'He was beheaded.'

She stopped cold. 'Beheaded?'

Li Feng started away from him, but was only able to move as far as the other side of the bed. She wanted to believe that she was afraid of nothing, but it was far from true. Her pulse pounded and the urge to run took hold of her.

'It was General Wang,' he said.

She hadn't stolen the jade out of greed or even out of necessity. None of them had. The theft was one act in a string of minor attacks against the warlord. The main goal was to disrupt Wang Shizhen's activities to keep him from seizing more power within the province.

The danger hadn't seemed real until that moment. At the time, the heist had seemed a grand challenge and that angry part inside of her had wanted to strike out at something to make up for all that had been taken from her.

At one time, she had believed deeply in the cause, but it was no longer her battle. Bao Yang, the leader of the rebels, had drawn her into his cause with his lethal charm. She regretted becoming so involved now.

Han watched her reaction. 'There was someone else at the head of it, wasn't there? If you were misguided or coerced—'

With every word and every action, he was testing her. She needed to understand where exactly they stood with one another.

'Are you still pursuing me over the jade?' she demanded.

'I'm interested in much more than that, Miss Wen,' he replied, keeping his eyes locked on hers.

She gave him an evil-eye at the double meaning. 'Scoundrel.'

The corner of his mouth twitched.

They were interrupted by a booming voice in the front hall. Footsteps marched downstairs. Han moved to the door and opened it just a crack before returning to her.

'Wang Shizhen's men,' he reported.

She glared at him. 'You brought them here!'

'I didn't—'

She was at the window without another word. The street below was clear and Li Feng let herself drop down, landing with knees bent and rolling on to her shoulder to absorb the impact. A moment later, the thief-catcher landed with a thud beside her, not quite as softly. She waited until he straightened, then sent a throwing knife sailing past his ear.

Han flung himself aside as the blade embedded itself into the post behind him. He stared at it, then back at her. 'She-demon!'

'I spared your life, thief-catcher. You owe me,' she said.

He frowned at her. 'What sort of logic is that?'

Overhead, soldiers tore through the pavilion, searching for her.

'Don't follow me,' she warned, backing away.

'If General Wang catches you, he won't be concerned about justice.'

'Then I won't get caught.'

There was no more time for talk. With a running start, she scaled the wall behind them and caught the edge with a hand to pull herself up on top of it. The manoeuvre was a little more difficult with the drag of the courtesan's robe, but she managed it. She crouched at the top and glanced back down at Han.

Scaling a city wall was a punishable offence. A single shout and Han could have the night watchmen and Wang's soldiers chasing after her. But he didn't sound the alert. He stood his ground and watched her with a grim expression.

Li Feng leapt from the wall, her feet landing deftly on the packed dirt of the alleyway. She continued through the city, slipping through spaces, finding handholds and footholds in hidden corners. Her movement was like water, shifting around and over obstacles, finding a path where others saw none. The ancient texts spoke *qing gong,* lightness training, but it had less to do with being as light as air than a sure-footedness that came from strength, balance and endless practice.

The silk of her robe rustled around her as she ran. There was freedom here, in the constant flow of motion. More freedom than she'd ever found in the open, quiet landscape of the mountains. She was walking on walls and flying over eaves, putting more distance between her and Han.

Thief-catchers were notoriously a corrupt lot, easy to deflect with bribes. Zheng Hao Han may be one of those rare men of honour and conviction, but she still couldn't trust him. He spoke of justice and truth, but for her, justice could only be found through the edge of a blade.

## Chapter Six

Memories were fragile and fickle things. There were minute details she remembered very clearly, insignificant as they were. Her hair had been tied in two little pigtails. The thread in her sleeve had come loose. It unravelled into a ragged edge that grew damp from all the times she'd wiped her nose across it. She remembered tripping and scraping her knee against rock in the dirt path. She remembered Mother having to pick her up and carry her.

Other details were hazy, as if seen through a veil of smoke. There were trees, hills, the sky was grey. She could sense that Mother was afraid, so she was afraid too. She couldn't remember if she'd ever seen the men who were chasing them. Perhaps she'd just recreated them in her own mind, making them more awful and fearsome in the years to come.

Wen *shifu* had told her about the mountain path he'd been travelling when he found her. When Li Feng had first returned to the province, she had gone to a place that seemed to fit both her fragmented memories and his description. There were trees, there were hills. The sky that day was blue, not grey.

She had even found an opening in the hillside, too high up for a small child to reach on her own. The crevice looked small and desolate and dark, but just large enough for a little girl to crawl inside and curl herself up into a ball while she waited for her mother to return. Li Feng had reached her hand inside the rock and closed her eyes. She wanted to believe that it was the place and by somehow coming back there, she could connect herself with what had happened in the past and, through it, what had happened afterwards.

When she opened her eyes, there were no answers for her. So she'd left the hillside to continue her search. She felt the same way now, her hand grasping for the past to have it disappear like smoke. She would listen to names of people and places and hope that one of them would contain the answers she longed for.

She was standing on the riverbank now, at a tiny river crossing waiting for a ferry. After escaping the brothel, she'd remained close to the river, navigating downstream according to the directions the courtesan Lotus had provided.

When Li Feng had arrived at the Singing Nightingale, Lotus poured tea for her and was eager for her story. The courtesan had a way of putting her at ease and Li Feng spoke of the jade pendant and her search for her parents as if they were long-lost sisters. Lotus had also been taken away from her parents at a young age.

'The family was poor. They needed the money,' she explained, though Li Feng caught the pang of wistfulness that crossed the courtesan's otherwise tranquil face.

Lotus went on to tell Li Feng of a man named Cai Yun who was the owner of the jade. Li Feng repeated the name to herself as a sampan boat floated across the river towards her. Had this man known her mother?

'Is there a settlement on the other side?' she asked the ferryman when the boat came to shore.

'There is a village up in the hills near the salt works.'

Li Feng thanked the man and handed him a copper coin before stepping into the sampan. The vessel had a long flat keel that sat low in the water. There was one other passenger on board who sat hunched at the back. His robe was dark in colour and a wide conical straw hat shielded his face from the sun. She went to stand before him.

'I don't need to see your face to recognise you,' she said drily.

The man lifted his head, two fingers pushing back the brim of the hat to reveal the rough square cut of his jaw. The sight of his familiar face made her heart skip. She was starting to expect these meetings between them, even to the point of looking forward to them. She had no sense, no sense at all, and deserved to be caught.

'It seems we are currently on the same path,' Han said as his gaze moved over her from head to toe. 'No longer wearing silk?'

Li Feng swallowed. Did she detect a hint of disappointment? She was dressed once again in her shortened tunic and leggings, her hair pinned in a simple knot. The grey, peasant colour allowed her to disappear in a crowd and the loose fit and shorter length allowed her to move quickly should she need to flee. She considered whether she should flee now.

'We are both looking for the same man. A man known as Cai Yun,' he continued.

'Why are you interested in him?'

'Because you are.'

She shot him a curious look.

'I sense there is some underhanded dealing here. If there's any corruption involved, I intend to uncover it.'

'You're no longer intent on bringing me before a tribunal?'

'I didn't say that.'

At least he wasn't trying to clamp irons on to her at the moment. If she knew nothing else about Han, she was certain he wouldn't resort to trickery to ensnare her, unlike some of her former acquaintances.

The ferryman dipped his pole into the river and Li Feng seated herself beside him, though maintaining a cautious distance. The sampan slowly floated away from the bank and into the current. The sun was at its highest point and reflected off the dark water.

'Why are you helping me?' she asked, lifting a hand to her eyes to shield them from the brightness.

'I'm not helping you,' he insisted. 'I just figured it might benefit both of us to combine our efforts... for now.'

Han untied the cord at his neck and took off the hat, holding it out to her. She stared at his outstretched hand. It was a kind gesture, done without any second thought. The man before her was very different from the Thief-catcher Han she had battled with several weeks ago. Not that Han had ever treated her with any cruelty. The connection between them had just changed so subtly. And there was no denying that they were connected, whether she wanted them to be or not.

'Thank you,' she mumbled, taking the hat from him.

'My father always insisted that one should not

aim to prove the guilt or innocence of the accused,' he said. 'Rather one should strive to seek the truth.'

'Was your father a thief-catcher as well?' she asked.

'No.' He was taken aback by her assumption. 'He was a county magistrate—at one time.'

A magistrate? As far as she knew, sons of magistrates didn't become thief-catchers. It was a lowly, dangerous and somewhat unsavoury profession.

The wide brim provided shade, but it also allowed her to take a long, hard look at him without seeming so forward. The sunlight washed directly over him. His skin was bronze in tone, darkened from many days out in the sun. Scholars and aristocrats tended towards paleness, but Han had the complexion and demeanour of a rugged and world-toughened individual, someone who had braved the elements and much, much worse.

The revelation did explain some oddities about Han. He'd always seemed overly dedicated to justice for a thief-catcher. The way he carried himself also set him apart from the other people of the street and now she knew the reason was his cultured upbringing. Along with training how to fight, he must have also studied. A combination of action and thought would make a formidable opponent.

'I still don't know how you were able to get Lotus to help you,' he said.

She shrugged. 'Men always talk about brother-hood among fighting men—why wouldn't there be sisterhood among women? Lotus saw that I was alone in the world and wanted to help. She has no particular loyalty to Cai Yun…or to you.'

Han stopped to consider it. 'Who is this Cai Yun to you?' he asked finally.

She stared at the patterns dancing over the water. The motion of the waves were disordered and chaotic. 'If I only knew myself.'

Han had proposed that they combine their efforts. Regardless of her training, it was dangerous out on the road alone. She was constantly seeking out shelter and finding fellow travellers, whether they were merchants or pilgrims or migrant labourers, to share the journey with. Out in the wilderness, she could hide away from danger, but she would be venturing into a salt farm and a village without knowing whether she would meet up with friend or foe. Han's strength and his skill with weapons seemed very desirable.

Perhaps desirable was not quite how she wanted to describe him.

She had no doubt he would drag her to the magistrate once he determined her guilt, but for now she needed an ally.

'I need to find out what happened to my mother,' she told him, never looking away despite how difficult it was for her to share this part of her. 'She was taken away by men with swords. The jade pendant is the one thing I have that belonged to her. I never saw her again.'

Han grew quiet, giving her admission its proper respect.

'How old were you?' he asked finally.

'Three.' She had asked herself the same question many times. 'Maybe four.'

She looked to the furthest shore. They were at a point in the middle of the river where it seemed they weren't moving at all, just drifting along without any progress in any direction.

'Wen *shifu* found me and took me to the foothills of Mount Wudang. It was a quiet, open place. He was a recluse, one of those Taoist masters intent on seeking immortality through meditation. Every day, he would commune with nature and reflect on the mysteries of heaven and earth, but all I could think about was those final moments with Mother.'

Duty to one's parents was a law that transcended both the world of rivers and lakes and the cities. Her entire purpose in life revolved around this one memory.

Li Feng had held on to the jade pendant. At the time, the carving had filled both her hands. Her mother had told her not to cry, but she did cry. Silently, as she waited for Mother to return for her.

'I have made up so many different stories of how she and I came to that hillside. I've learned that this jade is quite valuable and we weren't rich. There was a reason men were chasing after us... Perhaps she stole it.' Her mouth tightened with a forced smile. 'A tiger mother begets a tiger daughter, after all.'

It was an ill attempt at humour. There was no judgement in Han's expression as he regarded her, but he was very good at masking his emotions.

She breathed deeply and met his gaze without wavering. 'I know the story may not end well, but I need to know. But more than fifteen years has passed. There may be nothing left to find.'

'Everything we do, all that we touch, leaves a trace,' he said, sounding more like a philosopher than a hardened thief-catcher. 'We have knowledge that has survived from the first dynasty, over a thousand years ago. Fifteen years is not so long a time.'

They disembarked at the other side of the river and followed the dirt path that wound up through surrounding hills.

'The workers likely use this to transport the salt to the river to be loaded on to boats,' Han said.

Li Feng walked beside him. Even in the heat and on uneven ground, her step was light. It was the first time they moved together towards the same destination as opposed to one of them chasing the other.

The woods thickened around them as they travelled further away from the water. Soon the river was no longer in sight and they were surrounded by a dense growth of trees that blocked the sun, providing relief from the afternoon heat. Li Feng slowed as a bamboo wall appeared at the top of a hill.

'Soldiers,' she announced, slipping off the path.

Han followed her as she wove through the trees. Though it was unknown territory, she still moved with a confidence that enchanted him. He might have chosen to approach the gate directly if he was alone, but in this instance he was willing to follow Li Feng's instinct and remain hidden.

She stopped beneath a tree and looked up through the branches. The old roots crawled along the ground, twining up and over themselves like a nest of snakes. Apparently Li Feng saw what she was looking for because she ran a few steps up the trunk and grabbed on to the lowest branch. She swung herself on to it, stood and reached for the next one with the deftness of a golden monkey. In no time at all she was perched high above the ground.

He began his climb, which progressed much slower. Li Feng seated herself among the branches to watch him. She offered him her hand as he came near, but he had his pride. That, and he wasn't quite ready to release his grip on the tree.

'You never climbed trees as a child,' she observed.

'We grew up in the city.' He pressed his boot against a sturdy-looking branch and tested his weight against it before lowering himself down.

Li Feng had her legs straddled on either side of the branch. Her posture was relaxed, as if she didn't have any bones to break should she drop to the ground. He leaned back against the trunk and kept a hand on a branch overhead to keep steady.

'We?' she asked, completely casual and conversational. 'You have brothers and sisters?'

'One younger brother.'

The question, though simple, was quite personal. He rarely spoke of his family to anyone. Somehow he knew not to ask her the same as she nodded and turned back towards the view of the salt works.

There was an entire encampment inside the confines of the fence. Several towering rigs of bamboo had been constructed around the wells. A counterweight mechanism was used to pound a drill deep within the well, forcing brine water up to the surface where it was drained and collected in vats to be boiled down. The resulting sludge was spread out in shallow flats to be dried out by the sun. They could see workers collecting the white salt into buckets.

'A lot of guards at the gate,' Li Feng commented. He wondered if she was counting the guards and measuring the height of the bamboo wall.

'Local militia. Smuggling is a constant problem

at these outposts.' He had been assigned to similar watches in his youth. 'The guards are also needed to keep the work lines in order. Many of the labourers are convicted criminals sentenced to servitude.'

'As I might be...if the judge is merciful.' She glanced sideways at him. Her smile was syrupy sweet and sharp at the edges.

He should let her go. They would go their separate ways. As certain as he was of her guilt, he was also certain she hadn't stolen for greed or gain. That didn't negate the crime, but there were more dangerous criminals to capture.

Something inside him wasn't willing to turn away yet. He couldn't honestly discern whether he was here for the sake of truth and justice or because he wanted to see her again.

'Li Feng—' The words, whatever they were going to be, got caught in his throat and were lost.

'Don't worry. It won't be easy to capture me,' she taunted.

'I look forward to the chase.'

There was a group of men at the main building. Han crept forwards on the branch to get an unobstructed view. Li Feng did the same.

He pointed out the man wearing a blue robe. 'The tall one could be him.' Lotus had given him a description of a man of around forty years of age.

'Who is that beside him?'

'From the uniform and headdress, he's likely the agent from the Salt Commission.'

Lotus had spoken of private meetings between Cai Yun and the official from the Commission which had immediately made him suspicious. Corruption was rampant within the bureaucracy surrounding the salt trade.

The two men spoke briefly to the foreman before heading to the gate where the guards let them out. At the same time, a group of men entered the compound with a wagon laden with supplies.

'Provisions from the nearby village,' he concluded. 'It wouldn't be too difficult to get inside…if one were inclined.'

He had caught his share of salt smugglers and had learned a few of their tricks.

'Thief-catcher Han, are you planning an illicit activity?'

He turned to her. Her eyes were large in her face and alight with mischief. She was very, very close and her lips were curved in a smile that was both teasing and sensual.

'Only with you,' he replied.

Her eyes narrowed speculatively on him. They were dangling in mid-air, but she might very well be worth the fall.

A few hours later, they sat in the tea house in the adjacent village. An arrangement of dishes had been fanned out between them. Han watched as Li Feng plucked a morsel from each one into her rice bowl, wooden chopsticks flying.

'What is this?' She lifted a cut of meat from a pool of brown sauce.

'Snake,' he replied.

With a lift of her eyebrows, Li Feng placed the bite into her mouth. She chewed carefully before grabbing a few more pieces of snake into her bowl. Then she began to eat in earnest.

'You have a healthy appetite.'

'With Wen *shifu,* I ate rice and pickled vegetables every day,' she said between bites. 'Everything tastes so good in comparison. Besides, you never know when you'll need the strength to outrun someone.'

He turned his chopsticks over and selected a few items on to his rice before turning the sticks back to eat. Li Feng watched him, amused.

'What is it?'

'Even if you hadn't told me you were the son of a public officer, I would have guessed it from watching you eat.' She straightened her back and squared her shoulders to illustrate the point. 'You know there are places where your manners alone would single you out for trouble.'

'I can act the vagabond when needed,' he insisted. 'But I'm in the presence of a lady.'

That seemed to please her. She took a few dainty bites for show, glancing at him for approval. It was impossible not to smile.

The village was a secluded and tight community, though not unwelcoming to strangers. They saw a trickle of visitors from the salt activity as well as the occasional traveller stopping by due to the location near the river.

In the short time they had been there, Han had already found out that Cai Yun was not a local and that he and the agent were staying at the village headman's house.

'Our mysterious friend is likely involved in the salt trade. It's not difficult to guess why a wealthy merchant would send such an extravagant cargo to Wang Shizhen. It could be a bribe.'

'Or Wang could have bullied it out of him.'

He fixed his gaze on her. 'Why would you...would anyone steal so much jade if no one cared to profit from it?'

She shrugged. 'Perhaps so that warlord wouldn't have it.'

It was the most direct answer he'd got from her. Han had already given up trying to get Li Feng to reveal her accomplices. Loyalty meant everything to people who lived by the sword. He found it difficult to think of her that way. She lacked the hard-edged desperation of an outlaw on the fringe of civilisation. Li Feng had been raised outside the confines of society, as a child of the mountains and the open road. His own upbringing had been one of structure and discipline.

'We're outside Wang's domain,' Han said. 'This conspiracy spans across two separate prefectures. There's something underhanded at work here.'

'A much greater crime than the theft of, say, a few pieces of jade?'

Must she keep reminding him? Li Feng might be a talented thief, but she was far from a clever one if she wanted to evade capture.

'There is no such thing as an insignificant crime.' His father's words reached through the years to take control of him. 'Let's take, for example, the stealing of a horse. You may think it nothing, but for most families, a horse is their greatest asset and crucial to their livelihood. He is the only way they can take their goods to market or travel from city to city. They made sacrifices for that horse, buying and feeding and caring for it, sacrifices that you did not make.'

'But it was a state-owned horse,' she countered. 'One can say I was performing a spiritual service by releasing it from burden. Like freeing birds on festival days to promote good karma.'

'If one was attempting a very corrupted line of reasoning.'

Like his own faulty logic regarding Li Feng, a known thief with a dubious sense of morality.

'What did you do with that horse?' he asked as an afterthought.

'I gave it to a farmer.' She reached to put more food in her bowl. 'So he could care for it and feed it and take his crops to market.'

Han frowned at her while Li Feng continued eating, oblivious. When she glanced up, his arms were folded over his chest as he regarded her. He couldn't tell whether she was mocking him or telling the truth.

'You should have become a magistrate,' she commented, taking in his stern expression. 'Thieves would tremble before you.'

He relented and resumed the meal. As fast as she was with her chopsticks, he was going to end the night hungry if he didn't put up a good fight.

'Why didn't you pursue an office like your father?' she asked once the dishes were empty.

'It's not so easy being an official. There are studies and then the local exams, the provincial exams, the imperial exams in the capital to become *jinshi*. After that, one must catch the attention of the right people to get an appointment—'

Li Feng was leaning towards him, hanging on every word. He could see from the glaze in her eyes that much of it was foreign to her, yet she made an earnest effort to try to take it all in.

'I proved to be a very poor scholar,' he concluded, cutting his explanation short.

'How so?'

'Well, once for my daily lessons, I wrote out a single line that read, "I do not want to be a high ranking official".'

She choked back a laugh behind her tea cup. 'What happened then?'

'I was promptly beaten by my tutor. Twenty-five times with a bamboo switch. And when my father came home, I was beaten again. You like that, do you? Hearing about my suffering?'

Li Feng was laughing outright now. The laughter lit up her entire face and the sound of it wrapped around him and puffed out his chest. They were drinking tea, but he felt as if he were filled with wine, his spirits were so lifted.

As much as she challenged and teased him, she was an easy companion. Even when they were fighting, he felt more alive when she was around. It didn't make any sense.

He had grown silent without realising it. Li Feng was watching him curiously, so he lifted the teapot to refill her cup. It gave him something to do.

'You like me,' she said into the awkward lull in the conversation. 'But you don't want to.'

There was nothing to say to that so he drank his tea while her eyes continued to dance over him. He was not so easily lured by a pretty face, yet he was more than lured by her. He was utterly charmed.

He had liked Two Dragon Lo as well, when they had been drinking as strangers in a remote tavern much like this one. Had he been among outlaws for so long that he was starting to find kinship with bandits and thieves? This life in the grey border between civility and disorder was starting to become a new home to replace the one that he had left behind. Never was he in more danger of losing his way.

# Chapter Seven

The tavern doubled as an inn, or rather there was an area in the loft over the main room that the tavern keeper offered to them. Li Feng sat waiting inside the tiny enclosure while Han dealt with particulars downstairs.

The space couldn't quite be called a room. There was no door, only a passageway through which two wide and curious eyes were watching her. A little boy gripped the entrance with one small hand and peered inside, revealing the top of his head to the tip of his nose. Large brown eyes blinked at her.

'Ping!'

The boy went running downstairs at the sound of his father's voice just as Han appeared.

'I think he likes me,' she said.

The keeper's wife had brought a bamboo mat and an oil lamp before leaving them to their privacy. Han had fashioned a quick tale around them being a man and wife returning to his hometown. As much as she'd travelled, trading one set of companions for another, she was rarely alone with someone, let alone a man. It wasn't hard to imagine herself a young woman waiting for her husband and feeling the same hitch of anticipation in her chest as Han stood by the entrance.

He pulled off his boots and left them outside. Then he entered and settled on the opposite side of the mat, which wasn't far given the tight confines of the enclosure. Looking around, he stashed his weapon, which had been bundled in cloth, against the wall. He had hidden his *dao* before they had entered the village. The sight of it would immediately identify him either as a mercenary or some other form of rough character that would raise suspicion. She kept her own sword hidden beneath her sleeve for that reason.

'We'll try to find out more about our friend tomorrow,' he said.

'What if he leaves the village?'

'Then we'll follow.'

The relentless thief-catcher. Han had made this his new mission, determined to expose some grand scheme, but all she wanted to know was Cai Yun's connection to the jade and whether he knew anything of why the one pendant had come into her mother's hands. The answer was so close after all these years.

She wanted to break into the headman's house and interrogate Cai Yun that very night, but that would be foolish. It was possible, and highly likely, that this man was one more step along the path. She needed to adopt Han's sense of patience and bide her time.

Li Feng reached beneath her sleeve to untie the bindings that held the scabbard to her arm and set it down beside her. She could feel Han's gaze on her as she pulled the wooden pins from her hair. Heat rose up the back of her neck and she ran her hands through her hair to give her some time to compose herself. Then she took in a deep breath before turning around.

Han was reclined back on to his elbows. His eyes were dark as he watched her.

'Why did you leave Wudang Mountain?' he asked.

She didn't know what she had expected him to say, but it wasn't that. 'I wanted to find out what happened to my family.'

'But why at that moment? Was there something that happened that made you decide to leave?'

How interesting that Han would ask in that way. Something had happened to her.

'The mountain was a tranquil place, very quiet and solitary. There were days when *shifu* would barely speak.' Li Feng settled her back against the wall as she recalled the tale. 'I had always imagined how my life would be if I was with family. I wondered how it would feel to play with a brother or a sister. Then one day I heard the sound of someone playing a flute on the mountainside. It was the first time I had heard any music in a long time, other than the song of birds. The sound was so lonely and lovely.'

She could hear the melody now. The foothills where her *shifu* lived were open and empty. The sweet, piercing sound had travelled without any barriers to dampen the sound. She'd never seen who it was who had affected her so.

'I knew then that I belonged in a different place,' she admitted. 'A place with people and voices and music.'

Han remained quiet, his expression thoughtful as he absorbed her story. She had to look away. Her cheeks burned hot with embarrassment. The seemingly harmless tale had revealed too much about her feelings of isolation, of abandonment. The oil lamp was on the floor just beyond the bamboo mat. She leaned over to extinguish it and hide herself in darkness, but as she brushed past Han, he reached out and gently took hold of a lock of her hair.

He ran the strands through his long fingers as if testing the texture of fine silk. Slowly, as if he had all the time in the world. She could hear his breath deepening. Her own heart was beating fast as she faced him. Dark eyebrows framed his eyes, intensifying even the slightest glimpse of emotion.

When she lowered her mouth to his, he stopped her. He stopped himself.

'Coward,' she whispered.

'I didn't seek you out because of this.' Despite the denial, his voice was rough with desire.

So Thief-catcher Han was honest to everyone but himself.

She couldn't resist teasing him. 'I'm surprised to see such restraint, given your reputation in the bedchamber.'

He frowned, a deep crease lining his brow. 'That's nonsense. I have no such reputa—'

Boldly, she closed the space between them, fitting her lips to his. With their first touch, a shudder ran down her spine. Han tasted better than she remembered. His mouth was warm and sensual, yet he refused to yield completely. His hands closed over her shoulders and remained there. Han didn't push her away, but he wouldn't allow her any closer.

'Li Feng.' The way her name rumbled in his throat made her want to renew her efforts.

Instead, she fell back. She knew better than to fight force with force. If he was stone, she would be water. Han's eyes followed her every movement, his pupils as black and endless as the night. They both spoke at once.

'Why can't we—'

'We can't—'

'Stubborn man,' she muttered, blowing out the lamp.

Han tensed in the darkness, but she moved past him to lie down on the mat, her eyes pointed sightlessly at the ceiling. After a long, heavy pause, Han laid himself down beside her.

She could hear him swallowing to clear his throat. 'Who was it that—'

'Lotus,' she replied before he could finish.

More silence. She wriggled her toes restlessly.

He was the first to break their standoff. 'Lotus and I have never—'

'It doesn't matter,' she said hastily.

But secretly Li Feng was relieved. The courtesan was beautiful and elegant and charming. If Lotus was the sort of woman Han preferred, then no wonder he should overlook her so easily.

She'd had one lover before. Though the affair with Bao Yang had come and gone, she missed the moments of closeness. The feel of strong arms around her. And Han beguiled her with his manners and his careful regard. Laughing with her. Touching her hair. She wasn't expecting poetic declarations of love and longing, just….something to not feel so empty inside.

Infuriating and stubborn man.

If she touched him now, what would he do? But she didn't want to have him that way, pursuing him like a love-starved fox-demon.

'Li Feng,' he began softly. 'I can't take advantage of you.'

'How do you know I'm not the one taking advantage?' she challenged.

There was a pause. 'You grew up in a monastery on Wudang, sheltered.'

She made a face in the darkness. 'I didn't grow up in a monastery. I grew up by a lake in a hut that *shifu* built himself.' She nudged him with her foot as a reprimand. 'I was raised as a hermit, not a nun.'

They said nothing for the next moments. In the embarrassed silence, she felt Han turning one way. Then with a grunt, he turned the other way. She smiled. At least he was showing some signs of frustration.

'There were other girls at the Nightingale Pavilion besides Lotus,' she baited.

His pause stretched out for two heartbeats. 'I thought courtesans were supposed to be discreet.'

'Not to other women.'

'Such a headache,' he muttered.

'The accounts were favourable.'

*'Li Feng.'* He turned again in agitation, presumably away from her. 'Go to sleep.'

She chuckled, her mood lightened somewhat. Let him think she was a nun now.

\* \* \*

Li Feng woke up to the stroke of fingers over her brow. Opening her eyes, she blinked in the morning light and found Han leaning over her.

'How are you?' he asked.

His fingers came to rest on her cheek, as light as a butterfly. The gesture only irritated her after the missteps of the night before.

'What is this about?' She started to rise, but he pressed her firmly back down to the mat.

'You should rest...*wife.*'

She scowled at him, then saw the tavern keeper's wife standing by the door with a tray in her hands and a concerned look on her face. The tiny woman must have decided at that moment that Han's care was inadequate because she edged in between them and managed to push Han to the corner.

'Ah, Little Sister.' She knelt beside Li Feng and set down the tray. 'I brought a soup made of steeped wolfberries and longan. Very cooling.'

The wife patted Li Feng's hand like an older sister, enquiring about her comfort and telling her to be careful going down the stairs. Li Feng remained lying flat until the woman left them alone.

Her eyes darted to Han. 'What did you do?'

He had a hand over his mouth, but his eyes were bright with amusement. 'I had to tell them you were ill to give us a reason to remain in the village.'

'She thinks I'm with child!'

'I may have given enough hints for her to assume that.'

In addition to the herbal soup, the tray also held two generous bowls of congee along with a boiled egg to go with the rice porridge.

Han sat down beside her and arranged the tray between them. 'I'll be approaching Cai Yun today. See what I can find out about him.' He split the egg in two, putting the larger half in her bowl. 'For the child,' he added with a smirk.

He took his bowl in hand and spooned rice into his mouth, looking quite pleased with his ruse. She let her own bowl sit, growing cold as she regarded him accusingly.

'If I'm supposed to be ill, that means I'm confined here.'

'Only for the morning. You can claim to be feeling better later in the day. My mother was that way with my brother.'

She narrowed her eyes at him. 'You don't trust me.'

'I trust you enough to leave you with my *dao*.' Their weapons were still stowed away.

So much depended on this. She needed to know why her mother had left her, and who they had been running from. Without her past, she couldn't have a future. She was stronger now and faster, but in so many ways she was still that little girl.

'Hao Han, I've longed for this for over fifteen years—'

The words caught in her throat. How could she express how she felt to someone who was her constant tormentor, but also the one person she had confided in? The man who desired her, but refused to kiss her.

'Li Feng, I know.' He didn't say anything more.

The congee was still warm when she picked up her bowl. They ate together and the silence was almost companionable. She recalled how Han had sent food to her while she was locked up in the prison cell. Perhaps he had been paying her a compliment, a sign of respect that he didn't think of her as just another thief.

In the world of rivers and lakes, one showed the greatest regard towards the worthiest of adversaries. Han didn't seem like the enemy any more as he sat across from her. She truly hoped that he wouldn't have to be.

Han found out from the villagers that the distinguished visitor from out of town was drinking by the river with the government official. Throughout his travels, he had discovered that the local people were often more helpful when they didn't know he was a thief-catcher there to stir up trouble. His profession often dredged up animosity rather than support.

In these troubled times, local outlaws were often

treated like local heroes. Even worse was the case of privateers and smugglers. They were wealthy from illegal activity and appeared more respectable than a thief-catcher chasing an arrest warrant. He was almost certain Cai Yun fell into that lot, a merchant who bought his influence with bribes.

Han had followed the river bank and it wasn't long before he found Cai Yun and the salt agent sitting beneath an open pavilion, drinking wine. They were speaking casually to one another. Han stopped at a polite distance, far out of hearing range, and waited for them to acknowledge him with a glance. Finally the conversation halted and Cai Yun looked in his direction.

'Sir.' He bowed at the waist. 'This servant apologises for the intrusion.'

Cai Yun cast a disdainful eye at him. 'Who are you?'

Lotus had described him as thin and long, with a face that was always pinched as if smelling something funny. She had a way with words. He fit the description perfectly.

'I am here regarding the theft of a shipment of jade.'

'Well?' His tone was haughty. 'What of it?'

'General Wang Shizhen has apprehended one of the thieves.'

At the mention of the warlord, Cai Yun's eyes

widened with alarm. He glanced fearfully towards the salt agent before rising and pulling Han aside so they could speak privately.

'What does he want?' Cai Yun asked through his teeth.

Han kept his tone neutral. 'The general still seeks the jade.'

'Tell him—' He stopped himself, lowering his voice just above a whisper. 'Tell him we will need more time.'

Cai Yun must have assumed Han was sent by the general. Though Cai Yun said very little, Han assessed his mannerisms. The man's superior manner had disappeared and tension gathered along his jaw as they spoke.

'Wang Shizhen is not a patient man. Your master should know that,' Han ventured.

'He'll get nothing more out of threatening us,' Cai Yun retorted. 'Or interfering with our business here.'

'There is one other matter.' He hadn't forgotten Li Feng. 'A jade pendant engraved with a phoenix was recovered. There was speculation as to whether it was part of the shipment.'

Cai Yun stared at him incredulously. 'I have no recollection of what was in that chest,' he said impatiently. 'Do as you see fit. Find the thieves and save us some trouble.'

Han bowed in farewell and stepped back. Cai Yun

returned to the official and they resumed their conversation in much quieter tones, casting Han a few disparaging glances as he retreated back to the village.

His gamble had paid off. He now knew that Cai Yun was working for someone else. Han also had the impression that his master must be a man of some influence. As a servant, Cai Yun carried himself with the arrogance of someone who was used to being obeyed; someone who had a protector powerful enough to stand up to the warlord Wang Shizhen.

'We have a cat!'

Li Feng decided she had 'rested' enough and finally made it down from the loft to be met by the little boy at the bottom of the stairs. He was an irresistible creature, mostly head with eyes that took up most of his face. His hair was gathered into a little knot over the top of his head and he stared up at her expectantly.

'He catches mice,' he announced, when she didn't respond.

'He must be a very good cat,' she said.

The boy continued to stare at her, unblinking and utterly fascinated, until his mother called for him. He ran through the dining room on wobbly legs that carried more intention than co-ordination.

The tavern was relatively empty this late in the

morning. A group of elderly men sat in the corner, drinking tea and talking of this and that. There were several workmen moving about, carrying sacks and baskets into the kitchen.

The tavern keeper's wife came to Li Feng from across the room. The boy promptly wrapped his arms around his mother's knee as soon as she stopped. He peered out at Li Feng from his position of safety.

'Little Sister, you should be lying down.'

'I feel much better. Thought it would be good to get some air.'

In truth, her stomach fluttered with anxiety, wondering what Han had found out.

'It's almost time for the mid-day meal. We'll eat together.' She was already heading for the kitchen, making it impossible to refuse. 'My name is Yiyi.'

'Li Feng.'

'That's a grand name for you. You're so tall.'

At some point, little Ping transferred his allegiance over to Li Feng, tottering along at her heels as she trailed after Yiyi. The smaller woman slipped through the curtain that divided the kitchen from the main room and Li Feng followed her.

The smell of hot oil and spices assailed her. The kitchen was a bustle of activity in contrast to the quietness of the dining room. There was a large stove with several pots on boil atop it. The tavern keeper stood off to the side, overseeing the workmen as they stacked sacks of rice in a storage area.

'Oh, no!' Yiyi dragged her back out to the dining room and seated Li Feng at a table beside the window. 'You are a guest, Little Sister.'

There was little to do but sit dutifully and wait. The men in the corner paid her no notice. They seemed to be conversing about the boats on the river. The bamboo shutters had been propped up to let in light from all sides. Li Feng looked out to the rest of the village, hoping to catch a glimpse of Han.

It was a quiet and secluded place, though there seemed to be more activity than she'd seen the day before. Li Feng had always preferred the noise of the cities, for her ears to be filled with music and conversation rather than the solitude of her own thoughts.

The aforementioned cat made an appearance, sauntering out of some corner to wind between the legs of the bench. Its ears were black-tipped and its fur sleek in a pattern of white and grey. Given how the creature seemed to be loitering around the table with anticipation, it was likely he fed on more than just mice. Yiyi shooed the cat away as she reappeared with an armful of dishes and bowls. She set them out on the table and disappeared again, reemerging with more dishes and a pot of tea.

'Ping,' Yiyi admonished the boy when he started climbing on to the bench beside Li Feng.

'It's no trouble. Let him stay.' Li Feng helped the child seat himself. His legs dangled from the bench and his head barely reached the table.

'You like children,' Yiyi observed with a sly look.

'Yes. Yes, I like them very much.'

Was she supposed to blush? Smile proudly? Li Feng was a better dancer than she was an actress.

Yiyi ladled out two bowls of soup for the both of them and a smaller bowl for Ping. 'What does your husband do?'

Husband. Han was supposed to be her husband.

'He catches…fish.'

'No wonder he's so well built and strong. And so handsome too!'

Pretending to be married was awkward, but pretending to be married to Han was excruciating. She considered telling Yiyi, in a fit of ill humour, how Han tied her up and wanted to keep her locked away. Instead she took a spoonful of soup. It was a rich broth flavored with braised pork bones in a mix of wine and garlic.

'I've embarrassed you now,' Yiyi said.

'No, not at all.'

'I can see how he dotes on you.'

'Dotes on me?' she asked incredulously. Yiyi had to be teasing her.

'He spoils you so, you lucky woman.'

Well, of course Han had to appear to care for her. It was part of their ruse. Maybe this bit about being husband and wife was why she was becoming confused about them. They had only spent two days in each other's company, but their time together already seemed quite intimate and personal. She had never confided so much to anyone else.

'Your husband seems a very good man as well,' Li Feng replied.

'That oaf?'

At that moment, the husband came out of the kitchen. With a roar, he picked up Ping and swung the child into his lap as he sat. Li Feng could see that any complaint that Yiyi had about her husband was in jest. Li Feng's chest squeezed tight with longing as she watched them together. They were happy.

Yiyi made quick introductions. Her husband's name was Wei. He was broad shouldered and had an endearing habit of talking out of the side of his mouth. He had inherited the tavern from his father.

'The old man knew a hundred recipes for soup,' Wei boasted. 'One recipe has over twenty-five ingredients, some of them very rare.'

They ate together in harmony and Li Feng marvelled at the sumptuousness of the feast. It was even more extravagant than the parade of dishes she and Han had enjoyed last night.

'Really, you must allow my husband to pay you,' Li Feng said, happily volunteering Han for what was likely a substantial bill.

Wei raised his hand in refusal. 'Don't think of it. We've had some good years.'

'Things seem busy here today.' Li Feng watched as one of the workmen came out from the kitchen and exited the tavern.

'Tomorrow is loading day,' Wei explained. 'The salt from the wells is transported to boats to be shipped.'

'Good business for us,' Yiyi chimed in. 'But very busy.'

So they had been stocking up supplies to feed the hungry labourers. 'Is that also why the government official is in the village?' Li Feng asked.

Wei nodded. 'He's from the Salt Commission. Everything has to be weighed and recorded and loaded on to authorised boats. It's a long process…'

'They'll be working from sunrise to nearly sunset,' Li Feng reported.

After Han returned from his investigations, Li Feng had claimed to not be feeling well once again. Yiyi had dinner brought up to the loft and left them to their privacy.

'Everyone will be focused on transporting the salt and loading the boats.' She was quite proud to have gathered useful information, despite being relegated to the sick bed.

'That must be why Cai Yun is here,' he suggested. 'If he's made a deal with the agent, he might divert a part of the supply for himself. Sell it on his own for a greater profit.'

'I never realised there was so much money to be gained from salt.'

'A river of money,' Han said. 'And an ocean of greed to accompany it.'

He met her eyes with a determined, almost feverish look. Her stomach fluttered until she realised his gaze wasn't directed at her.

'I want to catch them,' he declared. 'Cai Yun and the corrupt agent from the Salt Commission. The agent is a public official, sworn to uphold his duty to the state, yet he's abusing his position. That makes him the worst of criminals.'

'What are you going to do? Report them?'

'There are severe penalties for bringing a false accusation before the magistrate. Let me think here.' That crease in his brow was starting to become a familiar sight. 'All salt production has to be carefully weighed and reported. There will be records in the main building of the salt works. I need to get inside that wall.'

'If the guards are concerned about smugglers,

they'll be stationed at the river to guard the boats tomorrow,' she reasoned.

'It has to be tomorrow then. I'll go in under the guise of one of the labourers.'

'Just you? We'll both go.'

'Li Feng, I'm not certain—'

'Are you afraid I can't protect myself?'

'That's not it exactly.' He rubbed a knuckle along his jaw, the answer sticking in his throat. Once again, he was being infuriatingly stubborn.

'What is it?' she demanded

'If you help me, I would owe you a debt. It would… it would confuse things. You already have me confused as it is.'

She liked the sound of that. Han prided himself on boundaries and his sense of restraint. She wouldn't mind if he found her a distraction. He should be tormented, just a little. She shouldn't be the only one so affected by their time together.

'So what did you discover today, thief-catcher?'

Han looked grateful to be back on a neutral topic. 'Cai Yun has been seen about the village once before and everyone assumes he's someone influential, but don't know anything about him otherwise. From his manner, he's acting on behalf of someone. Also he seems afraid of something, or someone. He flinched when I mentioned General Wang.'

'Everyone is afraid of Wang Shizhen,' she muttered.

The southern region of the province was even more remote and secluded from imperial control than the rest of the province. Wang had been seizing power city by city, growing his army so that no one dared to challenge him.

'And he doesn't know about the jade pendant. It appears the entire shipment belongs to someone else and he's acting on orders.'

She tried not to show her disappointment, but it must have shown anyway, because Han placed a piece of fish into her bowl to console her. Or maybe he just wanted her to finish up.

'I did find out where he comes from,' he said. 'A man like that doesn't travel alone. Cai Yun was rather tight-lipped, but his porters were drinking tea on the other side of the village. He's returning to Minzhou once his business is completed here. Whatever business that may be.'

'Minzhou?'

'A prefecture capital just west of here,' he replied, stuffing more rice into his mouth.

A strange look crossed his face when he mentioned the city. She had never been to Minzhou, but Han seemed familiar with it. He was so well travelled that he probably had past associations in many places.

Now there was silence. The rice was gone. There was nothing but empty dishes on the tray.

'You know it would be useful to have someone with you tomorrow,' she said finally. 'Why won't you just ask me?'

He gave her a half-smile. 'You might not want to help a thief-catcher.'

Li Feng turned her teacup around once in her hands. Maybe Han wasn't the only one confused.

It wasn't as if he were truly helping her in return. He just smelled some larger conspiracy and was doing his part to uphold justice and order. Yet her gut told her they were in this venture together. She had become involved with reckless undertakings before, with much less trustworthy people.

'Maybe I want you to be in debt to me, thief-catcher,' she said sweetly.

Her taunt made him pause. The muscle in his jaw flexed and she wondered how long his resolve would last if she did try to push against it. How long would hers last?

'We'll need to act as if we're leaving early tomorrow.' He tried to continue as if nothing had passed between them, but she could sense the minute tension that travelled along his spine. They were inescapably aware of one another. 'Cai Yun and the agent from the Salt Commission believe I was sent by General Wang. They'll be wary of doing anything underhanded while we're… Why are you making that face?'

She grimaced as if in pain. 'I told the tavern keeper's wife a different story.'

'What do you mean?'

'I told her that you were a fisherman.'

'A fisherman?' He made his own face. 'You couldn't make up a better profession for me?'

'There was a whole steamed fish on the table, looking at me. When Yiyi asked me about you, it was all I could think of. We've only been married for one day, you know.'

He blew out an agitated breath. 'No matter, we're leaving tomorrow.'

'But not really leaving.'

'Right.' He shot her a cross look. 'Fisherman,' he muttered beneath his breath.

# Chapter Eight

Han steered the wheelbarrow along the dirt path that led to the salt works. They had waited until late in the afternoon, at a time when most of the labourers were out loading the boats, to make their attempt. A pair of guards stood watch at the front gate which had been propped open due to all the traffic in and out.

'What is this?' one of the guards asked.

Han had replaced his robe with a long shirt made of hemp and loose trousers to blend in with the other workmen. '*Baijiu,* a gift from the gentleman from Minzhou.'

The guard lifted one of the jugs of rice wine and inspected the red label. 'Everyone will be quite thirsty after working so hard today.'

Han nodded and chuckled. 'Indeed.'

'Go on in.' He waved them through, conveniently tucking the jug beneath his arm rather than returning it to the wheelbarrow.

Spying from the trees had given them a chance to plan out their route. There was what appeared to be a set of storehouses beside the area where the labourers gathered for meals. Han settled the wheelbarrow behind the cover of the buildings, then shoved the wine jugs aside. A wooden slat had been fitted into the cart to create a hidden compartment. Li Feng wriggled out from it and handed him his *dao*. She took a moment to stretch out her limbs while he strapped on his sword belt.

'Only four guards at the gate,' he told her. 'The rest of the compound is nearly empty, but there's still a lookout up in the watchtower.'

'Wei said the loading work continues until sundown.'

They stayed against the side of the storehouses and crept between the buildings. The front entrance to the main building was easily visible from the gate or the watchtower, but Li Feng had targeted a second-storey window on the side. They stood below it now.

Han made a final scan of the area. 'Go,' he said.

She would have to make quick work of it. With a few running steps to lead in, Li Feng stepped up the wall, caught her first handhold, lifted herself, caught another one until she was pulling herself into the window. She moved as if weightless, with hardly any effort at all. He didn't even have time to blink.

A moment later, a rope snaked down the side of

the building. He gave it a tug before beginning his own climb. As soon as he was inside, he pulled the rope up behind him. The interior was still and quiet. A quick search showed that the top floor contained the private chambers and sleeping areas.

They moved downstairs. At the bottom, the sound of footsteps down the hall chased them into the dark corner beneath the stairs. They crouched there, listening and waiting. Li Feng gave him a sideways look as he crushed himself against her. Though she said nothing, her eyes carried all the reproach required.

The footsteps receded and he and Li Feng were moving once more. They slipped inside the front office and shut the door.

Han began rifling through the scrolls and papers on top of the writing desk. He could just make out the characters in the fading daylight.

'What are you looking for?' she whispered. Li Feng remained by the door, with an ear pressed to the wood.

'Records of some kind. Official documents.'

Han wasn't exactly sure himself. He found a thick ledger book and scanned the entries at the end. There were pages of figures stamped with an official chop. It would have to do. He wound a strip of cloth around the book and tied the makeshift pack around his back. With a nod to Li Feng, they retraced their steps back to the outside. Unfortunately, they returned to the storehouse to find their wheelbarrow was gone.

'Death take me,' he cursed.

Li Feng remained surprisingly calm. As if he didn't admire her enough already.

'You'll be able to walk out the front gate,' she said. 'I can find my own way out.'

'Absolutely not. We go together.'

She looked around the compound. 'All right, from the top of the storehouse, we might be able to jump on to the fence and then over.'

Han looked at the barrier sceptically. The bamboo fence was over two man-lengths high and cut at a slant to create sharp points at the ends. They would be impaled if they misjudged the jump and climbing on to the storehouse would certainly put them in sight of the lookout tower.

'I have a different plan,' he suggested.

'What would that be?'

'We go out the front gate, as you said.'

She frowned at him, but followed without protest as he went towards the tower of the nearest salt well. They stayed low and hid behind the extensive scaffolding at the base. He searched through the bamboo piping and found a set that led towards the brine vats.

'The wells produce fumes that can make the workers sick,' he explained, following the piping. 'The best way to be rid of the poisonous air is to burn it and then the workers use the flame to boil the brine. Don't breathe too deeply.'

Li Feng backed away as he broke open the bamboo pipe with the hilt of his *dao*.

'There's nothing there,' she said when he returned to her side.

'You can't see the poison.'

Han found a lantern and struck a flint to light it. Keeping as far back as possible, he threw the lantern towards the broken pipe. The paper shell ignited instantly. Li Feng let out a shout as plumes of flame licked out towards them.

By the time they returned to the storage area, the gong was already sounding from the tower. The few remaining workers rushed to the fire. As short-handed as they were, the guards at the front gate were forced to leave their post to see to the catastrophe.

'Now,' Han said.

They made their escape into the surrounding forest.

Hours later, they were situated in their temporary hideout, a makeshift shelter they had built in the woods. The area was removed from the road and situated outside the boundaries of the village.

The evening was upon them and the clack and buzz of night insects filled the air. Han scanned the ledger book by the meagre light of an oil lamp while Li Feng appeared to be searching the ground for snakes.

'I think it would be safer to sleep in the trees,' she said. 'I've done it before.'

'What if you fall? You could break your neck.'

'I never fall.'

Han turned the page and held it close to the flickering light, trying to focus on the reports.

'You can read all that?' she asked.

He nodded with an affirmative grunt. Reading was one thing, but comprehending it all was another. The book contained a meticulous log of operations within the salt works, complete with reports of official inspections, but if there was any evidence of wrongdoing, it was beyond him to decipher. The result was a headache and it didn't help that Li Feng watched him with such rapt attention.

'That's quite impressive,' she purred.

'What?' He held up the book. 'This?'

She touched a hand to her cheek in what might have been the most girlish gesture he'd seen from her. 'What woman doesn't dream of marrying a scholar?'

'Failed scholar,' he reminded her.

Li Feng laughed. The lamplight was warm on her

skin and set her face aglow. It was an easy sort of laughter. Genuine, not teasing or flirting or coy. It spoke of all they had just done together. Outwardly, it involved subterfuge and theft and the destruction of property, but inwardly... Inside, his heart was suddenly pounding. He turned a page and the characters faded before his eyes, forgotten.

He was in trouble.

'I'm afraid of you, Wen Li Feng,' he confessed.

'I didn't think Thief-catcher Han would be afraid of anything.'

Setting the book aside, he placed two fingers beneath her chin to tilt her face towards him. 'I'm afraid I'm going to become accustomed to having you by my side.'

Her lips curved and that smile was his undoing. If he kissed her now, he could capture it for eternity. At least he could claim this moment. He lowered his head towards Li Feng while she pressed closer to him.

The snap and rustle of movement in the woods stopped them both.

Li Feng bent to extinguish the lamp. Before the flame went to smoke, Han saw her touch a hand to her sleeve. With as little movement as possible, he ducked outside the shelter to see several lights floating in the distance. Lanterns. Someone was moving through the brush.

'Leave them. They won't find us here,' Li Feng urged as he straightened.

'I need to see what they're about.'

She made an impatient noise, but stood to follow him anyway. Li Feng was a rare sort of woman. Fearless. He had known during that first chase over the rooftops that she would be his match.

After a few minutes outside, his eyes adjusted to the darkness. The moonlight cast the forest into black against deeper black. The dark figures were moving towards the river. Han let them gain more distance before attempting to follow.

They stopped at a clearing long before reaching the water. It appeared the lanterns had been fashioned out of thick layers of paper to block the light. What filtered through was dimmed, but there was enough illumination to reveal six or seven men. Han could make out several carts packed high with sacks. The cargo had been placed there ahead of time, to be retrieved under the cover of night.

When he'd first started thief-catching, Han had assumed salt bandits were dirty thieves, lurking in the dark and raiding salt farms. He'd come to learn that the business of salt smuggling was much more organised.

He tapped on Li Feng's shoulder to signal a retreat. There was nothing more he could do here besides gather information. Apprehending a gang like this required some planning.

'Who's there?'

Han cursed at himself. He'd missed the presence of a rear lookout. Li Feng tensed beside him, but she didn't remain immobile for long. Together, they started for the forest while the smugglers gave chase. Han had no account of their numbers any longer, but from the shouts around him, he knew that he and Li Feng were being flanked. Not good. Beside him, he heard the whisper of a blade being unsheathed. Li Feng had her short sword in hand as she planted her feet to face the pursuers. He followed her instinct and drew his *dao*.

At the sight of the weapons, a few of the smugglers fell back. The men were meagrely armed with clubs and sickles, but they still had sheer numbers on their side. Brute force could readily defeat a skilled sword.

Han took advantage of their hesitation. 'Over here!' he shouted into the night, directing it towards his supposedly hidden comrades.

The simple ploy seemed to shake them. The smugglers broke formation, what little formation they had to begin with, and Han took the moment to charge. A cry of pain punctuated the darkness to his right. Li Feng had already drawn blood. A moment later, his *dao* also sliced through cloth and into flesh.

Trained fighters were rare among such gangs. These men were confused and lashing out in fear and blind instinct. Han repositioned himself and assessed the situation. Visibility was low, but it seemed their numbers had thinned considerably.

After fending off a few swipes from the crude weaponry, Han turned to search for Li Feng, but she had disappeared.

Li Feng sheathed her sword. There were two men chasing her through the trees and the gleam of metal could be used to track her. As she pulled away from her pursuers, the woods closed around her, looming with dark shadows.

She wasn't alarmed. In the night blindness, she started relying on touch—her footing on the ground, her hands scraping against the brush. She had grown up surrounded by mountains and wilderness.

After she had gained some distance, Li Feng launched herself up into a tree and settled behind the cover of the branches where she remained as still and watchful as an owl. The pursuers never even ran by underfoot. She had lost them.

She stayed crouched, waiting and listening. Her sense of direction was unassailable. The river was to her right, the village slightly north of that. She could find her way back to their hideout once she was safe. She strained to listen for the sounds of fighting, but she was too far away to hear anything. A knot formed in her stomach at the thought of Han fighting outnumbered in the darkness. He could be injured and helpless, bleeding out on to the ground.

Such an imagination! She had to trust Han to defend himself. These were untrained bandits, and not particularly stealthy ones. They were no match for Han.

Li Feng stilled as a lone figure passed by below her carrying a lantern. She couldn't discern his facial features, but she was certain that he didn't have Han's stature or build. He appeared to be heading towards the village.

Her fingers started to twitch. This was a dangerous situation and she had no business chasing after bandits. That was Han's obsession, not hers. She was safe up here. What she ought to do was stay put until daybreak.

Still, there was only one man. She had the cover of darkness and she had her sword. If there was any threat, she could disappear again into the trees.

Climbing down, she landed soundlessly on the ground and kept her distance. A lantern bobbed in the darkness ahead. The man was moving rapidly, but there was an unevenness to his gait. As she reached the far edge of the village, her heart seized. The bandit was sneaking into the tavern. Yiyi and little Ping were in there, asleep and defenceless.

Li Feng broke into a run, lungs filling with air and muscles straining. Drawing her sword, she entered the main room and prepared to strike first and strike hard. Her feet froze on the threshold.

The intruder was bent over a table. He propped himself up with one hand while the other was clutched to his side. His fingers were slick with blood. It was the tavern keeper.

Li Feng took a step forward. 'Wei?'

'There was a man with a sword—' He stopped when he saw the weapon in her hand.

She came forwards slowly. 'Where is this man?'

The tavern keeper gritted his teeth. 'He's coming.'

The prosperity of the tavern didn't come from the occasional travellers or the labourers from the salt wells. Wei and his wife were part of the salt-smuggling ring and Han was coming for them.

Li Feng was torn and the two halves warred within her. She and Han had come to this village wary of one another, but over the last two days, something had changed between them. Han was starting to trust her and she was starting to feel that she was worthy of that trust. *We go together,* he had insisted.

Wei's breath caught as he tried to breathe through the pain. When he looked up at her there was fear in his eyes.

'Miss Wen,' he pleaded.

This was no ruthless bandit. He was a husband and

father. His wife and son were sleeping in the back of the tavern and he was afraid for them.

She thought of Yiyi and her boy. Han might spare the two of them, but Wei had been caught in the act. Salt smuggling was worse than theft; it was a crime against the government. Ping would have to watch his father dragged away by a thief-catcher. Wei would be tried and executed.

No matter how many times Han explained it to her, Li Feng would never understand how a few sacks of salt could equal a man's life. Yiyi would be left without a husband and little Ping without a father.

'Is there somewhere you can hide?' she asked Wei. 'Somewhere safe and far from here.'

He nodded.

'Get ready now.' She looked to his wound. It would need to be bound before he lost too much blood. 'I'll go with you.'

She had to go in case Han tracked them down. Wei wasn't a trained fighter. He was no match for the thief-catcher.

Wei went to gather his family while Li Feng bolted the door. She considered asking Han to spare the tavern keeper, but she knew her effort would have been useless. Han believed in justice and order above all else. It would take more than what they had between them to persuade him.

Li Feng closed her eyes and rested her forehead against the door, listening for the pound of footsteps coming towards them. From the back of the tavern, she could hear shuffling and the sound of voices as Yiyi and her son awoke.

She and Han would have had to part ways sooner or later, she told herself. It wasn't as if she owed Han anything. Certainly nothing more than she'd already given. She had just assumed that when they parted, there would at least be a farewell. Instead she would disappear into the night and Han would know that she had betrayed him.

But there was no time for regret. Li Feng pushed away from the door and went to help Wei and his family.

## Chapter Nine

Minzhou was a city of hills and canals, hidden within the mountains which surrounded it on three sides: east, west and north. The old part of the city was located on top of a hill and protected by a stone wall. A newer section had cropped up in the lowlands to the south. The Min River flowed between the two halves and a wide wooden bridge connected old to new. Though it was the capital of the prefecture, its location within the valley made it seem remote and sheltered. At the same time, it was a sprawl of a city. Li Feng walked through lane after lane, engulfed in the crowd and the buzz of voices. How did one go about finding a single man in such a place?

Thief-catcher Han would know how.

She shoved the thought aside. There was no point in thinking about him every day. Or in yearning for his company. She was done with Zheng Hao Han.

It had been over a week since she had helped Wei and Yiyi escape from their village. She had made sure they were safe before continuing on to Minzhou. During that time, she had exchanged her peasant clothing for the blue-grey robes of a Taoist priestess. Her hair was pulled back into an austere bun.

Li Feng didn't know what she was expecting now that she was in Minzhou. Perhaps a sense of familiarity. Or of two pieces coming inevitably together, but she felt no more a sense of belonging here than she had anywhere else.

The bustling marketplace engulfed her and everyone became as nameless and faceless as she was. There were times when she sought this feeling of being lost in a crowd. She wasn't so alone in a place where no one recognised one another.

She found a stand that served sweet dumplings and spent some time chatting with the vendor. He happened to be a former clerk who had fallen on hard times. Now his wife made the dumplings every morning and he sold them to care for their small family with another child soon to be born.

'All things being said, Heaven has been good to me, Elder Sister,' he said.

The respectful address startled her until Li Feng remembered she was dressed as a priestess. She ordered extra dumplings to further ingratiate herself. This was a busy intersection and the dumpling seller was the sort who spilled secrets easily.

'Do you know of a man named Cai Yun?' she asked him when he brought the second plate of dumplings. 'He is supposedly from this city.'

'Cai Yun?' He scrubbed a hand over his chin. 'The name sounds familiar—'

Another customer piped up. 'Wasn't that the name of that man outside the tea house?'

'Him? Oh, was that his name?'

'Horrible!'

Li Feng tried to follow the exchange without success until the dumpling seller turned back to her. He lowered his voice gravely. 'If this was the man you're looking for, he's dead.'

The wind rushed out of her. 'Dead?'

'Right in the street, in daylight. They came upon him with knives.'

Others joined in the gossip. 'There were city guards right at the corner.'

'Nowhere is safe!'

The dumpling seller nodded. 'One can't be too careful.'

Li Feng was in shock. She had seen Cai Yun alive not ten days ago. 'What happened?'

'A man was leaving a local tea house when a gang of bandits surrounded him. He was with his attendants, but they were no use and were quickly overpowered.' He lowered his voice ominously. 'They slit his throat and left him there.'

'Heaven and earth.' She touched a hand to her own throat.

'He wasn't just any no-name,' another customer said. 'I heard he was the prefect's steward, in charge of his affairs.'

Li Feng stood, slightly shaken at the convergence of events. The man she was searching for had been ruthlessly murdered. Han had suspected Cai Yun was involved in corruption, but this was still unexpected.

'Did you know him, Elder Sister?' the seller asked.

She was listening with half an ear. There was a stranger at the end of the street, half in view, half hidden by the corner. His face was incongruous, his features slightly askew. His jaw was shaded by a rough growth of stubble. Something about him left an uneasy feeling in the pit of her stomach. Her gaze passed over him and he quickly turned away.

He had been watching her.

Hastily, she reached into her purse, placed a coin on to the table and turned to leave.

'Your dumplings, Elder Sister!'

She had to wait while he wrapped them in palm leaves. By the time he handed her the package, the mysterious man was gone. Li Feng murmured her thanks and slipped into the crowd, taking care to match the pace of everyone around her. After several streets, she glanced back warily. Nothing was amiss.

Was another thief-catcher after her? The weight of the stranger's stare sent a shiver up her spine. Whoever he was, the man was dangerous.

She crossed through a shaded area where a row of banyan trees had been planted. By the time she emerged on the other side of the park, the feeling of being followed had dissipated. She kept a hand close to her sword as she continued through the streets.

The rain came the next day, chasing all but the most stalwart of pedestrians from the streets. Li Feng had been expecting it, from the look of the sky, and had found refuge inside an abandoned Taoist shrine.

The front gate had been boarded shut when she came upon it, but she easily climbed the wall and landed inside the tiny square of a courtyard. Wild grass poked up between the rough stones that paved the garden and there was a small pond in the centre, though any fish that might be swimming in the murky waters were obscured beneath a layer of grime.

The altar in the main room was intact, leading her to believe the shrine's caretaker had left for a journey and intended to return one day. Statues of the Three Pure Ones, the old sages of Taoist legend, stood on the altar. A dusty spider's web stretched from the Jade Pure One's shoulder up to the rafters.

Perhaps the caretaker of this shrine had gone off on a pilgrimage. Taoist practitioners often preferred to meditate in solitude, reflecting upon life up high in the mountains. Statues and incense neither inspired nor enlightened them.

Li Feng lit a fire in the small brazier that was typically used to collect incense and then climbed on to the altar to brush some of the dust off of the three statues. The Supreme Pure One regarded her with a serene, yet someone amused expression as she cleaned his face. She wasn't one for idols either, but it was a small service to perform for her stay at the shrine.

'Elder Sister.' A deep voice cut through the rhythm of the rainfall. 'I didn't realise you had decided to follow the Way.'

It was Han. Of course it was Han.

She hopped from the altar, every muscle tense, as he stepped into the chamber. Water glistened upon his face and beaded on his cloak. The patter of raindrops upon the rooftop had covered the sound of his footsteps.

Her hand trailed to her sleeve. 'You found me.'

'I'll always find you.'

He didn't seem happy with that. Han shed his bamboo hat along with the heavy cloak that shielded him from the rain. His *dao* remained in his sheath while he looked over her priestess's robe curiously.

'Every time I see you, you've become something new,' he said absently before meeting her eyes. 'You disappeared that night.'

'It was time to go our separate ways,' she replied with her teeth on edge. Actually her teeth were close to chattering. It was cold inside and wet outside. The prospect of fleeing into the rain didn't please her at all. She was rather annoyed by it.

He looked out into the soaked courtyard, then back at her. 'Even though I'm blocking this doorway here, the frame on that window over there is pretty flimsy. I suppose you're fast enough to dive through it.'

'In one leap,' she agreed warily. 'And then I would be through the courtyard and up over the roof before you could turn around.'

'The rain would make everything very slippery. Are you sure you won't fall?'

He took a step into the altar room. By now he had to have discovered what had happened. Was she once again his quarry? Li Feng side-stepped along the wall to keep the distance between them. It was a precarious dance.

'I've tried the climb,' she insisted. 'I know exactly where to hold on.'

'You'll land in the alleyway out back,' he continued lightly. 'That's a dead end.'

'Not for me.'

'Ah, up another wall. On to another roof.'

'Walking on walls and flying over eaves,' she finished for him.

He smiled. It was a generous, genuine smile and, as always, it did alarming things to her insides.

'It seems you've escaped from me again then,' he conceded. 'If that's the case, we can both avoid the unpleasantness of getting soaked.'

He moved towards her, very much still in pursuit. Her heart was racing as fast as if she had run from him, even though she was standing still.

'One day, I'll find a way to get a hold of you,' he said quietly. He ventured closer and touched a hand to her waist, cradling gently with just the pressure of his fingertips. 'Is there a way to keep a hold on you, Li Feng?'

His mouth grew tight as she glanced over the broad features of his face, the strong cheekbones and broad jaw. He was seeking an answer with his eyes, his touch, but she had no answer.

'I searched everywhere that night.' His voice resonated beneath the cadence of the rain. She could feel it humming through her, inside her. 'At first I thought something had happened to you.'

He stopped himself, embarrassed at revealing so much. They were toe to toe, but still barely touching. It was hard to breathe freely with him so close.

She had never considered that he might be worried. That he might actually care for her. The thought flooded her with warmth.

'I saw that the tavern keeper and his family were gone the next morning,' he told her. 'I knew then what had happened.'

'It's just salt,' she argued.

'It is never just salt,' he corrected. 'And the tavern keeper wasn't the only one involved. I suspect the entire village had a hand in the smuggling.'

'You arrested the entire village?'

'No, that would be beyond my abilities. Such a serious accusation has to be carefully considered before being reported to the proper—' He stopped himself and regarded her with a determined expression on his face. 'This isn't why I came here,' he said, his voice rough.

'Why, then?'

His hands rounded her waist to rest against the small of her back. At first she stiffened, but his touch had the ease of familiarity. As if holding her was the most natural thing in the world for him. Slowly he pulled her closer, testing the bonds between them.

She braced a hand against his chest. 'This is impossible.'

'I know.'

He didn't kiss her.

With a heavy sigh, he lowered his forehead to hers. She had never realised how well they fit. Her height complemented his perfectly. It was a disconcerting thought. For a long moment they did nothing but stand together, breathing softly.

She closed her eyes. 'I'm only letting you do this because you're so warm.'

'Of course.'

He was more than warm. He smelled faintly of sandalwood, a clean, comforting smell that made her close her eyes and sink against him. His chest was broad, his shoulders strong and for once she enjoyed the feeling of being enclosed and held. It had been so long.

'Didn't you consider that I might have some compassion in me?' he asked her. 'I'm not made of rock.'

An apt comparison, actually.

'Justice is justice,' she pointed out. 'Your words.'

He fell silent. Li Feng pulled away and he let her slip through his fingers without a fight. Surely she was misleading Han to remain in his embrace, no matter how good it felt. She went to stand outside on the veranda. The tread of his footsteps on the wooden floor told her he'd followed her outside.

'Why do you continue to follow me, if not to arrest me?'

She stared at the endless fall of water. It was easier than looking at Han. She had allowed herself to be diverted once before from her quest and wouldn't let it happen again.

'I told you we would do this together,' he said.

'Why?' She turned and fixed her gaze on him. She wouldn't accept his deflections about truth and justice any longer. 'Why are you here?' she demanded.

He considered for a long moment before answering.

'Because we're friends.'

He managed to coax her back inside. They fed strips of wood into the brazier and warmed their hands over the fire as they sat on the bamboo mats that covered the floor of the shrine.

'How did you find me?' Li Feng asked.

'Does it matter?'

She tilted her head playfully at him. 'I want to know how the thief-catcher thinks.'

It was as if they'd never parted. All their meetings in the past weeks started to blend seamlessly together in his mind. And in the spaces in between, he'd done little else but think of her, looking over small details, things she'd said, done. Figuring out how he'd find her again.

He nodded. 'I knew you would come to Minzhou because it was where our friend Cai Yun was going. From our past altercations, I knew you favoured seeking out abandoned buildings. Then it was a matter of asking the right people about a woman travelling alone. You'll always stand out because of that.'

She made a face at him, her lips in a pout. She would always stand out for him because he couldn't take his eyes off of her. It had been that way from the first moment he'd seen her, sword in hand.

'Do you know that Cai Yun is dead?' she asked.

He blinked once. Twice. 'Dead.' He sat back, exhaling sharply. 'Dead?'

She shifted to find a more comfortable position on the mat, tucking her legs beneath her as she recounted the tale. Han noted that she was no longer in a position to leap to her feet and fly through the window. In response, he relaxed as well, leaning back and resting an arm over his knee. For the moment, they were companions again.

'An entire gang of bandits killed him out in the open and then disappeared?' he asked.

'They said a thief-catcher tried to hunt down the killers, but they beat him nearly to death and then escaped into the mountains.'

Outlaws were known to band together to attack transports along the rivers or merchants on the road. In remote areas, a group of thugs could overpower local authorities and try to take control of entire towns, such as in the case of Two Dragon Lo. The same problem had plagued the county where his father had served as magistrate.

'This wasn't mere banditry,' he concluded. 'This is intimidation.'

'The killers were part of the smuggling ring,' Li Feng suggested.

'Most likely. It stands to reason that a man who dealt with outlaws would die by their hands.'

'I also learned that he was Prefect Guan's steward,' she said.

Han stood and paced to the window, his mind racing. Guan He oversaw the administration of the prefecture.

'If the prefect is involved, then the corruption reaches far beyond the bribery of a few commission officials,' he declared. A fire rose within him. 'The entire salt trade within the region could be compromised.'

'Han.'

Li Feng's even, soothing voice disrupted his fervour. She regarded him with such a serious expression that he feared what she would reveal. As if she were about to confess to the murder along with ten other crimes, but it was nothing so dire.

'I know that it's your life's work to rid the world of outlaws and corruption,' she said.

He was taken aback. 'It's not—'

'But this, all of this that you're speaking of, it isn't my concern. This happened once before. I became involved in a conflict that had nothing to do with me. If I hadn't been so blind, then I wouldn't have got so deeply entangled with the wrong people. I wouldn't have thief-catchers chasing after me.'

She looked away from him. He could see the long line of her neck and the way a strand of her hair curved along her ear to grace her throat. His own throat went dry for no reason. Well, there was a reason. He was next to Li Feng and she didn't need to be dressed in a threadbare courtesan's robe to entice him.

'Maybe I should be grateful for your past transgressions,' he drawled. 'Otherwise I would have never been one of those thief-catchers with the privilege of chasing after you.'

Li Feng snapped back around, her gaze narrowing on him in cat-like fashion. Then she let out a short laugh. 'What is this, thief-catcher? Your method of courtship?'

He lifted one shoulder in a shrug. They regarded one another across the bamboo mat, her face lit with a smile and him grinning. This was better than courtship. Better than seduction.

All he knew was that even when they were on opposite sides of the law, he still felt a closer connection to her than anyone else in this world. What they had between them defied the boundaries of order and convention and he had never felt anything else like it.

Li Feng let out a long sigh. Her smile faded and

the fragile thread between them broke, or rather it was pulled thin once more.

'I only want to find out what happened to my family,' she told him. 'The jade led me to Cai Yun and now Cai Yun has led me to his master. I will continue my search with Guan He. The rest of this, I leave to you.'

She sounded almost apologetic. He didn't want to drag her into any cause. He had just taken for granted that their paths had become intertwined.

'I haven't forgotten what's important to you,' he assured her. 'Tell me what you remember about your parents.'

She looked up at him from where she knelt. 'Mother was a dancer. Father must have been one as well. We travelled with an entire group of performers. Maybe they came through here at some point. Or maybe we were from this city.'

'What's your family name?'

'I don't remember.' A look of pain flickered across her face. 'It's so infuriating! I remember some things, foolish things, so clearly. And yet something as important as this? Not at all.'

She threw a twig into the brazier. The low flame leapt, as if in response to her frustration, but it settled as the wood burned away. Han watched the slow dance of the fire, trying to understand the depth of Li Feng's loss.

His family was still alive, but in a way, they were lost to him as well. Or rather, he was lost to them. The difference was that he knew where his family was. They lived on a farm now, outside the city where his father had once served as magistrate. Even though he hadn't seen them in years, they were in his thoughts. If they were to suddenly disappear, he would be missing a part of himself.

'You said it was fifteen years ago that you were separated?' he continued.

Li Feng nodded. 'Yes, fifteen. Why do you ask?'

'I told you that my father was a magistrate. I must have still had my milk teeth when he tried to teach me about the law.'

She frowned at him, confused.

'This knowledge…it gives me certain advantages as a thief-catcher.' He didn't want to sound boastful, but he knew his upbringing gave him some insight into the inner workings of the tribunal and the magistrate's office. Part of his success came from being able to speak to appointed officials as well as the constables and common folk. 'You had mentioned the men who came for your mother may have been trying to arrest her for some crime. I can look into the case records in Minzhou. I can't promise anything, but I can try.'

She stared at him, her lips pressed together and her

brow creased in thought. 'Thank you, Hao Han,' she said finally, with a quiet sincerity that touched him.

They edged closer to the fire to enjoy the last of the warmth before it burned out. Even with the doors and windows shut tight, the small space inside the shrine grew chilled as the evening came. He had secured a slightly more hospitable place the day before and was going to suggest that they leave for more comfortable lodging, but Li Feng came and huddled against him with her head against his shoulder.

He would see about relocating tomorrow. For now, the rain outside could turn to snow and he wouldn't have moved from that spot.

Han wrapped his cloak around both of them and his arm slipped around Li Feng, settling around her waist. She steadied a hand flat against his chest, where she could probably feel how his heart had started pumping faster from having her so close. His entire body reacted to her, tensing, warming, wanting.

He did think of bedding her. Of course he did. He also thought of how he'd been a fool not to take her at the Singing Nightingale and again at the salt village. And right now. In his mind, he was already on to their second time together, let alone the first.

He lowered himself to the mat, bringing her with him the entire way. Li Feng settled partially over him and her head found the same spot on his shoulder in the darkness. He was breathing hard by now, though they had barely moved for nearly a quarter of an hour. His hand was cradled at the small of her back and he could feel the tension gathering along her spine. Li Feng had to be thinking along the same lines as he was.

'It would change everything,' he said to her, to himself and to the darkness.

'Would that be so bad?' She was drawing a lazy line along his collarbone with her fingertips. Heaven help him if it wasn't the most erotic caress he'd ever experienced. Just that slightest touch, nowhere near any significant part of his person, and he was already hard.

Every thud of his heart was telling him now. Now. *Now.* With the same insistence with which his thief-catcher instinct had told him to chase after her.

But despite her flirtatious tone, he sensed that it wasn't quite what Li Feng wanted. She seemed content to curl up beside him. Her breathing deepened as she relaxed into sleep.

The stars were not aligned. What else could he say? He knew that was a poor explanation, but it made as much sense as any other reason he could give. They were in a cold shrine, on a hard floor while rain poured outside. And there were unresolved issues between them.

Not eight days ago, Li Feng had run from him.

There was nothing that convinced him she wouldn't run from him again and, though he had lain with women before, he wanted more from Li Feng than that. And he wanted to be more than a moment of heat and passion for her as well, as sweet as that moment might be.

Li Feng burrowed against him and he clasped his arms around her so she couldn't get away. Not that she was trying to at the moment, but he held her tight to him anyway until she relaxed and settled against him. It was true that he wanted much, much more, but for now, this was enough.

## Chapter Ten

The front entrance of the magistrate's yamen was designed to be an imposing sight. Armoured guards flanked either side of it, with a long spear in hand and swords at their belts. Petitioners would enter through the blood red pillars to kneel before the magistrate. The vast compound contained the tribunal and the prison house as well as the various offices of the clerks and deputies that served beneath the county magistrate.

For Han, the towering gate held less intimidation and more of a sort of worn familiarity. When his father held office, the family residence had been located at the back of such a structure. Father would rise early each morning to go to the judicial hall and bureaus located at the front section and he would remain there until long after sundown. When his father was stripped of his title, the family had been evicted from the yamen.

The entrance courtyard was wide and the buildings set far apart to impress visitors with a sense of expansiveness and grandeur. Han found his way to the judicial hall and requested an audience with the county magistrate, citing that he was investigating a case.

'Name?' the senior clerk asked, with his brush poised over his ledger.

'Zheng Hao Han,' he stated.

'You're a thief-catcher?' he asked disdainfully.

Han nodded and debated whether he should claim his father's status as a magistrate in Nanping prefecture. Father would have certainly considered such an act unethical as well as a painful reminder of his dismissal.

'And what is this about?' the clerk asked.

'A private matter of great importance.' He certainly couldn't air an accusation of corruption out in public.

'Come back this afternoon.'

Bureaucrats tended to distrust all men of the sword, even the appointed constables who worked for the magistrate's office.

Han left for the streets, deciding to gather more information on the steward's murder while he waited. Some accounts indicated that there had been one killer responsible, others recalled two or three or as many as ten bandits involved. With so many witnesses involved and such an outrageous crime, it was impossible to get a straight story.

It had the mark of a planned assassination, Han concluded. A swift clean stroke such as this took a long time planning and the blink of an eye to execute. There was no chase through the streets. The killer or killers inexplicably disappeared.

As he walked along the lane, a woman crossing the street caught his attention. There was nothing particularly eye-catching about the way she was dressed. She wore a cotton robe that had been dyed yellow and her hair was tied back to fall over one shoulder. Her face was shielded by a parasol and he spied the smooth curve of one cheek beneath its shadow.

She leapt over a puddle of water left by the rain and Han found himself wishing Li Feng had accompanied him that morning. Not that it was practical, but she had her own ways of seeking out information that he had to admire.

The woman disappeared around the corner before Han recognised what had distracted him. What sort of woman would risk turning an ankle by jumping over muddy water in the streets? Not to mention how ill mannered it appeared.

Before he could start after her, an armed patrol shouted for all the pedestrians to clear the street. Han stepped aside and stepped back against the wall between two shops. He bowed his head with the rest of the crowd as an official litter appeared, hefted on the shoulders of four bearers. An entourage of armed guards flanked either side of the transport.

Han glanced up as the litter passed and had the misfortune of catching the eye of one of the guards.

'Weapons are not allowed on public streets,' the man barked. 'By official edict.'

Han raised his hands, palms faced outward, to show he meant no trouble. By then, the entire procession had stopped before him. Some of the younger guards had their hands at their swords, ready to draw.

A hand reached out from inside the litter to pull the curtain back. Half a face appeared. 'What's your name, my man?'

'Zheng Hao Han.'

'Ah!' The curtain swung aside to reveal a cheerful smile which was quite out of place with the grim countenance of his guards. 'The famous thief-catcher!'

The official ordered the bearers to lower the litter so he could step out on to the street. His belly sagged over his belt as he approached Han. His eyes and mouth looked engulfed by his rounded cheeks. His chin was small in contrast and adorned with a trim beard. He had the look of a well-fed, well-kept bureaucrat in every way. His state robe was made of expensive silk, but the style showed some restraint, being free of excessive embellishment.

'I'm known as Tan Li Kuo,' he introduced.

Han bowed. 'Magistrate Tan.'

He recognised the magistrate's rank from his headdress and the deep green of his robe.

'I'm glad that we had an opportunity to meet like this. I was going to get a drink down the street. Come sit with me.'

The guards scrambled to confiscate Han's sword, but the magistrate waved them away. He similarly refused to get back into the litter for the short trip to the drinking house.

'Let us show them we're not afraid,' he declared to the street in general.

Han assumed 'they' meant the bandits who had committed murder in stark daylight. He followed beside Magistrate Tan, matching the official's shorter gait respectfully.

'Some business there with Two Dragon Lo, eh? Good work there. Very good work.'

Tan was the sort that spoke with his hands. Even while walking, he would pause to turn and make his gestures visible.

'It was my duty,' Han replied.

'You're too humble, Zheng Hao Han.' The magistrate directed two fingers at him. 'And you speak very well for a man of the sword.'

As much as Han was trying to make his speech formal, the magistrate was working to speak informally. As if they were old friends. Han suspected their meeting might not have been accidental and that Magistrate Tan didn't typically break from his duties to drink in the middle of the day.

At the tavern, they were greeted by a hostess and immediately seated in a private salon. Tan poured the wine himself, holding the long sleeve of his robe back as he filled two cups.

'As you've likely heard, the bandit situation here has got out of hand,' the magistrate said, adopting the direct approach. Courtesy dictated they at least drink and speak of other matters for a few cups before coming around to the real purpose of the discussion.

'The murder of the prefect's steward?' Han ventured.

'They've become bold and incorrigible!'

As the son of a magistrate, Han had always assumed all men of that position had the same graveness as his father. The same steely-eyed look. A tight and disapproving thinness about the mouth. For the most part, his assumptions hadn't been too far off the mark. Magistrates tended to maintain a distance which allowed them to decide the fates of men. Tan was nothing like that. The magistrate appeared to be about ten or fifteen years Han's senior.

Quite young for such a position. His soft face had a youthful, innocent look. His expression was similarly wide-eyed and he was surprisingly quick to speak and act, almost to the point of impulsiveness.

'This bad element must be removed before it corrupts our city,' Tan continued. 'Which is why I am so happy to see the famous Thief-catcher Han.'

He lifted his cup and drank emphatically. Han followed his example and downed his drink. As soon as he set the cup down, the magistrate refilled it. It was strange to see a high-ranking official perform such a menial task and it made Han increasingly uncomfortable.

'I heard that another thief-catcher tried to hunt down the killers,' Han said.

'He was found trussed up in front of the yamen one morning, badly beaten. A strip of paper had been attached to him that read: "To all thief-catchers: Find us soon, or we will kill you all." Shameless of them, issuing a public threat!'

'The bandits left the thief-catcher alive?' Han asked.

Magistrate Tan nodded. 'To send a warning. The constables have been reluctant to go after them since.'

A dead man would have been warning enough. A very visible killing followed by the sparing of a thief-catcher? It made little sense.

'I hear that the man who was killed was very important,' Han said.

'Cai Yun had been with the prefect for many years. He was Prefect Guan's unofficial advisor in charge of his household affairs.'

If his steward was involved in salt smuggling, then the prefect was likely involved as well, which put Han in a very difficult position if he were to make a formal accusation. The ledger book was still in his possession as well as all the information he had gathered, but it wasn't as easy as dragging a thief into custody. Such a conspiracy was hard to prove and there were consequences for bringing false accusations, especially against someone as high-ranking as Prefect Guan. A false accusation here could be punishable by death.

'I've sent a petition to the local garrison that has yet to be answered,' Tan continued with impatience. 'And the city guards are under the control of Prefect Guan who has walled himself up in his estate—not to criticise my betters,' he added hastily.

The district was administered judicially by the magistrate's yamen. The magistrate in turn reported directly to the prefect who oversaw the administration of the entire prefecture.

'The magistrate will need to organise his own force then,' Han advised. 'Surely enough volunteers can be gathered to keep the city safe.'

'Very wise counsel.' The magistrate looked pleased. 'As Master Sun says, an army of thousands is easy to attain. But to find a man to lead them…'

The wine that was pleasantly warming him suddenly turned sour in his stomach. The overeager, slightly befuddled look disappeared from Tan's face to be replaced with a look of shrewdness. The magistrate wasn't seeking the services of a thief-catcher. He had lured and prodded and coaxed Han into a corner.

Han held up his hands. 'Magistrate Tan, you flatter me, but you have the wrong man. I'm not up to this task.'

'But your valiant capture of that notorious bandit Lo—'

Again with Lo. That one incident was turning out to be a curse.

'My head constable is getting late in his years. Most of his men lack extensive training in weapons or fighting,' Magistrate Tan prodded. 'Surely an upstanding, heroic individual such as yourself wouldn't turn his back on such a dire situation.'

'Honourable sir, there are others who are undoubtedly more qualified.'

'Now don't be so humble,' Tan insisted. He sipped his wine to allow some time to pass. 'I doubt there is anyone more suited to this job. What was it I heard?

Something about your father once holding an important office?'

His expression was mild. His gaze, however, was pinpoint sharp in contrast. Here was the shrewdness Han had expected. Tan Li Kuo wore the magistrate's robe in a different way from his father, but he was no less formidable.

'If the magistrate will excuse my ignorance,' Han began. 'I often hear rumors of gangs of bandits terrorising the countryside, but such outlaws prefer to attach themselves to a wide area and bleed it slowly, stealing from merchants when they were far from the protection of the city garrisons. In this humble thief-catcher's opinion, bandits don't murder prominent civilians for no apparent reason.'

'What are you suggesting? You can come out with it, we're friends here!'

Actually, they were far from friends. Han knew nothing about the magistrate's loyalties or if he was trustworthy, but Tan had taken the risk of criticising the prefect earlier. It was an obvious opening and perhaps Magistrate Tan was the ally he needed.

In the end, his upbringing wouldn't allow him to withhold information from a county magistrate. Despite the taint of corruption in Minzhou, Han still believed that a man of the law like Magistrate Tan would rise above it.

'I have some information that might provide some insight on the situation.'

He briefly described the activities at the salt well and the adjoining village. 'Cai Yun could have been killed by smugglers or associates he'd crossed. Or he could have been killed to be silenced,' Han suggested.

Tan listened carefully. 'Do you have any evidence of Cai Yun's involvement?'

'I can't be certain, but I do have records detailing the salt production at the well.'

'I'll need to see them.'

'Of course, sir.'

The magistrate seemed quite satisfied. 'You're a good man, Zheng Hao Han. An honest man. Our office can certainly use your experience hunting down these killers in the meantime.'

'I will do what I can.' How could he refuse? He had started something and intended to see it to its end, with the smuggling ring as well as Li Feng.

'There is one more thing,' he said as Tan was finishing his wine. 'If I may be allowed to look at the local case records.'

The magistrate raised his eyebrows. 'A thief-catcher who likes searching through records, eh? Is this another scandal I need to know about?'

'No, sir.' Han bowed humbly. 'Just a personal matter.'

'He asks for so little. The mark of a true hero.' Tan gave a small wave of his hand. 'Consider it done.'

The magistrate drained his cup, concluding business neatly over the space of one pot of warmed wine.

# Chapter Eleven

Han had warned her that morning to stay away from Prefect Guan. He was an appointed official and a powerful man. Han had also pointed out that with the recent murder in the streets, the guards would be patrolling vigilantly. Li Feng had nodded at him, telling him that she understood, but she prepared to leave as soon as he was gone.

Li Feng did understand the risks, but she also sensed her answers were finally within reach. *Shifu* had tried all her life to teach her patience, preaching action through non-action, but she had failed to absorb that lesson. She would go mad waiting inside that tiny shrine for Han to return.

The rain had given her a reprieve that morning and a hint of sun appeared from behind the clouds. She replaced the grey Taoist garb with a modest cotton robe from her pack and took a parasol with her. Today she was a young woman on a morning stroll.

She wanted to take a look at the prefect's residence, that was all.

As she walked the muddied streets, Li Feng took note of the placement of buildings and walls, paying attention to not just what was visible from down low, but on high as well. In her mind, she marked out the lanes and avenues. It was a habit she'd formed upon first returning to Fujian province. The sprawling cities were less intimidating to her once she'd mapped them in her mind's eye.

At the river, she located a dock and waited for the ferry to take her along the water. Her first glimpse of the prefect's residence was from the river. All there was to see was the surrounding wall, which enclosed a spacious mansion. An array of winged rooftops rose just above the brick barrier.

Later Li Feng approached the house on foot, with her head ducked beneath her parasol to peek at it like a shy admirer. She had been holding on to so little for so long: a piece of jade and her fragmented memories. Now the Guan mansion loomed before her, so large and real that she wanted to believe she was close. She wanted to put her hand against the grey brick to mark the moment, but there were guards in front. Another squad patrolled the perimeter.

She considered calling at the front gate and presenting the jade. Mother must have given her the pendant for a reason. Was Prefect Guan somehow related to them? Had Mother been running from this place or running to it?

In the end, Li Feng passed by the gate without stopping. The place had a discordant feel to her, a bad energy. It was barricaded like a fortress and the guards were less than welcoming. Instead she shifted her attention from the front gate to the wall. It rose five or six *chi* over her head and the brick-work provided grooves and a roughened texture that would make it easy to find footing.

Li Feng could easily evade the patrols. She could scale the wall with a running leap and be over in one breath.

But what would she do once she was inside? Maybe she would find old memories there, long discarded and waiting to be recovered. Or maybe there was nothing to see beyond the empty shell of a house.

Whatever she was going to do, it had to wait until dark. She left the mansion before the guards recognised that she had been skulking about.

On a whim, she made a few enquiries and fol-lowed the directions to a neighbourhood where the streets were narrow and the houses worn and shabby in appearance. A school was located at one corner. There was no door on the front gate and Li Feng was able to peek into the courtyard to see a group of ten young girls practising dance drills. The youngest of them appeared not much older than four. They lifted their right arms overhead in unison, keeping a graceful rounded curve, fingers shaped in lotus position. Next they raised the left arm to create a mirror image, then both arms gradually down, hands fluttering like falling leaves.

Li Feng watched them, transfixed by the unity of movement, until the rap of a bamboo switch against the gate snapped her back to attention. A middle-aged woman stood before her. She wore her hair in a severely coiled bun and wore an even more severe expression on her face.

'Why are you here?' the headmistress demanded.

'I was trying to look for a dance troupe,' Li Feng began.

'This is a school. We only train children.'

There were many such schools for orphaned and abandoned children throughout the province. Li Feng might have gone to such a place if *shifu* hadn't taken her in. The girls glanced over at the disturbance, but immediately returned their attention to their drills.

'I apologise for the intrusion, madam.' She started to ask whether the school worked with a performance group that toured the province, but the woman cut her off.

'You go on to the courtesan district,' she suggested sharply. 'There's no use for you here.'

The whole endeavour was a waste of time. Li Feng left the school, her initial feeling of anticipation draining out of her. She had thought she might find a familiar face, but fifteen years was too long. The troupe her family had travelled with would be scattered to the four corners of the Earth by now.

As she returned to the main avenue, she sensed movement off to the side. She whipped around to stare at an empty alleyway, but there had been someone there just a moment ago, she was certain of it. She darted between the two buildings, eyes searching the shadows, her sleeve sword close in case she needed it.

'Zheng Hao Han, are you following me?' she demanded, directing her question to the surrounding walls.

It was just like the thief-catcher to sneak after her, but there was no answer. If it wasn't Han, then someone else was stalking her. A stranger had been secretly watching her in the market the day before. Two occurrences were too much of a coincidence.

When she turned the corner, the hairs on her neck rose. A set of fresh footprints was visible in the mud. They led to a wall where the prints suddenly ended. Whoever had been spying on her had disappeared by going up and over, as easy as if he were walking.

The clerks in the magistrate's office certainly kept meticulous records. Han spent hours scanning through book rolls, searching through a list of thefts and disputes for any case that resembled the circumstances Li Feng had described. Something involving a dancer or a group of vagrants coming through the city. He was also paying special attention for any case that might mention Prefect Guan or his steward. After a good ten book rolls, nothing had caught his notice.

As evening approached, Han requested a lamp which the clerk provided. Han pressed his knuckles to his eyes. The endless columns of characters were beginning to swim before him. It had been nearly ten years since he'd ended his studies, to his father's disapproval. It was much, much easier chasing down bandits than reading casebooks.

He blinked away the cobwebs in his head and resumed his search. By the end of the next double hour, he was thinking his efforts were for nothing. All the cases started sounding like one another. Li Feng hadn't even been able to give him a family name to search for. Han switched to a list of arrest warrants.

Halfway through the scroll, one of the descriptions sent a tremor down his spine. It was for the arrest of a woman who had fled the county after her husband was imprisoned. Han jumped as the clerk's voice rang out.

'The records hall will be closing soon.'

Urgently, Han checked the warrant numbering and date and returned to the case records, using a finger to keep track of the columns. He could hear the clerk's footsteps approaching and his heart was beating as fast as it had in any hunt.

Then suddenly it was all there before him with startling clarity. A crime that had occurred at the prefect's residence fifteen years earlier.

'Honourable sir.'

The clerk stood over his shoulder as Han read through the case report as fast as he could.

'*Sir,*' the man repeated, sharper and more insistent. 'The yamen gates are closing for the day. All of the functionaries are to leave the premises.'

Han nodded and quickly wrote down the case information with his ink brush. The clerk, who was at least ten years his senior, was busy rolling up the scrolls and packing them back on to the shelves.

'Don't you know there's a very strict curfew in effect? In another hour, the city patrols will be hassling anyone on the main streets.' The man snorted impatiently. 'My home is at the far corner of the East Gate neighbourhood. Who has the money to hire a carriage?'

The clerk snatched up the final scroll just as Han finished inking the last character.

'You best get going yourself,' he huffed. 'The patrols will be even less understanding with an outsider. You might find yourself back here after all, spending the night in a holding cell.'

It was good advice, despite the clerk's brusque attitude. Han retrieved his weapon from the constable's station and left through the main gate, which the guards promptly barred shut behind him.

The main market area to the south of the yamen had closed as well. He had enough time to get to the shrine where he and Li Feng had spent the evening, though he hoped to convince her to return to his lodging instead, as scandalous as it might seem. The room he'd found was considerably warmer and they'd moved beyond the lines of propriety long ago.

There was a man selling charcoal on the street and Han stopped to purchase some, just in case they were forced to spend another night at the shrine. As he continued towards the plain wooden gate at the corner, his stomach knotted. He didn't know how to tell Li Feng what he'd discovered. Even though he had read through the case briefly, his gut told him he had found the right one.

He pushed open the gate and entered the courtyard. The windows of the altar room were black like the hollowed eyes of a skull. When Han peered inside, only the lifeless statues at the altar stared back at him.

Li Feng's absence struck him like a physical blow. After holding her close through the night, he'd as-

sumed she would be there waiting for him. He should
have known it was against her nature to stay still for
so long, especially when she thought the answers she
was searching for were somewhere within the city.

Han lit a small fire in the brazier and waited, but
as the end of the hour neared, he knew she wasn't
coming. He hoped that Li Feng would be careful,
wherever it was that she had gone. The incident he'd
read about hadn't involved theft. It had detailed a
crime of assault and murder.

An unbroken string of drumbeats sounded at the
start of the Hour of the Dog. It was followed by three
strikes of the gong and then another string of drumbeats. The pattern was repeated at several stations
throughout the city. Curfew.

An edict had been declared after the violent killing just a few days ago. No weapons were allowed
in the open. Administrative buildings were heavily
guarded and all public officials were to have an
armed escort out in public. Shortly after sundown,
the city patrols swept the streets, pushing stragglers
into their respective neighbourhoods. The sentries
had the authority to imprison anyone suspicious who
was found outside.

Li Feng avoided the first stream of armed guards
she encountered by squeezing into the narrow space
between two shops. Once the patrol had moved on,

she slipped onto side streets and back alleys to navigate her way back to the prefect's residence. The path of the river provided an easy landmark for maintaining her direction. If there was a wall in the way, she leapt over it.

At the Guan mansion, there was an additional set of guards stationed around the perimeter. The lanterns were still on inside the walls so she pressed back into the shadows to wait as the lights were extinguished, one after another, until only a few faint glimmers remained.

By that time, it was deep into the night and the stars were out. The three-quarter moon cast a translucent glow over the residence and Li Feng waited for clouds to drift over the face of it to begin her climb. It appeared as if the guards circled every quarter of an hour. She would have to move quickly as soon as they cleared the corner.

A flicker of movement down the street stopped her just as she was about to make her run. Someone else was also staking out the residence. Or worse, someone was watching her.

Blood rushed to her limbs as her body prepared for flight. Li Feng breathed steadily to calm herself as she stepped back into the shadows, into the maze of lanes and alleys. The curfew had left these corridors quiet, dark and empty. She could see the haze of a lantern just beyond the end of the street, hidden behind the black outline of the buildings. The night watch.

She stopped and remained still, head tilted to catch faint sounds. There were footsteps padding towards her, gaining speed, their distance closing. There was more than one person.

As the pursuers closed in, Li Feng spun around. She drew her sword and struck at eye level. A cry of pain answered her along with a pressure that travelled through the blade as steel cut through flesh. Not deep, but deep enough. The first figure fell back against a second one. It was time to run.

She ran towards the lantern light. Her stomach plummeted as the men shouted out to others. The shadows came alive ahead of her and two others emerged, blocking her way.

They had four to her one. What she needed to do was go up, up and over, but the space was too narrow to manoeuvre. She was forced to fight force with force, which was a losing proposition. Li Feng positioned her back to the wall and glanced at the men on either side of her. Raising the short sword with her right hand, she slipped a throwing knife into her left.

'Lower your sword, girl. The Black Eagle wants to meet you,' a voice grated in the darkness.

She absolutely would *not* lower her sword. 'I don't know anyone who goes by that name.'

'You won't be harmed,' he promised.

She looked over the men again. Their clothes were mismatched and ragged. Their beards overgrown. One had a new gash cutting across his nose, just missing his eyes which now glared at her murderously, but no one made a move as they waited for her answer.

She didn't trust them, but they could have overpowered her had they chosen to and there was nowhere to run. She could have called for the city guards, but they might very well cut her throat at that point and leave her in the alley.

'I keep my sword,' she said. 'And you keep your distance.'

'By all means.'

There was disdain in his tone. These men weren't afraid of her. Li Feng considered running once again, but she had a feeling that, if she was caught, these men would not be so accommodating after the added trouble.

'Where is this Black Eagle?' Her lips curled around the lofty moniker.

'Outside the city.'

'The gates are closed.'

'We know of other ways.'

They led her into what appeared to be a garden in an abandoned property. There was a well at the corner of it, which she was told led to a tunnel. Li Feng took the rope after the first two had disappeared into the blackness. She forced herself to breathe as she sank past the stone ring. The old fear rose up her throat like bile as she was surrounded by stone and rock. She tried to quiet her mind as Wen *shifu* tried to teach her, but instead of calm, she found a chilling numbness that deadened her fear along with the rest of her. It would have to do.

At the bottom, the water rose up past her ankles. The space was just big enough to walk through at a crouch. Li Feng held her hand against the dirt walls as a guide and an anchor. The rest of the gang followed in behind her and together they shuffled blind through the tunnel.

Whoever these men were, they were organised. She was reminded of her time among rebels. Perhaps that was how she was able to hold back her fear as they took her into the unknown.

As soon as the passage widened, her lungs opened and her muscles relaxed. They emerged in a shallow cistern outside the city borders. The suffocating enclosure of dirt and rock was replaced by clean night air.

The leader retrieved a lantern hidden behind a pile of stones. They had planned this, she realised as he lit the lantern and beckoned her towards the nearby woods. The gang kept their distance as promised, but they formed a ring around her as they ventured into the wilderness.

She wondered who this Black Eagle could be and why he would be intent on speaking with her. Though the men dressed and acted like outlaws, there were signs of discipline among them.

The air grew cool and damp as they continued on foot. The whisper of open water cut through the hum of insects and other night creatures. She tested the ground, checking for her footing against the springiness of loam and moss in case she needed to run. Out here, they no longer had her trapped. She could escape and hide among the brush and the trees if there was any threat.

A lone figure waited inside the tree line with his back to them. He was long-limbed and lean of build. When he turned, his eyes immediately sought her out. The dim lantern light revealed features that were hawkish and well-defined, a mouth that was a bit on the harsh side and eyes that were set deep and pierced into her. His jaw was covered by a rough growth of stubble. His long hair was tied back, but that didn't make him look any less feral. He looked more like a stray wolf than an eagle.

He swallowed nervously, the knot at his throat lifting and lowering. 'You don't remember me.'

'You were following me that morning in the market.'

It wasn't the answer he was looking for. His posture was tense as he regarded her. 'Li Feng,' he began, his voice rough with emotion.

She was startled to hear her name on his lips.

'Little Sister.' He tried again. 'I'm your brother.'

Li Feng sifted through memories. As always, there was the running, her mother shutting her inside the rock. Before that moment, her mind was a blur of disconnected images. There was another presence beside her. Someone bigger than her. She remembered reaching for a hand. She remembered someone pulling on her braids. She remembered laughing together.

*She had a brother.* It was a truth she had known without knowing. After searching for so long, after hoping against hope, she'd found what she was looking for.

'How did you know it was me?' she asked finally, in a whisper.

He smiled, looking happy, looking sad. 'You look like Mother.'

Li Feng followed her older brother to a shallow part of the river, crossing it in several well-placed leaps from one rock to another. It was like a game, so much like the ones they must have once played.

'Black Eagle is a silly name,' she called ahead to him.

He was without shame. 'Who knows how these nicknames come about?'

His feet made a splash at the edge of the bank. She cleared the jump without any problem, landing on soft grass and springing after him. They regarded each other once again, not yet knowing how to be with one another. This man had suddenly become the closest person in the world to her. Such was the pull of blood, of family. But they were still strangers.

'I don't even know your real name, Brother.'

'It's Liu Yuan. Our family name is Hua.'

Hua Li Feng. Hua Liu Yuan. The names felt right on her lips. She took them into her heart.

They had left the others behind as they went deep into the woods, winding around the tall and straight tree trunks which gleamed pale in the night. The surrounding hills engulfed them, blocking out the moon and the stars. Their final destination was a cavern beneath an outcropping of rock. Inside, Liu Yuan lighted an oil lamp and placed it on a flat stone which he used as a table. He produced a gourd and poured the contents into two ceramic cups.

She was at a loss. Here was a brother she barely remembered. A man who clearly lived as an outlaw. She sat down obediently at the table and struggled to find something to say. Liu Yuan seemed similarly lost. He raised his cup wordlessly to her, before downing it. She did the same.

The brew seared her throat and brought tears to her eyes. It was raw, harsh, with a taste that was earthy and medicinal. She felt vindicated as Liu Yuan choked back a cough as well, before grinning at her. She smiled back, feeling foolish. Feeling happy.

'Little Sister,' he began.

'Elder Brother.' She tested the feel of the address on her tongue.

'Do you remember when I tried to lift you on my shoulders, the way they do in those acrobatic routines?'

She shook her head as he refilled her cup. This time, she took a much smaller sip, barely wetting her lips.

'You were all the way up there. Standing.' He gestured with both hands over his head. 'And then suddenly you started wobbling. I started yelling, "Don't move! Don't move!", as I tried to regain my balance, but we both ended up falling.'

Li Feng stifled a laugh behind her hand. 'So we were troublemakers!'

He nodded. 'You hit your head on a rock and started wailing. By the time Father came, you were bleeding so badly. I was so scared.' He looked up at her and the lamplight danced in his eyes. 'I don't know why I think of that time so often. I should apologise now, hmm?'

'No matter. I'm sure it didn't hurt that much.' She tilted her head towards him, teasing.

'You were afraid of nothing, Little Sister. Ever since you could walk, you wanted to fly.'

He finished his cup and she felt obliged to do the same. The liquor burned a little less this time and her cheeks were beginning to tingle with warmth. She wished she could remember the incident more clearly.

On a whim, she reached up to feel the spot just above her left ear. There was a small scar there, hidden beneath her hair. She'd always had it, but had never known how she got it. Her brother's story found its place inside of her and she had that feeling she had longed for all these years, of the pieces of her life falling into place.

A knot formed in her throat and she didn't know whether to laugh or to cry. She became hungry for more memories. What other games had they played? What were the cities they'd visited? What was Father like?

'Father played the flute,' Liu Yuan said.

The flute. The beautiful sound that floated through to her on the mountainside. A lightness filled her. There was pattern, a will, a rightness to the world that had led her to this moment.

Her brother went on, 'He had an instrument made

of bamboo and would play it at night when we couldn't sleep. I tried to learn, but...'

His voice trailed off and he looked away.

The moment of joy began to fade when she noticed Liu Yuan was no longer speaking. He was staring into his cup. This time when he drank, it was as if he was forcing the bitter brew down.

He brushed the back of his hand over his mouth, pausing to search for words. 'When we were separated, I never thought—'

'Everything will be all right now,' she said. 'We've found each other.'

When he met her eyes, his look was bleak. It was the same look that had frightened her the first time she'd seen him, when she hadn't known he was her brother.

'Li Feng, so much has happened. I brought you here so we could at least meet. So you could know who I was.'

'Don't talk like that.'

'You can't remember what it was like.' He scrubbed a hand over his mouth again. It was an agitated, frustrated gesture. 'I was with Father when they came to arrest him.'

Where had she been? She was with Mother. Li Feng remembered hiding in a boat and her mother telling her to be still, be quiet. She wasn't sure if she wanted to know the rest of it now, but she had to find out the truth. She couldn't be afraid of it any more.

'What did they do that was so wrong?' she asked, dreading the answer.

'Nothing.' Liu Yuan laughed and the sound was awful in the night. 'Nothing, Little Sister.'

The story came out in a flood. Mother was a dancer. Father was a musician. They travelled together with a troupe of performers who were like family. The band would move from city to city throughout the province, making enough to survive at each stop. It was a carefree existence.

'Then we came to Minzhou,' Liu Yuan explained. 'There was a special performance for the Full Moon festival. It was a great success and everyone was so happy. Father brought us moon cakes.'

'How old were we?' she asked.

'I was eight at the time. You couldn't have been more than four.'

She had been half his age. He would remember the events clearer than she did, though still through the eyes of a child. Liu Yuan was the key to everything she'd been searching for.

'There was to be another performance the next night. A private one.' At that, his jaw tightened. 'The prefect had taken a liking to our mother and it was impossible to deny such an important official such a simple request.'

She tensed as if preparing for a physical blow. 'What happened then?'

'Father and Mother went to the prefect's mansion with several other members of the troupe. No one is certain what happened, but after the performance there was a dispute. I was later told...' He paused, gathering his breath. 'Much later, I was told by the troupe master that Guan He propositioned Mother after the performance. He tried to drag her into a chamber where they would be alone.'

'She fought him.'

'Of course she did!' Liu Yuan said vehemently. 'Our father saw them and struck the prefect. A blow to the head. There was blood everywhere, they said. He nearly killed that bastard.'

Li Feng dug her nails into her palms. She didn't need to ask what happened then. The court would think little of the prefect attempting to violate her mother, but the crime of striking an official, committed by someone of such low birth, had to be punished.

'I wasn't allowed to watch when they executed Father.' For the first time his voice broke. 'They killed him like a dog in the street.'

He took another draught and hid his eyes from her. She drank as well. The burn of the liquor down her throat covered up a pain that was sharper and deeper.

The rest of her brother's story was full of a seething anger. Liu Yuan stayed with the troupe. The first time he tried to leave, he was caught stealing, but was young enough that the authorities had sentenced a beating with the light rod before returning him to the troupe leader. He grew older, stronger and angrier before he left again. When he was caught this time, the beating was with a heavy rod and they'd inked a tattoo on to his hand so honest men would know not to trust him.

'I learned how to use the knife out of necessity,' he told her. 'And turned to banditry because there was nothing left to lose. They had already marked me as such.'

He held up the back of his right hand to her. A black character had been etched near his thumb.

'Thief,' he read aloud. 'Such a mark ensures that I can never walk among honest society. I knew this life would kill me or teach me to kill. One or the other, I didn't care.'

'Liu Yuan,' she murmured softly.

Her heart ached for him. She wished she could offer some comfort. Her life had been easy in comparison. *Shifu* hadn't treated her with the warmth and affection of a parent, but he'd been caring and patient and tried to teach her in his own way. He had taught her how to channel her restlessness into the study of the sword.

'I was sentenced to labour once, building ships on the coast. But wherever they sent me, I always knew I had to return to this place. I had left something unfinished in Minzhou.'

'I feel the same way, Brother,' she said in a near whisper.

His sentiment echoed the emptiness that Li Feng had felt in her own soul.

'I never knew what happened to you or Mother,' he said after a long pause. 'There was no way to find you.'

'They caught her as well.' She couldn't say more. Her throat had closed up.

The finality of what had happened shook them both. Li Feng finally had her answers. Her father was dead, executed for crimes committed. Mother was gone as well.

'They said Father fought when they arrested him,' her brother continued. 'He cursed the magistrate and the prefect at the trial. He was unrepentant. His spirit is still here, Little Sister.'

The thought of Father's spirit wandering the city as a hungry ghost chilled her. She'd been neglectful as a daughter. 'We'll set up an altar and light incense to send him our prayers.'

Her words didn't seem to reach her brother.

'You carry a sword.' Her sleeve had fallen away

and Liu Yuan stared at the hilt of the weapon. 'Do you know how to use it?'

'Yes.' She pulled her sleeve back and rearranged it carefully to cover up the sword. A sense of unease stirred inside her. 'I know how to use it.'

'Mother was a dancer and our father played beautiful music. Now look at us. Funny, isn't it?'

Despite his words, there was no amusement in his tone.

'You killed the steward,' she said, her stomach turning.

'With my very own hands,' he replied with cold pride.

'But he was innocent.'

'Innocent?' His mouth twisted. 'Cai Yun was the one who came to the troupe leader bearing gifts to show off his master's wealth. He demanded a private performance.'

*Gifts.* She pulled the jade from her sash and showed it to Liu Yuan. 'Mother gave this to me before they took her.'

Liu Yuan stared at the jade, but would not touch it. 'That scoundrel brought that to our mother. "My master is a great admirer," he said. Like a damned procurer for a brothel. I don't know why she kept it.'

A knot formed in the pit of her stomach. To wealthy pleasure-seekers, dancers and entertainers were little more than prostitutes.

Only now did Li Feng make sense of these fragments of her memory. Mother had tried to sell the jade. She had tried to go to shopkeepers and even begged on the street for someone to buy it from her. She was desperate for the money, but no one would take the jade. It was too fine, too expensive.

Why had her mother given the jade to her, then? Was it to provide for her the only way she could? Li Feng had held on to the pendant for so long. She had traced the lines of the carving and held the stone close to her until it became warm against her skin.

Jade changed over time, as it took in the essence of its wearer. For the first time, she noticed there was a thin vein of red along the bird's wing as if it had been wounded. Even this reminder of her mother was now tainted.

'They owe us blood, Li Feng.' The words rang eerily, surrounded by darkness and the lonely flicker of the candle. 'They owe us blood. They owe us blood.'

With each repetition, Liu Yuan's voice grew stronger. The darkness of the cave became heavy around her until it seemed once again she was in that tiny hole in the rock, suffocating with dread.

They'd both been children, helpless and unable to do anything, but Liu Yuan had the burden of being the eldest son. The responsibility for taking care of their parents fell to him, in body once they grew old and frail, and in spirit once they had passed on to join their ancestors. But Father and Mother would never grow old.

For him, blood was the only way. How else could he ever atone for a line that was broken? For lives that were wrongfully cut short?

Part of her rebelled. She wasn't the same as her brother. Liu Yuan was a man of violence. He killed his enemies. He cut their throats and left them lying in the street. She remembered the fear and the loss of being abandoned, but she also knew that life was both pain and happiness, that the world was light and dark and opposing forces. These were the teachings of Wen *shifu*. This was the Tao.

But what enlightenment the teachings provided her at this moment of darkness was no more than the flicker of a candle.

'Revenge would mean your death as well,' she said, trying to remain calm.

'But we're already dead, aren't we, Little Sister?'

His eyes were black and empty. The search for her past had consumed her, but now she had been reunited with her brother, the only family she had. Finding him should have brought them both happiness. Instead she was rendered as cold and dark inside as he was.

# Chapter Twelve

Han was up with the sun the next morning, ready to search for Li Feng for the rest of the day if needed. He shouldn't have been so worried. He found her a few streets away, walking down the street and absently browsing the morning market stalls.

The grey robes of the Taoist priestess were gone, traded for a cotton robe dyed in the warm colours of a spring peach. The skirt was shortened, falling just past her knees. Her hair was pinned carelessly and she was turned away from him, but he still recognised her. The sight of her locked into him as it always did.

He could sense her through distance, through crowds. He didn't need to see her face or hear her voice. He was aware of her beyond sight and sound. Han would have liked to boast that it had something to do with superior thief-catching instincts, but it was nothing like that. He was always finding her because every part of him was always searching for her.

She turned and saw him. They met in the middle of the street while the crowd flowed by on either side of them.

'Li Feng,' he greeted.

'Hao Han.'

'I was looking for you.'

'I was looking for you too…for once.' Her faint smile was for her own benefit, not his.

He should have been relieved that she hadn't once again disappeared, but the tightness in his chest remained. One day he would no longer be able to find her. She would be lost to him for ever and the thought of it left him gutted.

'What…' He paused, looking at the dark circles under her eyes. Her ivory complexion was as pale as milk. 'What happened?'

She didn't answer, but her expression appeared haunted. Searching amongst the food stalls, Han selected one with benches where they could sit and settled in opposite her, folding his legs beside the low table. Li Feng watched listlessly as a steaming bowl of chicken and ginger soup was set before her.

Usually Li Feng was a joy to watch. There was a perpetual fire in her eyes and she was like a hummingbird, never holding still. This morning, her usual spirited manner was locked away. Something had changed.

'I went to the prefect's residence last night,' she confessed. She spooned some of the soup into her mouth, her colour returning a little as she ate.

'What were you hoping to find?'

'It doesn't matter,' she said, her tone sharpening. 'I didn't go inside.'

Li Feng spooned soup into her mouth. For a while, he just watched her.

'Not hungry?' she murmured, seeing how he hadn't touched his food.

He'd been stalling, trying to work out the best way to tell her what he'd learned. 'I never asked you what you planned to do after you found what happened to your family,' he said, still stalling.

She regarded him for a long time before answering, 'I don't know. I haven't thought of it.'

The search had consumed her. It was the reason behind everything she'd done, right or wrong. Han knew how a single goal could consume a person. He had investigated and searched for Two Dragon Lo for months, convinced that the bandit was growing more dangerous with each passing day and needed to be stopped. By the end of it, he couldn't remember when he'd become so intent on hunting Lo down. He was also left without any purpose once the bandit was dead.

'You've discovered something about my mother,' she realised, looking deep into his eyes. 'Something about me.'

'There was a case in the city fifteen years ago involving a musician.'

Her expression was unreadable. 'Go on.'

This was about Li Feng's family and her past. He had no right to keep it from her.

'Prefect Guan was hosting a banquet at his residence and hired several performers,' he began. 'The musician and his wife were caught in the house, attempting to steal. Guan He discovered them and the husband attacked him. The prefect was struck repeatedly, but that wasn't the worst of it. A servant came to the prefect's defence and was left dead in the courtyard, bleeding from a wound to the head.'

Li Feng's mouth pulled tight, but she said nothing, waiting for his report to continue. He had always known she was strong, but there was something unnatural in her silence. They were surrounded by the clatter of dishes and the conversations of the other customers. Han wished he had waited until they were alone to tell her everything.

'After the musician was arrested, he wouldn't confess to the theft, but he did take responsibility for the servant's death, claiming it was an accident.'

'Admitting his guilt,' she said.

'I'm sorry, Li Feng.'

Her face remained blank of emotion, though her hands were folded in front of her. He could see the struggle within her as she clasped them tight.

'Do you believe all of that?' she asked quietly.

'It doesn't matter what I believe. This is what was recorded.'

He was trying hard to be impassive, even continuing to speak of the man and his wife as if they weren't Li Feng's father and mother. But it was impossible to remain detached. His own father had always insisted on objectivity, but Han wasn't like his father.

'You don't need to soften the blow. Tell me everything.' Her demeanour remained too calm for all that she had heard.

There was no easy way to say it. 'The musician was executed for the death of the servant and for striking a government official.'

'What of his wife?' Her bottom lip trembled as she spoke. For the first time during the conversation, a sliver of emotion pierced her armour.

'She fled the city and was later captured. The casebook records that she was sentenced to death and allowed to commit suicide.'

A small tremor moved along her jaw, but she bit down against it. Despite the public setting, Han reached for her, but Li Feng rose to stand. She straightened her spine and lifted her chin proudly.

'Whatever that report may say, my father and mother were not thieves,' she insisted. 'They weren't sentenced because they tried to rob the prefect. They were executed because they dared to disobey.'

With that, she pushed out into the street, weaving with a dancer's grace and strength through the crowd. Pedestrians were left staring at this girl who dared to move with such audacity.

Han chased after her, but Li Feng broke away from the street to climb on to the bridge that spanned the main canal. She gripped the wooden rail with one hand and in the next breath she was up and over, disappearing over the side. Cursing, Han ran to the bridge to see that she'd landed safely down below. He climbed on to the rail and dropped on to the embankment beside her.

Unimpressed by his dramatic manoeuvre, she turned away and headed towards the bridge. He caught her by the arm to swing her around, then immediately regretted his forcefulness when her eyes flashed fire at him.

'I know this must be difficult for you. This is a great tragedy.' He struggled to find the right words, but his tongue was thick in his mouth, his words stiff and stilted.

'We are finished, you and I.' In contrast, Li Feng's words lashed out with all the emotion she'd tried so hard to keep hidden.

'We're not finished. Far from it.'

He followed her as she strode beneath the arch of the bridge. They were enclosed in a cool, mossy darkness away from the noise of the city.

'I know what you want,' he began.

'You don't know anything.' She kept on walking and refused to face him.

'You want what anyone would want. To set things right.'

Li Feng did turn on him then. 'None of this means anything to you,' she accused, her voice trembling. 'My mother and father broke the law and they were punished. Justice was served.'

'That isn't what I think—'

'You would never understand,' she went on vehemently. 'The meaning of family. Of loyalty.'

'You don't know what you're speaking of, Li Feng.'

His voice barely rose, but his face flushed hot with anger. She had gone too far. He knew about the importance of family. He'd sacrificed everything for his.

'Your family is alive, yet you've turned away from them. You've chosen to be alone.'

He froze beneath her onslaught, but this wasn't about his family or his loss. It was about hers.

'Li Feng, don't run away. Just—just stay for once.' He was angry at her, angry for her. He didn't know any more.

'I know who you are, Zheng Hao Han,' she challenged. 'You believe in upholding the law, yet you've taken a liking to me. So you've told yourself I must be innocent, because how could Thief-catcher Han ever befriend a common criminal?'

He could feel her slipping away as she pulled out of the shadows and back into the sunlight.

'But I'm not innocent,' she declared. 'Don't follow me any more. We go our separate ways from here, Han. This is the way it has to be and you know it.'

Han trailed Li Feng at a distance, always keeping her in sight. Usually Li Feng moved with efficiency and grace, but today even the way she carried herself was unbalanced and off-centre. She wandered the streets for a while, as if lost, before leaving the city through the main gate.

When she strayed from the road, his instincts told him to turn back. Family was a deep and private matter and she was mourning for something that had been taken away from her fifteen years ago. But he couldn't leave her to feel such pain alone. At some point she would slow down and they could talk.

He meant every word when he told her they had become friends. What had his life been before Li Feng? He had no illusions. The life of a thief-catcher wasn't a glorious one: chasing down one criminal after another and collecting coins for it. Killing treacherous men until one of them killed him. He sent the money home for his brother's studies along with letters to his father and mother, yet he'd avoided returning himself.

Li Feng had seen that part of him that he had refused to admit. She made it sound as if he'd denied his family. As if he were ashamed of them, when the truth was very much the opposite. Han stayed away to protect his family. His father always insisted on order and discipline within the household. Arguments over Han's dangerous profession would upset the peace and cause strife amongst them. It was best for everyone.

He had become a thief-catcher because something needed to be done. The family could no longer support themselves, certainly not while their eldest son focused on studying the classics while earning nothing. So Han had made a decision and gone out on his own.

Han waited for Li Feng to cast a glance over her shoulder, but she never did. She was moving deep into the woods now and it was quickly becoming apparent that she wasn't escaping to some secluded place to grieve. His thief-catcher instinct awakened, all senses becoming alert.

He let the tangle of brush and vine swallow him as he continued to track her. Emotion drove him now, not strategy or reason. Li Feng was pushing blindly through the trees. Branches scraped and snapped over her and she swiped at them viciously, as if fighting an invisible foe.

She was going to meet someone.

His stomach turned at the thought, but Han fell back so he could continue to follow her undetected.

At the river, he waited until Li Feng skipped over the stones to disappear behind the trees before making his own crossing. It wasn't too difficult to recapture her trail given how haplessly she tore through the wilderness.

Li Feng had done questionable things, he knew that. But he had also come to know her. Li Feng was right that he believed in justice, but so did she. Her code of honour was different from the one he'd been taught. In Li Feng's world, material possessions held no value, but loyalty was priceless. She believed in protecting the weak. She was also so starved of contact that anyone who helped her was quickly taken in to her circle of trust. Even if he was a thief-catcher.

As he reached the shadow of the hills, he heard Li Feng calling out to someone. His suspicions were correct. Han quickened his step, then crouched low when he caught sight of her silhouette through the brush.

A man came out from what looked like a cavern in the hillside that was partially hidden by bramble and rock. Li Feng ran to him. Han's blood boiled as she clasped the stranger's hands.

'Liu Yuan, let's go together. Somewhere far from here.'

Han could hear the desperation in her plea. From the way she addressed him, the stranger could be a close friend. Or a lover. Bitterness rose in his throat.

The man was half a head taller than Li Feng and slight of build, though from what Han could see he was wiry with strength. For a bandit, he looked the part. His clothes were patched and fashioned from hide and leather. His skin was swarthy from the sun.

The bandit took hold of Li Feng by the shoulders. 'Little Sister, you're not alone.' He aimed his gaze in Han's direction. 'I'm not alone either.'

Li Feng swung around, her eyes searching him out through the branches.

'Run,' she commanded.

More men dropped from the trees. Others seemed to sprout from the earth. Their clothing was discoloured, blending in with the surroundings.

Han veered to the left and shoved through the brush like a wild animal. The way back to the river was blocked and the bandits were in close pursuit. There were more of them than the magistrate had reported and they didn't seem willing to spare yet another thief-catcher.

If he was a true hero, Han might have stood his

ground and drawn his *dao*. He could go down fighting and Li Feng might weep for him. Not likely, he realised bitterly. Considering how intimate she and that bandit had appeared.

The incline rose as he trudged on. His heart pounded like a war drum signaling an impending battle. His lungs were burning. His muscles strained against the rise of the ground. It was time to stand and fight while he still had the strength.

He drew his *dao* and turned to charge at the closest pursuer before more could gather. His opponent held a knife in his right hand, which Han sliced across the knuckles. The knife fell to the ground. So did the man once Han kneed him in the groin.

Han left him rolling. The next two were upon him while two more approached immediately behind them. They wound through the trees to circle him.

Sword against knives. Advantage. One against four. Distinct disadvantage.

'Come on, dogs!' he goaded. Because that's what you did in a fight.

The bandit who headed the attack had what looked like a fresh cut across his face. Han struck at him, keeping his attack controlled. Han split his attention to the other bandit moving in behind him. These men were accustomed to fighting together. Han was accustomed to avoiding this sort of situation. At least he had been until he'd met Li Feng.

A thrust came from in front, low and aiming just beneath his ribs. The man at his back closed in as well. Han had to jump out of the way. He cut as soon as his feet found purchase. He smelled blood and felt the graze of steel against flesh. The rear bandit clutched at his forearm and his hand came away red.

Contact, but not enough. Han attacked again, aiming for the man who was already injured. The others were moving into position. Killing was slow, maiming was quick. He needed to disable elbows and knees. Eyes were good. An exposed throat would be best, but these bandits weren't as easy as that.

A familiar voice interrupted the fight. 'I told you to *run*.'

Li Feng came flying into the circle, blade flashing. She cut two of the bandits before they could regroup.

'Fox-whore,' the scarred one roared. She threw a knife at him.

Han and Li Feng were then on the run together, charging uphill side by side. The outlaws labored behind them.

'We can defeat them.' Han was breathing hard and certain that the fight would be easier than this climb.

'No.'

'I've seen your sword skill.' Exhale. Inhale. 'You've seen mine.'

'Stop wasting your breath,' she panted, sliding the blade back into her sleeve. 'Come on.'

Li Feng picked up speed. She was moving like air, as if the earth had no hold on her.

'Don't slow down,' she shouted over her shoulder.

'What?'

He was a few strides behind her. As the ground leveled out, he saw the edge of a ravine drop off in front of them.

Her words drifted over the wind to him. 'If I can do this, you can do this.'

Li Feng reached the edge and continued forwards. A surge of energy pulsed through him and suddenly the ground disappeared from below him as well.

He was falling, flying. Practitioners of the fighting arts spoke about feeling and not thinking. He certainly wasn't thinking when he'd leapt after her. He wasn't thinking of how far the other edge was or how high up they were. Strange how time can stretch on for ever and yet stand still. Was this the mind of birds and dragons as they soared on high?

His mind and body joined back into one as he crashed hard against the earth. The impact jolted through his legs as the ledge gave away beneath him. For a heart-stopping second, he slid downwards. His hands clawed over dirt and rock before digging in enough to hold on. Li Feng dangled beside him over the ravine. Panting and huffing, they pulled themselves up over the ledge.

Han rolled on to his back once he was on solid

ground again. Relief flooded him. For a moment, they merely lay there in the grass with the sound of the river flowing below.

Li Feng turned her head to him. Her hair fanned out in the grass like black water and her eyes were bright with surprise and delight.

'You made it.'

'You didn't have any doubt about it on the other side,' he accused.

'I knew how far I could jump and since you're bigger and stronger—'

'And heavier,' he interrupted her excited chatter. 'I'd fall faster and harder.'

She turned her face up to the sky and laughed. Han realised, looking over the flush in her cheeks, that he didn't quite know her as well as he thought. Maybe he would never know her, but he wanted to. She was the most fascinating woman he'd ever encountered. There was something not quite safe about Li Feng.

Her laughter rang free and child-like in the forest, intertwining with the driving rhythm of his pulse. His body still hadn't recovered from the jump and Han was at once angry and elated and uncommonly aroused. He rolled himself over her and kissed her.

She sighed into his mouth. Her lips were warm, soft. Her body curved against him as he pressed her gently into the grass. She was a live and wild thing and he was mad with the taste of her. He broke the kiss to frame her face in his hands. He ran his thumbs over the shape of her cheekbones and kissed her again, claiming her in the only way he could.

Her heartbeat skipped against his chest, resonating into him, through him. The rush of the jump was still in their blood, headier than the strongest of liquors. The chase freed her from her ghosts in a way nothing else could. The chase freed him as well, taking them past the boundaries of law and society. It was no mistake that they found each other in it.

'Li Feng.'

'Hmm?'

His fingers curved around her face to tilt it towards him. She touched a fingertip to his chin in answer. Her cheeks were tipped in pink like a ripened peach. Every bit of her glowed warm and enticing. He had the urge to drag clothing aside and sink his body deep inside her.

But they were in the woods. They'd just been chased. And he'd seen Li Feng practically in the arms of a bandit.

'Who was that you were with?'

She tensed beneath him. 'An interrogation? Now?' Her fingers curled into the front of his robe. 'This is why we can't be friends.'

He stood and offered his hand to her. She took it without too much ill humour and they stood side by side, looking across the ravine. Despite her earlier laughter, Li Feng's expression was one of turmoil. Blood rushed through his veins. Every part of him was awake and acutely aware of the woman beside him.

'We're not friends, Li Feng,' he said, breathing deep to take in the grass, the sunlight, the moment. 'We're much, much more than that.'

Han should have thought much harder before leaping after her, but he feared any attempt at caution was far too late.

# *Chapter Thirteen*

They returned to the city, walking side by side with hardly a word between them, but in her mind, Li Feng was still running. When her brother had sent his men after Han, she couldn't hold back. She had spared Liu Yuan a single glance before setting off, knowing this would strain the tenuous bond they had just formed.

No matter how strong the ties of family were, Zheng Hao Han wasn't meant to die in a thoughtless ambush in the woods. It went against the code of honour of the rivers and lakes. It also went against everything she had started to feel for him, emotions that had remained unspoken because she didn't have the words for them. Li Feng could only speak through action.

There was a rightness in fighting beside Han. He moved well, fought well. It had felt good to run with him, to fly blindly through the air without a care. And then the kiss. *The kiss.* Han held her as if he would never let anything get to her while he thoroughly devoured her, caressing her with lips first, then tongue. Their teeth met as the kiss deepened, the brief clash sending a primal thrill down her spine.

That kiss had promised things. But the moment she had returned to earth, her brother was still a murderous bandit and the man that she desired was still a thief-catcher. She was torn in two and needed time to gather the pieces of herself back together.

So she continued through the gates and let Han lead her past shops and taverns, back into the shelter of the city. It was a place where she could hide, but only for so long.

Han took her down a side alley and into the back door of a restaurant. The kitchen was evidently a busy one with bowls clattering and the hiss and crackle of food being cooked. His hand rested at the small of her back as he led her down a shallow staircase. It was a lightly possessive touch. More promises.

And just like that, she was inside a small, bare room and alone with her thief-catcher. The furnishings were sparse: a woven pallet that served as a bed, a bare wooden table, a single cabinet in the corner. A window had been cut out of the exterior wall and covered with a roll of bamboo slats. There was no lock on the door as there was nothing to steal.

She began a circle around the room. 'This is your place?'

'I paid for this cellar when I first came to the city. Although for the last few days, some seductress lured me to an abandoned shrine.'

'She sounds wicked.'

'I was weak.'

Li Feng smiled, but it felt forced as did the rest of the conversation. Usually their words flowed together effortlessly, but not now. There was something unfinished between them and from the dark look in Han's eyes, he knew it as well. She didn't let her gaze linger on the bed, though her throat went dry at the thought of Han in it.

'Something amuses you?' He sounded very close though he still remained at the door. Her every sense had become keenly aware of him.

'I never imagined that you actually went anywhere once I escaped from you.' She cast him a slanted look. 'I just thought you disappeared, like some demon.'

'I shut myself in a room every time and brood about letting you escape. Then I scheme and plot about how to capture you once more.'

She completed her circle to end face to face with Han again. He was grinning at her with one shoulder against the doorframe and his arms folded over his chest. He was a handsome sight with that hard jaw and startlingly soft mouth. Those eyes that laughed and wooed her. He was beautiful in the weathered, untamed way that mountains were beautiful.

Heated air wafted in from the kitchen above, making the atmosphere tepid. She wiped the back of her hand over her brow.

'It's hot,' she said. Which wasn't particularly clever. Her heart was beating too fast for cleverness.

Han pushed off the wall with a shrug of his shoulder. 'Wait here.'

A moment later he returned carrying a basin with a tray balanced over the top. A washcloth was draped over his arm. Han set the basin down and lowered the tray beside it. He took two cups from the tray and arranged them side by side before picking up the wine flask.

'That man was my brother,' she said abruptly, in answer to his earlier question.

Han paused mid-pour before continuing. He handed her a cup before taking one for himself. It was rice wine, the taste of it slightly sweet. Han downed his in one swallow and set about pouring himself another.

'I didn't know you had a brother,' he said.

'I didn't know either, until now.'

It was pointless to hide it now that everything had changed. She watched for his reaction, but as usual Han was as unmoving as a stone lion. He was an experienced and intelligent thief-catcher. He had to know by now that it had been Liu Yuan and his gang who murdered Cai Yun. There was no way he could let that go.

'He tried to kill me,' Han said.

'Liu Yuan is family,' she insisted though her throat tightened. 'He felt threatened when you appeared. My brother is like that. He's been cornered and beaten so often that he lashes out.'

It was pointless to defend a killer to a thief-catcher, but Liu Yuan was her only family left and she had been alone for so long.

'We're bound by blood.' There was nothing more she could say than that.

'Yet you're here,' Han said. 'With me.'

'For now.'

Only for the moment. Han narrowed his gaze on her, weighing her words before coming forwards. Gently, he pried her fingers from her cup. She hadn't realised how tight she'd been gripping it. He poured her more wine and she sipped it slowly, pulse racing. Every action suddenly seemed like it was an act of fate, a step towards the inevitable.

They were indeed friends, but they were also adversaries. Between the wine and the excitement of the shared escape and the way he was looking at her, they were likely to become lovers before the night was even upon them. But that was all they could be—lovers for one night.

Han rolled up his sleeves and dipped the washcloth into the basin. The muscles in his forearms tensed as he wrung out the excess water. In the moments that passed, they had reached a tacit agreement. No more questions.

'You have a smudge here.'

His knuckle caressed her cheek before he handed her the washcloth. The seemingly casual gesture sent a rise of heat up her neck that had nothing to do with the swelter of the kitchen. She ran the damp cloth over her face, letting the cool water slide over her skin. Han averted his eyes to allow her some privacy as he finished his wine.

When she handed the washcloth back to him, he paused with his hand on the cloth. His look focused keenly in on her. Han extracted the cloth from her fingers and dipped it once again into the basin. 'Here, let me.'

He smoothed the damp cloth over her forehead and down her cheek, taking much more care than she had given to herself. She blinked as water dripped over her eyes, but she didn't dare close them. Han was watching her face with such intensity, his breathing growing heavier with each pass.

She held her breath as a trickle of water ran down her throat to disappear into the valley of her breasts.

Her pulse throbbed beneath Han's fingertips as the cloth followed the same downward path. His eyes were still focused on hers as he parted her tunic. Her breasts were wrapped under a plain swathe of cloth. Han's fingers slipped deftly beneath the material to tug it loose. The tip of his thumb grazed lightly over her nipple and she shivered. A delicious ache formed low in her belly.

This was for her. For her and for Han and no one else. She was selfish to want it, but she wanted it all the same.

Han peeled away her tunic and let it slip to the floor. Her bindings followed soon after and she was bared from the waist up. Han caressed the washcloth over her breasts, his hand separated from her by a thin layer of material. The cool water brought her nipples to a hard peak and she inhaled sharply, her throat tight with desire. Her heart pounding. Li Feng closed her eyes and longed for Han to kiss her. She longed for him to do so much more.

He finally did kiss her. A passionate, insistent kiss that parted her lips. There was no more washcloth, only his strong, sure hands rounding her breasts and stroking her stomach. She moaned around his invading tongue, sucking gently. He responded with a low, almost feral sound as his arousal pressed hard against her.

The rhythm had changed. Her heartbeat was like

a drum beating faster to urge on the next act. His breath was hot and ragged in her mouth. He pushed her back on to the pallet and eased her trousers down past her hips. At the same time, she dragged his robe open and ran her hands over wide shoulders and the lean, sculpted muscle of his chest. He was hard all over, his skin smooth and warm.

She was naked while he was partially undressed above her. Han pulled his trousers down just as much as he needed to free his erect organ. Li Feng stared up at him. His brow was damp and furrowed as if in deep concentration. He tugged her roughly downwards to position her beneath him. Her body quivered with anticipation. She had been waiting for this for a long time.

His fingers moved over her sex lightly as he positioned himself. It was enough to make her back arch with pleasure. Then he pushed his hips forward, exhaling forcefully as he came into her. Li Feng clutched at his shoulders. The initial shock of penetration took her to a precarious edge. Nothing else was like this moment of first discovery of how their bodies fit together.

He repositioned his hand at the back of her neck, the possessiveness of it unmistakable, and thrust deep. The completeness, the fullness of accepting him overwhelmed her and her flesh convulsed around him as she was consumed with heat and a rush of elation. She squeezed her eyes shut as the climax drained her of all thought and resistance.

'So quickly,' he murmured in astonishment.

His breath was hot against her ear. He was gloating a little bit, but she didn't mind. Not when her body shuddered with so much blinding pleasure. Not when he was holding her tight against him. He continued holding her as he brought himself to his own peak and continued holding her afterwards, never letting go.

'I did steal the jade,' Li Feng confessed.

Han's hand played along her spine. 'I know you did.'

She lifted her head and propped her chin on to her hands so she could look at him. His eyes were half-lidded, drunk from an afternoon of lovemaking. He regarded her with an indulgent expression.

Han proved to be an energetic lover. They had joined together once again and she was now stretched out languidly on top of him, skin to dampened skin. She enjoyed the steady rise and fall of his chest beneath her. He was a much more comfortable mattress than the threadbare pallet and the hard floor beneath it.

'Well?' She tapped a finger against his chin and he made a half-hearted attempt to capture it in his lips. 'You don't believe I should still be punished?'

'Certainly.'

She yelped as he dealt her a stinging slap on her rump.

'There,' he said, quite satisfied.

*'Scoundrel.'*

She reared up and pinned his shoulders to the mat. He met her glare with a lazy smile.

But she knew him. Han wasn't so stupidly male that he'd cast aside his beliefs after a few moments of passion.

His smile faded into seriousness. 'I know you've been involved in questionable activities in the past, Li Feng. But I've come to know you beyond that.'

'That's a very open-minded sentiment for a magistrate's son,' she murmured.

He stiffened beneath her. 'In many circles, thief-catchers aren't thought of much higher than the thieves we bring in.'

'But you're no ordinary thief-catcher.'

A slow, satisfied grin spread across his face. 'No?'

'I meant what I said beneath the bridge, Han. We are opposites, you and I.'

'Yin and yang.'

She shot him an irritated look. *'Not* yin and yang.'

Han was being purposefully thick-headed—or maybe he wasn't. Han was regarding her with that same earnest expression that always got the best of her. He wielded a sword and fought like a warrior, but his heart and mind was that of a scholar.

'I don't want you to have any illusions about me,' she warned him. 'Or about this.'

She hadn't always been forthcoming with him, but she wanted honesty between them for these last moments. And it had to be farewell afterwards.

'I'm not as honourable or heroic as you believe,' he said in all seriousness. 'I joined up with the local militia at fifteen because I had no skills for any other profession. I didn't become an officer either. I was a common soldier, working with my hands.'

He propped himself up on one elbow and she slid alongside him, their legs still entwined.

'A couple years after that, I started hunting down fugitives for no other reason than the money,' he explained. 'It wasn't considered very reputable, but it was work that needed to be done.'

'But you did this as a sacrifice for your family.'

Even when Han lowered himself, it was for noble reasons. He might not see it that way, but she certainly did. She was willing to sacrifice everything for family as well, but there was nothing noble about Liu Yuan or about her. The events of fifteen years past had shaped her and Liu Yuan into what they were: angry and fighting against the world.

She had made a choice in the forest, siding with

Han against her brother, but it was a temporary one. Family was life's blood.

'You asked me what I would do once my search was over.' She thought of her brother and of the tragedy that had taken their parents. Han listened patiently as she struggled with her next words. 'I don't know what happens now.'

She couldn't bring herself to say the last part, that this was farewell.

'I know what happens,' Han assured her.

The intensity of his gaze sent a flutter to her stomach. He rolled on to his back and is hands stole to her hips to lift her over him. His organ stirred and reawakened against her. Not stupidly male, but male enough. She shot him an admonishing look, even as her flesh warmed to him. She needed simple answers right then and this was the simplest, most basic truth there was.

He touched her, opening her soft flesh intimately as he positioned himself at her sex. Her own fingers grazed against his as she moved to help him. They said nothing in that sacred moment. The only sound was a deepening of his breath and the catch of hers as he slid inside.

She closed her eyes as her body accepted him. How quickly a new lover became welcome and accepted, in this one most invasive act. He thrust slowly while she ground her hips downwards, seeking the small, subtle pleasures of soft flesh against hard contours.

In the absence of sight, there was only the sensation of their joining and the heat of the day around her. She felt the roughened tip of his finger caress against her just above the juncture of their bodies, focusing her pleasure. She became his creature, straining towards his touch, her head thrown back and helpless as he stroked her.

'You're so beautiful,' he said huskily.

Her eyelids fluttered open and her chest squeezed tight when she saw that he had been watching her the entire time. His mouth was tight, his face nearly expressionless except for the fire in his eyes.

'Stay,' he said. His gaze bore into her. 'With me.'

Her breathing was ragged. *'Here?'* Passion blurred her vision as she looked around the room.

With a grunt, Han wrestled her beneath him, keeping his hard length inside her.

'She-demon,' he growled. 'Not *here.*'

Laughter bubbled up inside her, but at that moment he pushed deeper, fitting himself completely within her until she could no longer move, or speak or even breathe. All her thoughts were of him and how he felt. How all of him felt.

'I want you to stay with me. Like this.'

All the while he moved in her, touched her, made

her feel so good that she wanted to weep and scream. She did both.

He couldn't know what he was saying. It was only lovers' talk, vulgar and profound all at once. Her heart fluttered regardless.

Han bit her neck and the sharp nip of his teeth sent a shiver down her entire body that curled her toes. She pressed her face against his shoulder, tasting the saltiness of his skin as she wrapped her legs tight around him. He groaned as the angle of his body inside her shifted.

She had no doubt Han would marry a proper girl one day, but right now he belonged to her and she wanted him to remember. The next moments stretched out exquisite and unbearable until finally they reached the peak of their desire—her first, then Han shortly after. Even here in the torrent of pleasure he was chasing after her.

Evening came and one of the kitchen boys arrived with bowls of rice and soup along with other odds and ends from the cooking pots.

'This must be how kings live,' Li Feng said, stretching out her arms on the pallet.

Han lit an oil lamp and the meagre flame danced shadows around the empty room. He wore only his trousers. The night was only slightly less warm than the day. They would need another bout of rain to beat back the oncoming heat of the summer. He stared at the curve of Li Feng's back as she slipped her tunic back on, tying the sash in a loose knot around her waist.

All he had to do was glance in her direction to appreciate the perfection of gently rounded thighs and well-shaped calves. Her figure was a combination of grace and strength and he could watch her for ever. At that moment, he certainly felt like a king.

Li Feng regarded him as she spooned some soup. 'Tell me about your family,' she said. 'You said your father was a magistrate.'

'In a county of Nanping prefecture.'

'And your mother?'

'She was very kind and soft-spoken. Loathed to harm even the tiniest of ants, Father would say. She used to raise songbirds.'

Her eyes brightened. 'Really?'

He nodded. 'She taught me how to whistle like a lark.'

'Show me.' Li Feng waited eagerly with her arms folded over her knees.

'It's been a while,' he warned her, cupping his hands together and blowing into them to create a high-pitched trill.

She laughed with delight. Han didn't think his chest could puff out any further.

'What does she do outside of tending birds?'

'The usual things that women do, I suppose. Embroidery?'

'I don't know what those usual womanly things are.' She wrinkled her nose at him and he had the urge to kiss it.

'Nothing involving a sword,' he teased, receiving a punch to his shoulder in return.

A sobering thought crept in. He had left within a year of his father's dismissal from office. Visits home after that had been infrequent. Considering that it had been nearly five years since Han had returned to the farm, everything would be different from what he remembered.

'My family and I have spent too many years apart,' he admitted. 'I should go back to see them.'

'Why did you stay away so long?' She set aside the empty bowl and curled on to her side on the pallet, propped up on one elbow. 'You must have missed your brother.'

'I returned often at first, but one starts losing track of time. Years blend into one another.' Han stopped himself. He sounded like he was giving excuses.

With a sigh, Han moved to sit cross-legged at the corner of the pallet. Li Feng waited for him to continue while he was tempted by a glimpse of ivory skin where her tunic parted. Her knees were bent and her toes pointed even though she was only before an audience of one.

He could have guessed she would be so comfortable in her skin, even in the bedchamber. She wasn't one for blushing and fluttering eyelashes. Where other women were soft and delicate, Li Feng was toned and supple, with a force and presence that never completely yielded to his touch. Even in surrender, in the depths of pleasure, he could feel the strength in her.

'What happened between you and your family? Did you quarrel?' she asked when he was silent for too long.

'We did not quarrel. At least not openly.'

Li Feng would have never asked such a question were she raised in polite society. Such matters were private, barely spoken of between family members, let alone an outsider.

It was easy to confess secrets after joining one's body intimately to a woman's, but there was more than that between them. Only Li Feng knew who he truly was, with no illusions of what he should have been. Han had never felt so close to anyone.

'When Father had been removed from office, it was a devastating blow,' he explained. 'This was during the famine years, which my family was shielded from due to our wealth. There were grain shortages throughout the prefecture which culminated in a violent outbreak in the city. A group of rebels raided several storehouses and set them on fire along with several government buildings. After the provincial army marched in to quell the uprising, Father, who was head magistrate, was dismissed as incompetent. He had failed to instil a sense of discipline and authority over the populace.'

'It hardly seems like that could be his fault, or at least his fault alone,' Li Feng remarked.

'Someone had to take the blame. Father had no control over the management of grain stores, which seemed to be the root of the unrest. Yet he never protested his dismissal. He accepted judgement without complaint.'

'Like a warrior suffering a wound in silence,' she suggested.

As a performer, Li Feng certainly demonstrated a liking for the dramatic. Han had never stopped to think about how stoically his father had behaved throughout the scandal. He had taken his father's response as a matter of course. Father always conducted himself with the same stiff-jawed forbearance.

'Father decided we would stay in a farm just outside of the city borders rather than return to his native town in shame. He wanted me to continue my studies and pass the imperial exams. It was the only way to restore our family name,' Han recounted.

'But instead you became a thief-catcher.'

'Instead I became a thief-catcher,' he echoed.

'When I left, I defied my father's wishes. In my heart, I always thought he understood that I only did what had to be done, but that wasn't enough to earn his forgiveness. Not that I earned his condemnation either. All of Father's hopes of scholarship transferred to Chen-Yi and we don't speak of things that would upset the peace.'

Han wasn't ashamed of being a thief-catcher. He seemed to have a talent for hunting down criminals and he was able to occasionally send money home, but there was always that unspoken rift between him and his father.

'How old is your brother?' Li Feng eased the question into the tense silence.

Han looked upwards as he added on the years. 'He must be sixteen or seventeen this year. Heaven and Earth, last time I saw him he was just a boy.'

'I apologise, Zheng Hao Han.'

His eyebrows rose at the sudden formality. 'For what reason?'

She sat up, straightening her shoulders to mark the seriousness of her words. 'I accused you of not valuing your family earlier. I apologise.'

'Perhaps when I go home, you could accompany me.'

Li Feng's eyes widened and her lips parted with surprise. He had no idea where that thought had come from, but it would be the coward's way to back down now.

'You never did answer my question,' he reminded gently.

She avoided his gaze, hiding her face behind the dark curtain of hair. 'Don't talk about things that cannot be, Han.'

A fist closed around his heart. At that moment, he realised that all of this, all that they had shared, changed nothing for her. All the lightness and warmth between them fled with those few words between them: his entreaty, her denial.

Li Feng was still trying to escape.

She trusted him enough to set aside her sword. She even trusted him enough to wrap herself around him as they lay naked, but that was only her body. He knew she still didn't trust him. Han didn't know if Li Feng could ever completely trust anyone.

'Han.' She spoke his name in a single exhale. 'Even if you could overlook what I've done, I know you would never forgive my brother. Liu Yuan killed Cai Yun for his part in luring my mother into Prefect Guan's mansion.'

He reached out to draw her against him, but she was stiff in his arms, refusing to look at him.

'Why did you even come with me, then?' he asked quietly.

Anger wouldn't solve anything. He needed to focus and understand her before he lost her.

'I couldn't let Liu Yuan kill you.' Her voice sounded small and distant. 'You have nothing to do with his vengeance. And you were right. Things were unfinished between us. I knew—I knew I would miss you in the days to come.'

A knot formed in his throat. 'So this was only one night for you?' he demanded.

There was a pause before she nodded. Once, brokenly. He wished she would turn around so he could see her face. Han leaned forwards, his body curving around her.

'You're wrong,' he said against her ear.

She took in a breath and he could feel the shudder of tension along her spine.

He pressed the momentary advantage. 'Your brother is dangerous, Li Feng. You can't go to him.'

'We'll disappear, he and I. We'll go far away,' she insisted.

'He won't stop so easily. He wants blood.'

Li Feng swung around to face him, the movement dislodging her from his hold. Her expression was sharp enough to cut through bone. 'Wouldn't you?'

He listened as Li Feng recounted the same story, but from a different perspective. The prefect had tried to force himself on her mother and her father had intervened. It was possible. He knew nothing of Prefect Guan's character other than that he was in hiding. He could have easily coerced his servants to testify to his version. But where was the truth? Somewhere in between. But there was one thing Han did know.

'Your brother is a killer. He's dangerous to everyone around him, including you.'

She wouldn't answer.

He pressed on. 'Vengeance won't resolve anything.'

'This isn't about resolution,' she replied coldly. 'It's about a debt that needs to be paid. You have to understand. We were left with nothing, nothing but fear and anger. He turned to thieving and violence, but I'm not so different.'

'He's lost to you,' Han said.

Li Feng fell silent. Han knew he was fighting a battle he could not win. Han tried to put himself in her brother's place, into the mind of a son who could do nothing but stand by while his father was put to death.

'We only have until morning before I have to go,' Li Feng said finally. 'Let's not waste our time arguing.'

The earth would have to open up before he accepted that.

Han pulled her closer and pressed his mouth to hers desperately. She returned the kiss with equal desperation. He could already feel her slipping from his grasp.

He broke this kiss abruptly. 'That only means 1 have until morning to convince you,' he said, his voice rough.

'Hao Han.' She touched a hand to his cheek. There was sadness in her eyes.

'I won't let you go.'

He didn't take her then, though he wanted to. He would lose himself inside of her and she would sigh and shudder against him. Then she would forget. And he would forget. But by morning, she would still be gone. He had made the mistake before of assuming that her acceptance of his body inside her was an acceptance of him.

Instead he took her face in his hands. He wanted all of her, not just her cries of pleasure in the dark.

'I know what sort of men your brother has surrounded himself with. You don't belong with them.'

'It wouldn't be the first time I've been among outlaws.'

She had previously mentioned Wang Shizhen and the rebels she had been involved with. With every word he was losing ground.

By the end of the double-hour, the oil lamp had burned out, leaving them in darkness. The restaurant above them was finally silent. Han was on his back with Li Feng beside him, her head on his shoulder. He was out of arguments, but at least she was still there with him. That had to mean something.

The night was ending so differently from how it had begun. Though her warm weight moulded to him, though he could feel the soft fan of her breath against his neck, the passion between them had receded into a quiet resignation. He was even afraid to hold her, as if she were a fragile shell ready to break. So they lay together at an impasse, unable to see one another, but feeling every shift and sigh with a heightened awareness.

He was not ready to give up.

'Tell me about Two Dragon Lo again,' she said sleepily.

With all that was happening around them, she wanted to talk about that old tale? 'That story is told too often as it is.'

'You don't like speaking of him.'

'Thunder and lightning split the sky with every strike of our swords,' he said, resigned.

'We're lovers now,' she chided. 'Indulge me'

He ran his hand along her arm. 'What do you want to know?'

'What was he like?'

'Like?'

'Was he clever? Cruel? Did he ambush you?'

He was taken aback. Everyone wanted him to talk

about the notorious battle, but no one seemed to care who Lo had been behind the legend.

'He was an educated man. More so than me.'

'Educated? I've never heard that before.'

He liked the way she sounded, so soft and close. They were nothing but two voices with no pasts between them. He wasn't a thief-catcher and she wasn't a sword dancer. He could be completely honest with her.

'He took the imperial exams several times, but never passed.'

'You could tell that from a swordfight?' she asked, incredulous.

There were legends of great warrior-scholars who could read an opponent's entire soul in how he wielded his sword. Han could tell a lot about someone from how they fought. He had recalled his first match with Li Feng countless times, reliving the memory over and over. In this case, the answer wasn't so ephemeral.

'We spoke. Over wine,' he replied.

He had been tracking Two Dragon Lo, but believed he was still far from the bandit's lair. He had reached a remote drinking pavilion in the mountains and stopped to rest. Another traveller had happened by as well. It seemed untoward to sit at different tables, so they shared wine. The stranger had knowledge of classics, of history, of poetry. Han was so accustomed to dealing with the lowest of society that the discussion reawakened an ember within him. He called for more wine.

Eventually they came to the topic of law. Han's studies had ended at the age of fifteen, so he was lacking in all those other areas. But in this topic, he was able to at least provide some lively debate.

'We disagreed on everything,' he told Li Feng. 'But the stranger had such well-formed arguments and he was passionate about them. The way Father would be whenever he lectured us over dinner. I was certain I had stumbled upon some wandering scholar.'

*'What's your name?'* he had asked the stranger. He was ready to concede defeat in the debate and drink to his opponent's honour.

*'I had another name where I came from, but now everyone calls me Lo.'*

'He finished his wine, but from the look he gave me as he set the cup down, I was certain he had known the entire time who I was.'

Li Feng held completely still as she considered his story. 'He came to challenge you.'

'I don't know for certain.'

'Were you frightened?'

He placed his lips against her hair. She smelled like rain. 'Yes,' he answered. 'Two Dragon Lo deserved to die.' He'd told her the same thing once be-

fore and he still believed it, but there was one thing
that he'd never admitted to anyone. 'I didn't want
to kill him.'

'You've killed men before Lo.'

He nodded in the darkness, but she seemed to
know his answer.

'Then why regret his death?'

'I don't.'

She was silent after that, which meant she didn't
believe him.

'He wanted you to be the one to kill him,' she said.

'That's not true. Lo didn't come to surrender. He
fought with everything he had.'

'You didn't hear me correctly.' Li Feng drew a
senseless character over his chest. 'He didn't want
to die, but he wanted you to be the one to kill him.'

He tried to bring back the last moments of the
battle. It was grey outside the pavilion. All Han remembered was the killing stroke. Lo was on his
knees. Han was also bruised, bleeding. His last blow
had torn into the bandit's shoulder and Lo's weapon
was gone. His hands were stained with blood and
dirt. Han's shadow had fallen over him and Lo had
looked up with eyes that were unblinking. Han
ended it quickly after that.

What he didn't realise until after the battle was
that Lo had studied the sword the way a gentleman
studied. His technique was centred on perfecting

sword forms which were intertwined with symbolism and philosophy. He was proficient with the sword, even skilled. But Han, the failed scholar, had been trained as a soldier. He'd fought for his life against murderers, smugglers and rebels—desperate men with nothing to lose. His skill had been earned through survival.

'I don't know why I won,' Han confessed.

This was the mystery of war and battle. Was it truly valour that determined who walked from the battlefield alive?

'You weren't the only one hunting him. There must have been others.'

'The provincial army was preparing to move against him. After his death, they raided his lair and his gang was apprehended.'

'Then Two Dragon Lo would have been beheaded as a traitor,' she pointed out.

It was a trial by ordeal, an ancient tradition that he and Lo had even debated over wine. If Lo had defeated him, the bandit leader would have considered it a sign that it wasn't his time and continued on with his rebellion until the next opponent came along.

'I never considered that Lo wanted to die as a gentleman.'

'He wanted to choose his own death,' she concluded.

The world of rivers and lakes glorified honourable death just as it made heroes out of rebels and outlaws. Han didn't like the dark turn of the conversation or Li Feng's fascination with this underworld.

'Don't go, Li Feng.' He couldn't make it any plainer.

'There is no other way.'

She started to move away, but he reached out to take hold of her hand.

'There is.' He could be just as stubborn as she was. 'I already spoke of it. Stay with me. We'll find a place where we can start a new life.'

'And both give up the thing we've longed for the most? You would turn back around long before I would.'

'You're not making sense,' he said impatiently. 'What would I be giving up? I'm a thief-catcher, Li Feng. A man with a sword and nothing else. This isn't a life.'

'Hao Han.' There was a bitter hint of laughter in her voice. 'You don't really think that?'

'We're better together,' he said fiercely. 'Do you remember the salt village? It felt right with you at my side, step for step, planning every move together.'

'Shortly before I abandoned you,' she reminded him.

*'Li Feng.'* He sighed. There was nothing he could say to sway her.

'I remember the look in your eyes when you discovered the salt-smuggling ring. You looked so determined, so intent on setting things right and seeing wrongdoers punished. It was the look of someone who had found their rightful place. I've never felt that certain about anything.' She sounded almost envious. '*That* is what you cannot leave behind.'

He tried to form an argument, to find some weakness in her attack, but there was none. He stared up into blackness, letting her description of him sink in. Li Feng was right. He would never take the imperial exams or serve as magistrate, but he was trying to uphold the ideal of justice the only way he could. The same ideal his father had upheld.

She spoke again. 'You must have felt the same as you hunted down Two Dragon Lo. You were doing what you were meant to do.'

On this point, she was wrong. He had never felt more lost than when he had faced the bandit Lo. 'None of this convinces me we cannot be.'

'This is fate without destiny,' she said.

'No. It isn't.'

Li Feng sighed and shifted against his side, as if seeking out a more comfortable spot before settling back again. Her hair tickled against his cheek, but he didn't brush it away.

'Sleep now,' she urged. 'Let things be peaceful between us for once.'

He couldn't sleep, but he did remain silent as she grew soft and heavy against him. He didn't have to ask Li Feng about what she longed for most. She had listened to the stories of his family, of strangers she had never met, with such wistfulness.

His arm tightened about her possessively, his thoughts not at all peaceful. Li Feng dreamed of reclaiming the family she had lost, but what Han wanted most was her.

## Chapter Fourteen

Han didn't know how long they had slept, but in the still hours of the night, he woke enough to reach out for Li Feng and pull her beneath him. His body was more awake than his mind was as he kissed her. She responded sleepily, her mouth slow and sweet against his.

The room was completely black. He moved on touch alone, his hands caressing over her shoulders, finding her breasts and letting the shape of them fill his palms. Her breath deepened as he stroked her nipples, her back arching slightly to him. Her head was still clouded with dreams, yet his body aroused and gripped with an urgency that traced back to the last of their conversation.

He whispered to her. 'Is this—?'

'Yes.'

Their hands moved between one other, shifting layers of cloth aside. He positioned his hips on either side of her, felt her damp flesh beneath his fingertips and entered into her. A sound of surrender escaped from her throat and he laid his head on to her breast in surrender, his mouth pressed against her throat as the heat of her flesh accepted and enclosed him.

He thought there could be nothing better than this moment when their bodies finally joined, but he was wrong. Her legs curved around him, deepening his penetration into her and making him groan. How could she be so intent upon leaving when every part of them fit so perfectly together?

He thrust slowly, not trusting himself to move any quicker. Li Feng dug her fingers into his hair, dragging his mouth to her with tender violence as her pleasure deepened. Too soon, his climax rushed upon him. His control slipped away as he pushed himself feverishly into her.

As the rush of blood through him subsided, he could hear the pant of Li Feng's breath. In the blindness of release, he had no knowledge of whether she had reached her peak, but she still clung to him. Every muscle within her vibrated with tension.

Lethargically, he reached between their bodies. She gasped, her flesh contracting around him as he found the pulse point of her sex. He stroked with his fingertips and she arched gratefully against him, her hands digging into the muscle of his shoulders.

He felt clumsy and graceless as he willed her towards her own release, but he needed her to feel this now. With him.

Soon her breath caught and she shuddered before her limbs finally relaxed, going as pliant as wax. The joining of bodies was something corporeal and primal. It wasn't enough to convince her of anything, but why couldn't it be?

Han stayed up for a while afterwards, listening to the sounds Li Feng made in her sleep. She shifted restlessly on the pallet, back and forth. He reached out to stroke her brow and it seemed to calm her. What did she dream of? Did she leap and fly over walls even in her sleep?

Finally he did fall asleep again.

When he woke, he had that unsettling feeling of not knowing whether ten minutes had passed or an hour. He reached his hand out blindly and met nothing but emptiness.

'Hao Han.'

Relief flooded him. Li Feng was still there.

He turned and propped himself up, his limbs still awkward and heavy upon waking. She had lit a candle, the light framing her in a tiny orb. Her face was set with deep shadows. She was already dressed.

Her voice cut through the fog in his head. He was still caught in the memory of their last joining.

'I was going to leave while you were sleeping, but

I couldn't bring myself to go. But now that I've seen you to say farewell, I think I can do it.'

'Li Feng—'

She extinguished the light and he could hear the sweep of the curtain as she left.

The death of all things. He cursed as he fumbled for his clothing.

Was it morning? Was it night? He dragged on his robe in the dark and staggered towards the stairs. Only when he left the cellar did he discover that it was indeed morning. The kitchen was stirring with activity and when he pushed out the back door into the alley, the light outside was grey.

The lane was despondently deserted. He swung his gaze upwards to the rooftops. Also empty. Li Feng had the advantage on him and she could move through a city like the east wind. It would be impossible to catch her, but he had to try.

Han scoured through the hidden alleyways first and then roamed the streets in a final, futile effort. As the city gong sounded the sixth hour, he was still empty-handed, standing dishevelled as the market crowd surrounded him.

He ran a hand roughly over his chin, reassessing. He'd wasted too much time. If he couldn't find Li Feng, then he had to find her brother. Liu Yuan was bent on revenge and the only way to keep Li Feng safe was to stop him.

Han set out towards the yamen. Before entering the gate, he ran a hand over his robe in an attempt to straighten his appearance. He located Magistrate Tan's office, requested an audience and was informed that the official was overseeing the morning tribunal. He would be finished at the end of the double-hour.

Han waited impatiently in the main courtyard on a bench, taking in the offices and administrative halls that surrounded the space. His father had meant for him to serve in such a place as a ranking official.

A steady stream of petitioners had entered the hall of justice. Occasionally, he had seen a prisoner being led in restraints to be brought before the tribunal. After what appeared like a busy morning, the tribunal had adjourned and Han was summoned into the inner offices.

'Thief-catcher Han!' Magistrate Tan welcomed him eagerly into his study. He sat down behind his desk.

'Sir, I have information regarding the bandits responsible for murdering Guan's steward.'

'So soon! I knew you would not disappoint.'

The easy praise made him a little uncomfortable. 'The bandits are hiding in the hills just north of the city. I encountered eight or nine of them, but there could be more.'

'Well, they must be eradicated for the safety of our

city,' the magistrate said with resolve, but then let out a sigh. 'However, our constable isn't prepared to confront so many. And with the city guards protecting the prefect, there's hardly enough men to protect the streets. Now, if someone had experience with bringing in such undesirables.' Magistrate Tan regarded Han expectantly.

He was too involved to retreat now. 'The area is spread out and there are many places to hide. We'll need to send out several parties, but keep in close contact. How many volunteers does the constable currently employ?'

Tan looked quite satisfied. 'Not enough, but I trust you can find good, capable men for the task. I'll bring in Constable Guo immediately.'

'Thank you, sir.'

He needed to move quickly. They might not be able to raise a large enough force to capture all of the bandits immediately, but the patrols would scatter them from the surrounding areas and keep them away from the city until reinforcements arrived from the local garrison. At least that was Han's plan.

As they waited for the constable, Magistrate Tan spoke again. 'Your father was a magistrate in the Nanping prefecture, was he not?'

'Yes, sir.'

'I've heard admirable things about him.'

Han raised an eyebrow. Either Tan was lying or he was being overly kind.

'Oh, I've certainly heard about the unfortunate events that occurred,' the magistrate added. 'Cruel fate, you know.'

'It was a long time ago,' Han said, hoping that Magistrate Tan had enquired out of politeness and that was the end of the matter.

Unfortunately it wasn't.

'Now, you've accomplished great things as a thief-catcher, but I wondered if the son of a magistrate wouldn't have aspirations of taking the civil exams one day. Perhaps following in the steps of his illustrious father.'

He hadn't been in the city for more than four days, yet Magistrate Tan had taken the time to discover his family history. The quickness with which he was able to find information was both remarkable and disturbing.

'It's been a long time since I have studied the classics,' Han replied humbly. 'My younger brother has taken over the burden of being the family scholar.'

'Ah, so you have a younger brother studying for the exams? What's his name?'

'Chen-Yi.'

'Zheng Chen-Yi. Very good. It would be beneficial for him to come to Minzhou,' Tan suggested, relentless in his interest. 'The yamen library has copies of all the classics. There might even be a clerk who needs an assistant. No better way to learn, wouldn't you agree?'

'Sir, this is—' Han was caught completely off guard. 'Magistrate Tan is being very generous, but this isn't necessary.'

Tan waved away his objections and pulled out a sheet of yellowed paper. 'Too humble, too humble. I'll write a letter to your father. Let him decide what's best, hmm?'

Han couldn't escape the feeling he was being bought, but he was being bought for something he felt already duty-bound to do and for a price that benefited not him, but his family. He watched silently as the magistrate's brush flowed over the paper.

'You do our city a great service, Zheng Hao Han.' The brush continued to move steadily without pause as he spoke. 'If your brother is half as right-minded and honourable as you, then he would make a worthy representative for Minzhou as a candidate for the exams.'

The magistrate was as slippery as an eel. His friendly, easygoing manner hid a shrewd thinker, but Han needed the man on his side if he was to hunt out Liu Yuan and his gang of bandits.

Li Feng would never forgive him for plotting against her brother. Family was blood. Family was everything, even if it meant one's own destruction. Last night together might be their first and last, but Han had to make that sacrifice to protect her.

It had been hard to leave that room. Li Feng had fled as fast as she could, ignoring the stinging at the corners of her eyes and that sick, wrenching feeling in her chest.

She didn't see Han behind her, but she couldn't let down her guard. He had a way of finding her and right now she was too weak with emotion to withstand him. It would take time, she told herself. Time and distance.

Li Feng turned to lose herself in the city. She paused at the corner in the busy market, not knowing whether to turn left or right. People walked by without stopping. Faces she would never see again. Han and his relentless pursuit had become something to look forward to in a world where she was constantly surrounded by strangers.

Her last image of Han had been of him just awakening, naked in dim light. The shadows had highlighted the contours of his body and she wanted to remember him that way, that private vision that she could keep within her soul.

That wretched feeling came again, as if she were being torn up inside. She pressed a hand to her mid-section, willing herself to let go. But it seemed she would need a lot more time, a lot more distance.

A man came from the opposite direction and she nearly crashed into him.

'Pardon, miss.'

'Sir.'

She averted her gaze and tried to step aside, only to find he'd done the same, ending up in front of her once again.

'Miss, are you not well?'

She hadn't given a thought to how she must look. She was blinking rapidly against the threat of tears.

'I'm fine,' she said curtly, willing the stranger to go his way.

The man wore a dark-coloured tradesman's robe, modestly cut. He looked to be about forty years of age and his beard was neatly trimmed around a square face that carried a calm and serious demeanour.

'The lady appears flushed and her breathing irregular.'

She stared at him, startled by his impertinence.

'This servant apologises for his improper introduction! Wu Song is a humble physician. His herbal shop is across the street.'

Just a tradesman scouting for business. She allowed herself to relax. 'I wish your business great success then.'

She bowed and attempted to disengage herself, but he was insistent. 'Wu Song sees that the young miss is new to our city. Please come into the shop for some tea as a form of welcome.'

There was an open sincerity in his eyes. Reluctantly, she found herself following the physician. Maybe it was a good idea to get out of the street and compose herself. She also needed to be certain that she had evaded Han before seeking out her brother again.

The herbal shop was small, but well lit. The walls were lined with red-pine cabinets and rows upon rows of tiny drawers, each labeled meticulously. Physician Wu directed her to a table positioned to the side of the front room. He sat down next to her and held out his hand. Li Feng was taken aback by his forwardness, but his confident and somewhat impersonal manner disarmed her. She stretched out her arm, now more than a little curious. Wu folded back her sleeve and placed two fingers over the pulse point in her wrist. Then he bent his head as if in deep concentration.

Li Feng held her arm still and tried not to fidget. The physician's eyes were closed and a slight crease formed at the bridge of his nose.

'Good pulse,' he pronounced. 'Your *qi* is strong, though slightly imbalanced. Something is disrupting the proper flow of energy. Perhaps some strengthening of the liver would do you some good.'

He replaced her sleeve with the same meticulous care and stood to go to the medicine drawers, pulling out one after the other. He extracted an assortment of roots, powders and dried herbs which he piled on to a square of paper. Li Feng was still uncertain of whether Wu Song was a very aggressive businessman or a well-meaning physician.

'Sir, I have no money to pay for your kind service,' she called out to him, determined not to be swindled.

'No payment required. The young miss is my guest.'

Li Feng bit into a piece of candied ginger from a fish-shaped dish on the table. The sharp tang of it numbed her tongue as she watched the physician pour the mixture of herbs into a pot. He glanced out the window before placing it on to his tea stove. He added more charcoal beneath it and then returned to the table.

'The tea will take a few moments to boil.'

She nodded. It would be impolite to leave now.

The physician was pleasant enough. Perhaps she was too long away from polite society. Surely she could sit for a minute and enjoy the company and it delayed her departure for just a moment longer.

'One of the disciplines of a physician is the reading of faces. Does the young miss believe that there are only a few types of faces in the world? That the same patterns are repeated over and over?'

He was looking over her features as he spoke and the glance suddenly didn't seem so professional or impersonal. The back of her neck heated under the prolonged scrutiny.

'I don't know, sir. Maybe we're always searching for similarities. To find some trace of kinship, even if it's from generations past.'

He looked impressed. 'Well said, young miss.'

He stood to check on the tea and Li Feng lifted another piece of ginger. The exchange was becoming a bit strange and she was eager to drink whatever brew he offered and take her leave.

'There is something this servant should tell the young miss.' The physician was looking out the window again. 'Someone is following her.'

Han. Her breath lodged in her throat. He'd come after her. If the physician had been holding her wrist then, he would have felt her pulse racing wildly.

'He isn't any trouble. He's a…a friend.'

As she tried to figure out how to evade him again, Wu stepped away from the window and approached her, teapot in hand. 'There are several men, actually.'

'Several?' Li Feng sprang to her feet. 'How many?'

'It looks to be about five or six, miss. This physician suspected she was being followed before inviting her into the shop, but he wasn't certain until now.'

'Is there a back door?'

'Just beyond the storeroom.'

She didn't bother to glance out the window. It was a waste of time and she didn't want to alert whoever it was that she was aware of them. The men could be city guardsmen or more thief-catchers, but she had a feeling they were much more dangerous than that. With a hasty apology to the physician, she ducked through the curtain into the workrooms in back. A glance outside the door showed the lane was clear.

Li Feng found a narrow alleyway and began her climb upwards, leaping from corner to wall to balcony. In no time, she was up on the roof with the sun shining down on her. She stepped over to the shaded side and anchored herself against the roof ornaments, crouching low to keep watch over the alley below.

It wasn't long before a man came into view. She didn't need to see his face to recognise him. He was dressed as a wealthy merchant in a brocade robe with gold accents, but she knew him for what he was. Bao Yang, the perpetrator of the famous jade heist, scanned both ends of the alleyway before shifting his gaze upwards. He would know she was more likely to be up high than on the ground. She moved to the edge of the roof and dropped down behind him, rolling to absorb the impact. The sleeve sword was in her hand as she stood.

Bao Yang swung around. His gaze dropped to the blade before returning to her face.

'I suppose this means things are over between us.'

'Are you here to kill me?' she demanded.

A frown creased his brow. 'Why would you think such a thing?'

His features were angular and his nose slightly off centre, but there was something compelling in his imperfection. At least she'd always been enthralled by it.

He started towards her, but halted mid-step when she raised her weapon. Bao Yang feared nothing and no one. She should take it as a compliment that she was considered dangerous enough to be treated with caution.

'You left so quickly without a word of farewell.' He didn't sound particularly saddened by it.

'You always warned me that your work was dangerous. I had to keep quiet and it meant life or death.'

He was watching her, assessing her. 'It wasn't meant as a threat,' he said quietly.

She affected a mock smile for him. 'I don't entirely believe you.'

He smiled back, a genuine one. Apparently there was still a tiny bit of warmth between them, but it was the last embers of a fire that had burned hot and fast and was now gone.

'If you're not here for me—' she began. Bao Yang

lifted an eyebrow at that and she was reminded of how she'd been lured in by enigmatic expressions and secret glances. 'Why are you here?'

'Wang Shizhen is coming to the city.' His focus shifted behind her and she heard the approach of footsteps. 'And we are here to kill him.'

The rest of his cronies had found them. She recognised her fellow jade thieves as they closed in, forming a net around her and Bao Yang. They appeared harmless for the most part. One short, one thin and tall. Chang-cheh always seemed to have a grin on his face, but he could throw a knife faster and truer than she could. They were dangerous, dedicated men and she was once again among her kind.

## Chapter Fifteen

With an efficiency that unnerved her, Bao Yang brought her to a private banquet room at a drinking house near the eastern edge of town. He was posing as a wine merchant, had already made connections under his assumed identity and likely had more informants within the city no one would ever know about.

He cleared the room so they could speak privately. The others would make a sweep of the outside to ensure no one was spying on them. Bao Yang was always very careful.

'Why did you leave so suddenly after the heist?' This time, the tone of his question almost sounded personal. Intimate.

She kept her response impassive. 'I never wanted to be part of any rebellion.'

'This is no peasant uprising. Wang Shizhen is a tyrant and he must be stopped.'

Li Feng had never discovered exactly who Bao

Yang was or where he'd come from. She'd fallen into bed with him as she supposed many women had, drawn by his intelligence and charisma. During their brief period as lovers, she'd discovered an impenetrable wall around him. The sense of mystery that at first seemed so appealing quickly transformed into something cold and threatening beneath the surface.

'Tell me something.' She met his gaze. There was an intensity there that she'd once mistaken as passion. 'Did you know what I was capable of before you came to me?'

When they had first met, they were in a tavern. Wang's soldiers were taking up several tables and acting drunk and rowdy. One of them had tried to grab her, but she'd shoved him away.

Bao Yang took a moment before replying. 'I saw you reaching for your sword,' he admitted.

He had defused the situation by stepping in with his gentlemanly manners, claiming to be her brother, and had ushered her away with a deftness that had stunned her. They had begun their affair on so little beyond that and it had been ill fated from the start.

'You used me,' she accused.

'You wanted to stand up against General Wang. You hardly needed any convincing.'

Bao Yang was so clever in his persuasiveness that she always felt as if she were doing exactly as she wanted. But then again, she had always been looking for a fight.

'I knew that you would keep asking for more,' she said. 'Then one day, I would be in too deep to turn away. I knew you weren't content with disrupting General Wang's operations. You wanted him dead.'

He regarded her quietly, as if testing her defences for a weakness. 'That is exactly what I have come here to do,' he said finally.

'You? Or your loyal followers? Do you know Wang Shizhen executed Ma Shan?'

She recalled what she'd heard from Han about their former companion being publicly beheaded.

His jaw tightened. 'I do know of this.'

'And of all of us, it was me that the thief-catchers came after.'

'That wasn't my intention. I would have protected you—and Ma Shan if I could have. I don't take pride in sacrificing others. Everyone was a willing participant.'

'But we are expendable while you are not. You're too cunning to ever be implicated yourself.'

'That is not true.' A muscle ticked along his jaw. 'I have come here to ensure this is done properly. With my own hands, if I must.'

The vehemence of his response startled her. It wasn't the first time she'd suspected there was something personal in his hatred of the general. The more she questioned, the more he'd retreat.

Bao Yan watched for her reaction as he spoke. 'Wang Shizhen is coming here to pay his respects to Prefect Guan, a man I believe you have some interest in.'

It was the prefect who had sent that shipment of jade to General Wang. The two of them were connected, but she wasn't sure how. The warlord had taken military control over city after city. The prefect had to be aware of that, yet why then would he allow a tiger like Wang into the gates? The general would usurp his authority as he had done all the other districts under his control.

As Li Feng considered what she and Han had learned about the prefect and his corrupt dealings, a few small pieces of a vast puzzle came together.

'I never knew what the source of your wealth was, but it's quite easy to see now,' she said to Bao Yang. 'You're a salt smuggler, aren't you?'

His mouth twisted into a half-smile. 'I prefer to call it trading. The private salt trade. As they say, the mountains are high and the Emperor is far away.'

Bao Yang possessed an endless supply of money. He'd even given her enough for her journey in silver before they parted ways. Though she had been raised outside of Fujian province, she was learning quickly how the illegal sale of salt created wealth and power.

'Well, you and Wang Shizhen can fight out your battle. I don't want any part of it.'

Li Feng needed to return to her brother, to family, and leave this power struggle behind. She had to leave Han behind too. She and Liu Yuan would never be free if they remained in Minzhou.

Bao Yang let her go, despite all they had discussed. It was a testament that he did indeed trust her to remain quiet. How had she fallen for a man she never completely trusted? Or rather, she thought she had fallen. Li Feng tried to tell herself that it had been different between her and Zheng Hao Han, but they'd only shared one night. She had wanted that memory of being in the arms of someone good and honest who wanted her for herself.

Part of her was afraid she couldn't feel any deeper than that. Maybe she'd been wounded and broken since her family had been torn apart and scattered to the winds. And everything, all of her own mistakes as well as the crimes committed fifteen years ago, were finally coming back around.

Li Feng left the city by the late afternoon and hiked into the surrounding hills to the vantage point that Liu Yuan had pointed out to her. He was waiting for her there and acknowledged her arrival with neither surprise nor anger. She took his side and followed his gaze down to the former site of his camp. She could see movement below, through the canopy of the trees. Here and there, she caught the glint of metal. There were men sweeping through the area with swords and cudgels drawn.

'The thief-catcher.'

It was the first time they had spoken since she'd escaped with Han. There was no reproach in his tone, but she could sense it in the stiffness of his posture as he stared down the ledge.

'I know who he is,' he told her. 'He's the Thief-catcher Han they tell stories about. What is he to you?'

It was the same question she had been asking herself all morning. What was more important, her duty to her family or her own heart? The answer was easy. What she wanted didn't matter. She had lived for no one but herself for too long.

Liu Yuan was a head taller than her, but he wasn't nearly as strong or imposing as Han. She hoped the two of them would never meet.

'He means nothing to me.' It pained her to say it. She tried to close off her heart and make it true. She had left with only a single farewell, hadn't she? And without a single tear.

Maybe she was cold. She discarded places and people and memories as if they were nothing more than leaves floating by. Maybe she was a shell of a woman, unable to trust or to love. But she loved her brother, even though they had just been reunited. She knew it without knowing why and she couldn't bear to lose him now.

'Liu Yuan…brother.' It was the first time she had called him such. 'We should just leave. The past is done and gone.'

She had asked the same thing of him yesterday. Had it been only a day? The chase, the leap across the ravine and the long night in Han's embrace had seemed an entire lifetime. A cycle of death and re-birth.

He didn't answer. All she could see of him was the hard cut of his profile. His eyes were fixed on the valley below where Han was hunting for him, but his gaze was distant.

'Leave the prefect to his own fate,' she pleaded. 'We can honour our parents through their memories.'

'Have you seen the prefect's mansion?' Every muscle in his jaw tensed as he spoke. 'He has three wives. Meat with every meal. Fate *rewards* men like Guan He.'

'Revenge won't bring back Father and Mother.' It sounded empty even to her own ears, but she couldn't let him sacrifice himself.

'I can't, Little Sister,' he said.

A knot formed in the back of her throat. She blinked furiously, holding back tears. 'I don't want to lose a brother too.'

The wind over the ravine made a howling sound. Even the air seemed heavy around them.

His tone softened. 'When you were little, you were always very stubborn. Mother would say you were that way from the moment you were born,' he continued. 'You had your own mind about things and once you had decided, nothing could sway you.'

She recalled a foolish, childish tantrum in the rain. She had been so angry about something and refused to come out of the cold, out of spite. Despite that, it was a warm memory now. Every time Liu Yuan spoke of the past, she was able to recover a little more of herself. How much of memory was exactly this? Turned vivid and real only by being shared with others. With her brother, she had a connection to everything she had lost. Maybe if she just gave him some time, he would reconsider.

She smiled a little, for him. 'You seem very stubborn yourself.'

'I think you always knew you would come to this one day. That there would be a time for retribution.'

'I never—'

'You studied the sword,' he pointed out.

'I learned many things from *shifu*,' she protested.

'But you chose to learn how to fight.'

She couldn't deny it. *Shifu* had taught her to become strong and fast to defend herself, while teaching her about harmony and peace. But she'd accepted the physical lessons so much more readily than the spiritual ones.

Liu Yuan wasn't finished. 'Do you know that in ancient times, when a criminal was executed, they would also put his entire family to death? At least his sons would have to die. Because if any son was allowed to live, he would have no choice but to seek revenge. A son who does not avenge his father is not a son.' He turned away from the ledge to look at her. His eyes were vacant as if his spirit were trapped elsewhere. 'I have to do this, Little Sister. There is a reason that I could never leave Minzhou. And there is a reason why you found your way back.'

For as long as she could remember, she had dreamt about going back to that moment when those soldiers had taken her mother away. In her dreams, she wasn't small or slow or weak. She didn't stumble and she didn't need to be lifted and carried. She was strong, strong enough to protect her mother.

'This can't be what they would have wanted for us,' she said in desperation.

He raised his hand to stop her. He frowned, the lines of anger cutting deep into his face. 'You have been on your own all these years, Li Feng. You've experienced too much for me to treat you like a child or a helpless woman. That is why I won't ask you to stand aside, Little Sister. Give your brother the same respect.'

She stood there, stunned and shamed by his words.

This wasn't his burden alone. They had both been children, both helpless to stop what was happening to them. But they'd both come back stronger.

Prefect Guan was in hiding behind a horde of guards and Han was searching for her brother. And even if Liu Yuan managed to kill the prefect and survive, what then? Could he ever start a new life? The mark of a thief had been inked upon his skin, but deeper than that, his heart had grown black with anger. Her brother wasn't thinking of survival or a future. So she had to think of those things for him. She owed him that much. She owed it to her mother and father, who she now knew had gone to be with their ancestors a long time ago.

'We do this together then,' she said, linking her hand with his for the first time. 'Brother and sister.'

Liu Yuan stiffened at her touch, but held on to her with a tenuous grip, as if she were made of fine porcelain. If they were still alive when this was over, they would be fugitives, but they would be fugitives together.

## Chapter Sixteen

Han returned to the room below the restaurant late in the evening after the tenth hour gong. The oil lamp cast long and lonely shadows over the room.

All of the empty dishes and bowls had been taken away. Only the cups had been left behind, a reminder that Li Feng had been there with him. He drew his finger through the last dregs of rice wine.

Li Feng was gone. She'd returned to her brother. Han had spent the entire day searching for Liu Yuan, directing the constable's men through the woods. They had found several caverns stocked with a few meagre supplies, but there was no sign of any of the bandits.

Exhausted, he removed his boots and unbuckled his sword belt. Han arranged his few belongings near the pallet and left his *dao* close at hand. With the lamp still burning, he laid back fully clothed and imagined Li Feng's clever hands working his sash free and tugging away his outer robe. She whispered something softly into his ear, but he couldn't hear the words.

Han blew out the candle and let sleep drag him downwards. His muscles were sore from hiking through the hillside and there had been little rest the night before while Li Feng had had her legs wrapped around him. Even in his bone-weary state, the sense memory was close and visceral enough to send blood pumping through his veins until he was restless with desire. Wanting her. Missing her.

Li Feng had gotten beneath his skin and into his blood. She had become his mirror—the only way he could truly see himself was in her eyes.

He turned on to his side. When that didn't work, he sprawled on his stomach, agitated with himself, with Li Feng, possibly with the entire world. His hand strayed to the edge of the pallet and brushed against something solid tucked underneath.

Han pulled the object free. A silk tassel tickled against his wrist and the rectangular shape fit neatly in his palm. He ran his fingers over smooth stone, tracing the curved wings of the Vermilion Bird in flight.

Li Feng had left her jade pendant. It couldn't have been an accident. The jade was precious to her.

Could it mean she meant to return to him? The thought made his pulse race. Han was filled with foolish hope until he realised it would never happen.

Li Feng hadn't been able to say the words aloud, but this was her farewell to him. Her search for the past, the part of her life that he had been allowed into, was over.

The constable's volunteers assembled before him just as they had for the last two days. Han divided them into squads of four, assigning them to sweep from the woods into the mountains. The instructions were the same each day.

'Stay close together. Seek signs of shelter or cooking fires. Raise the alarm to gather the others as soon as you see anything,' he reminded them before dismissing the men to their tasks.

Guo, the head constable of Minzhou, stood by as the men departed. He had the arms of a blacksmith and carried a sword with a good amount of wear in his belt. His stout form, though a little worn with age, was still strong. He stroked his beard thoughtfully as he regarded Han.

'You were in a regional army, weren't you?' he asked.

'For a short time,' Han replied.

'I can tell!'

'I don't mean to undermine your authority, sir.'

Guo chuckled. 'Not at all. You young and spirited fellows can do all the hard work. I can take all the glory.'

'How many years have you worked under Magistrate Tan?' Han asked.

'Ten years or so. I worked for him even before he came to Minzhou. He offered me the choice of another turn in the salt wells or honest work as a constable.'

Han frowned at that, which amused Guo even further.

'Magistrate Tan said I had been arrested so many times and knew so many constables, I might do a reasonable job of acting like one.' He rolled back his sleeves to show a web of scars along his arms. 'That was in my undisciplined youth. You know how it goes. The more civil magistrates restrict punishment to arms and legs only, but some constables get carried away.'

'The magistrate took you off the streets?'

Guo nodded. 'Fortunately, I was a better constable than I was a thief. Now look at me. A wife, two sons to take care of me when I get old. Tan Li Kuo is a good man.'

The magistrate certainly knew how to instil loyalty. Han couldn't escape the feeling that Tan was trying to buy him as well. The magistrate's offer to help Chen-Yi wasn't exactly along the lines of promising wealth or trading influence for bribes, yet Han couldn't deny it would be a great benefit to his family. Perhaps Magistrate Tan was clever enough to figure out exactly what would tempt him—or maybe Han was becoming like Li Feng, seeing corruption in every public official.

He turned his attention back to the problem of the bandits.

'Perhaps they've fled,' the constable suggested.

Han shook his head. 'Those scoundrels know every cave and hole in the mountains. The surrounding terrain is too rugged for us to do a thorough search with our numbers. All the bandits need to do is hide out and wait for us to tire.'

The volunteers were indeed getting restless. After the initial sweep, there had been no further sign of the bandits in the mountains and a meagre day's wage was not enough to keep them on hand, even with the promise of a reward for every successful arrest.

Han hadn't found any sign of Li Feng or her brother. He sincerely hoped that she had convinced Liu Yuan to forget vengeance and leave Minzhou. If she was arrested among outlaws, there was nothing Han could do to save her. Though he hadn't seen her since they'd parted that morning, something told him she was still close. It was emotion, not logic.

'Constable Guo, what was the name of the tea house where Cai Yun was murdered?'

'It was in the street out front. The place was called the Seven Bowl Tea House.'

Han thanked him and left the yamen. He had been

directing the volunteer patrol to search the surrounding hills and mountains, but what if the bandits weren't hiding outside the city?

The report had indicated the suspect had mysteriously disappeared. There was no chase. Han had also noted how the murder was executed with precision. It had been well planned by someone who knew the streets.

What if the bandits had a hideout within Minzhou? They would be commonplace to the locals and often seen around the tea house before the crime was ever committed. Perhaps they were even regular customers and had spied on Cai Yun from within, marking his routine and habits. Liu Yuan had slipped in to kill the steward while his cronies stood guard. Then they had blended into the local crowd.

Han needed a full accounting of who had been in the tea house as well as in the street. Not just anyone who seemed out of place. In fact, he would place emphasis on repeat customers or people who had business being in front of the tea house and were expected to be there that morning. The interrogations ate up the first half of the day.

It was afternoon by the time he left the tea house with a new list of suspects. As Han stepped back onto the street, his heart stopped. The crowd around him faded away and his focus narrowed in on a woman walking along the shops at the opposite side of the road. She was wearing a pale-blue tunic with a wooden comb in her hair. Her slender figure disappeared maddeningly behind the line of the crowd like a carp beneath a pond's surface.

He chased after her. It had to be Li Feng. There was no mistaking the way she moved, like wind and water. There was no mistaking the way his body reacted to her, deep down inside.

The woman reappeared in front of him, no more than ten paces ahead. A group of pedestrians grumbled at him as he shouldered past. Just before he reached her, his instinct soured. He touched a hand to her arm anyway, but something in him already knew.

The face that turned to him was unfamiliar. The girl stared at him while an older woman, presumably the girl's mother, smacked at his hand.

'No manners!' she scolded. She took her daughter by the arm and dragged her away.

Han stood in the street and watched the young woman go. The sight of her was a placeholder—a poor, pale substitute for the real woman he longed for. Li Feng and his ever-present awareness of her had been so strong. He could practically taste her in the air, which made his sense of loss all the more palpable.

Li Feng pressed herself flat against the wall of the alley. Her heart beat frantically in her chest, the rhythm of it flooding her veins with heat. Han was still standing in the middle of the street. She could see him in profile, but he appeared strange to her. His gaze was unfocused and his usual imposing stature had sunken.

She had to struggle to catch her breath there in the shadows. If he turned right then...if he looked to the narrow alley between the shops, would he see her? Her muscles coiled in anticipation while her skin flushed warm and her palms began to sweat.

If Han saw her, she would have to run—but she didn't know whether it would be towards him or away. Funny how fear and elation and desire all felt the same inside. How could the mind sort things out if the body couldn't?

Her heart cried out as she edged away, but she ignored it while slipping into the back streets. If Liu Yuan continued with his own plans, he'd end up dead. He didn't seem to care, but she did. So she had told him she knew of someone who could help them seek revenge.

Bao Yang was still at the same inn where she'd met him before. The salt privateer received her in a sitting room adjacent to his chamber. He had little visible reaction to seeing her beyond a pleasant smile.

'You knew I would come back,' she remarked.

'It could be said that I was hoping to see you again.'

She glanced about the chamber, refusing to reply to his suggestive remark. These rented rooms were extravagant in comparison to Han's small cellar below the kitchen. She realised Bao Yang was scrutinising her every action, so she turned back to him.

'I'm here on someone else's behalf.' She debated whether to reveal anything more to him, but it didn't make sense not to. What she was going to propose meant life or death for all of them. 'I have been reunited with my brother.'

His eyebrows lifted. 'Your brother?'

'Guan He killed our father and our mother. He owes us a debt of blood.' Li Feng was surprised at how impassive she sounded saying such a thing aloud. Yet her insides churned until she was sick with the thought of it. 'You mentioned that Wang Shizhen and Prefect Guan would be together.'

'By tomorrow evening.'

Could they be ready so soon? They would have to be.

'I've seen the mansion. We can enter late at night,' she suggested. 'There are guards surrounding it, but the walls aren't high.'

Bao Yang leaned back, fingertips set together as he considered it. 'We would then need to search through all the chambers for our two targets. How do you intend to do that without alerting the entire household? And if Guan He is not alone? Are you willing to execute some unfortunate concubine to keep her silent? Or some servant who happens by?'

Her throat tightened. 'If it comes to that.'

Bao Yang fixed a hard look on her. For all her brashness, it was gravely apparent that, deep down, she wasn't like him. The thought of striking like an assassin, unseen in the dark, made her stomach turn. This was a matter of honour, an act that should be done in the open, so Guan He would face his death and know what he had done.

She could never think the way Bao Yang did or be as unfeeling. He was an insurgent and a rebel, but he was also a strategist. That was why she needed him.

'There may be a better opportunity for us,' he proposed. 'One with a greater chance of success. I have learned that Prefect Guan is throwing a banquet for his honoured guest in his residence and bringing in entertainers. Both men will be out in the open. We can rely on a targeted, direct attack.'

'How would we get into this banquet?'

'I have a connection on the inside.'

Li Feng considered asking him who this connection was, but Bao Yang would never reveal his contacts.

'I can get a small group in, but too many would be conspicuous,' he continued. 'A simultaneous attack from outside the gates would create confusion and disrupt the guards. It will give whoever is within the walls a chance to escape.'

She would be face to face with Guan He. The bastard could no longer hide behind walls and armed guards. Once she was before him, all that would be needed was a quick and steady hand.

'After the initial attack, we would be trapped in the courtyard with armed guards all around us,' she reasoned. 'We would be going to our deaths along with the enemy.'

'That is not my intention. It will be night-time. The attack at the gate will disrupt the guards and there will be confusion and panic amongst all the guests. There's a chance of survival if one can remain calm through it all and have a plan.' He spoke without emotion, all the pieces fitting together soundly in his own mind. 'I have no illusions, however. I know this feat will be difficult, nearly impossible—which is why I thought of you. There is no other sword I would want by my side.'

'Your side?'

'I will be heading this attack. Wang Shizhen is mine.'

The cold intent in his tone took her by surprise. She had never seen a weapon in Bao Yang's hands.

'My brother and I will be there.'

The heaviness of the decision pressed down on

her as soon as the words left her lips. The situation was so much like the one Guan He had used fifteen years ago to lure her parents to their deaths. It had to be a sign.

'Are you truly ready to die, Li Feng?' Bao Yang asked softly.

'I won't fail.'

He watched her face with such intensity that her cheeks began to heat, but she refused to look away.

'Do you still believe that I used you against Wang Shizhen?' he asked.

'No,' she admitted. 'I was already looking for a way to rebel, just like I came seeking you today.'

'I always liked that about us. Our common purpose.'

He reached for her hand. The gesture was too casual, lacking any true affection, and she flinched away from him. For a long moment, Bao Yang watched her, looking deep into her eyes.

'There's someone else.' His lip curled. 'Someone close to your heart.'

He waited for her to deny it, but Li Feng refused to answer. She stood, irritated at the way he always prodded and tested her, pushing against her boundaries.

'What does that have to do with anything?' she demanded.

'When the time comes, you'll be thinking of him

instead of what you need to do. It will turn your blade.'

She was thinking of Han now. He was inside her, a part of her. And Bao Yang was right, the thought of him made her want to turn back while she still could, but she had to do this for the sake of her family, for her brother.

*They owe us blood.* She kept on hearing Liu Yuan telling her that over and over. She had to do this for her sake as well.

'Once we're inside, any hesitation could cost all of us our lives,' Bao Yang warned. 'It will all be for nothing.'

'There's no one.' She looked fiercely into Bao Yang's eyes. Let him challenge her again if he still doubted her resolve. 'I can do what needs to be done. There's no one.'

# Chapter Seventeen

The upper room of the Seven Bowls Tea House served expensive tea to higher-class customers while the lower floor and courtyard had tables crowded with labourers and porters. Han continued his investigations the next day, discovering that a good portion of them worked at the many docks along the river, loading and unloading the transport boats. It seemed a reasonable place to focus his effort, given Cai Yun's salt-smuggling connections. Unfortunately, there were hundreds of boats and the Min River wound throughout the entire city.

By the afternoon, he knew he'd have to enlist more help. Han approached the yamen gates with thoughts of petitioning Magistrate Tan for additional men to assign to the task.

'Magistrate Tan is not present,' the clerk told him.

'This is an urgent matter. If I could enquire where I may find him.'

The man glanced worriedly about and gave a look

to the other attendant who promptly disappeared into the back. A moment later, a deputy magistrate appeared flanked by a pair of armed guards. Constable Guo showed up at the same time to wave them down. Han should have known to go to Guo first. He wasn't known to the bureaucratic arm.

'You're Zheng Hao Han, the thief-catcher?' The deputy magistrate looked him up and down.

'Yes, sir.'

Han knew the picture he presented. A thief-catcher was nothing more than a common labourer to the scholars and officials in the magistrate's office.

'Magistrate Tan received an invitation from Prefect Guan and has left for the day,' the deputy said.

Invitation? The prefect had been locked inside his residence for over a week, refusing to see anyone. 'This matter involves the prefect as well,' Han began.

'Prefect Guan is hosting a banquet for an important guest, one Wang Shizhen. Surely any business can wait until tomorrow.'

The name struck Han like a blow to the face. He had mentioned the salt-smuggling ring, but hadn't yet revealed the connection between Prefect Guan and the warlord to Magistrate Tan.

'I need to get to that banquet. Immediately.'

The prefect had spared no expense for the feast. The orders came to the local restaurants for roast pig and duck. A newly appointed steward ordered an entire wagon of Bao Yang's special wine.

'Had we known, we might have poisoned the casks and saved ourselves some trouble,' Bao Yang remarked drily, but she found the idea of poison highly unsatisfactory after the wrongs these men had committed.

They entered the mansion under the guise of a martial-dance troupe. Bao Yang and her brother would perform a lion dance, operating the head and tail of the costume. Li Feng would perform an ever-popular sword dance, a favourite of General Wang's.

The prefect's bodyguards searched through their stage items. The men only gave a cursory glance at her sword, an obvious show sword with its dulled edge and tip. They spent more time staring at her costume. The turquoise material flowed over her like a second skin, allowing for movement. She glared at their backs as they moved on to the other performers.

'Careful,' Bao Yang warned, though he didn't refrain from casting a dark look at the guardsmen either.

The entertainers were separated from the banquet by a paper screen stretched over a bamboo frame. From behind it, she could make out the silhouettes of attendees sitting at low tables. A constant flow of music from a pipa accompanied the event.

The prefect and the general would be enjoying the feast at the front tables. She tried to focus on them, but they were nothing more than blurred shapes amidst the buzz of voices and laughter. Guan had likely invited a few distinguished poets and scholars to toast their accomplishments. Courtesans were present to pour wine and liven the conversation. They would be distracted when it was time to strike, full of wine with beautiful women in their laps.

Behind the screen, the performers waited for their time.

The performances started after the first dishes were served. There was an acrobatic tumbling routine, a graceful ribbon dance. The lion dance would follow and Li Feng's sword dance would be the last act.

Bao Yang and her brother were dressed in black. The lion's head rested at their feet. It was painted in bright colours of red, green and gold with large yellow eyes. A long striped canopy trimmed with black fur draped down from the lion's head to serve as the body. Their weapons were hidden inside the hollowed shell of the head, sealed behind layers of paper pasted over the rattan frame.

As the guards moved away, Liu Yuan broke into the hidden compartment and slipped Li Feng her short sword. A shiver wormed through her as she took the weapon in hand. The blade promptly disappeared beneath her sleeve.

A rising drumbeat signalled that it was time. Her heartbeat thudded to the same rhythm as the men slipped into the lion costume. Her brother pulled the head over the top half of his body. He aimed the painted eyes at her and the lion bowed his head and shook his mane. Its mouth gaped open in a smile that appeared ghastly under the circumstances. She almost wanted to laugh, but it would have been a harsh, flat sound. She had no joy left in her. She left all thoughts of happiness behind to focus on what she needed to do.

The acts finished one after another as the shadows danced on the other side of the screen. Then it was time for Liu Yuan and Bao Yang to begin, parading out in the lion costume to join the world of silhouettes.

The movements of the traditional lion dance required strength and co-ordination as the two men acted as the front and hind legs. The lion pranced and leapt, a celestial beast at play. They had spent the afternoon practising so that they could at least enact a mimicry of the popular dance. Their real purpose was to present a diversion as they moved into position.

Li Feng gripped the prop sword. She closed her eyes to gather her thoughts.

Their parents had performed for the last time in this very place. Mother had twirled around and around on nimble feet. Father had piped out a happy melody on his flute. Their spirits would be watching now over son and daughter. Soon they could rest. They could all finally rest.

A cymbal clanged and she opened her eyes. It sounded once, then paused. Then two more times. She moved into position and took in a deep breath. The moment the drums began again, she started her run. Each beat propelled her forwards. Thump, thump, thump. The feel of the ground pushed up into the muscles of her legs. The drumbeat became her pulse. She sprung on to her hands just before the screen and burst through the paper as the audience gasped with wonder.

Her tumbling pass continued. The world spun around her in swirls of colour as she flipped from hands to feet to hands. With the last flip she twisted around in the air and landed, her feet whisper soft.

The world shifted back into focus and she raised her eyes to the man who had destroyed her family. She expected such lewdness and greed to show on a man's face. It would drag down his mouth and sink his eyes into an ugly portrait. But the man she looked upon had aristocratic features. His face was elongated, his nose high. His hands were raised in applause, but they had stilled mid-clap. His smile was similarly frozen.

He recognised her.

She didn't know how that was possible. She only knew it was time to act.

Rearing her arm back, Li Feng launched her sword like a spear towards the main table. General Wang leapt aside and his guards sprang into action the same time Bao Yan and her brother cast aside the lion costume, knives in hand.

These next moments meant everything. She closed the distance to the prefect, slipping the real sword from her sleeve. The dramatic costume made the sheath easy to hide.

Guan He didn't move as the blade came for his throat. He was too stunned. Let him die with that fear choking him. Her own heart pounded within her, forcing blood to her limbs and resounding hard through her skull—louder than any drumbeat.

A shadow flew from the corner of her vision as she drove forwards. Another blade connected with hers, deflecting it with a force that jarred her arm to the bone. Zheng Hao Han had emerged from nothingness to stand in the centre of the courtyard. That bastard Thief-catcher Han.

He grabbed a handful of the prefect's robe and shoved the man to the corner.

'Li Feng.' His dark eyes never left her face. 'Don't do this.'

A surge of emotion filled her at the sight of him, but she forced it back down to the darkness within. It was too late to stop.

A cold smile curved her mouth. 'Han,' she acknowledged, with the softness of a lover. 'Don't hold back.'

With that warning, she released the catch on the sleeve sword to extend the blade and attacked.

A fist clenched around his heart. He meant nothing to her.

Han raised his *dao*, prepared to defend against Li Feng's thrust, but she'd misdirected him. Her attack was directed to his left. It was Prefect Guan she wanted.

He shoved the low banquet table into her path. The obstacle provided only a moment's distraction. She stepped on to the tabletop and leapt, using the added height to bring her blade down on him. He dodged just in time and positioned himself directly between her and Guan. She would have to fight through him.

All around them, other fights broke out. Han gave the other attackers a cursory glance before focusing back on Li Feng.

She drove back in, closing the distance, moving deep into his stance. Her sword pointed at his heart.

He stepped out of the way, but Li Feng shifted her weight and flowed back into him, her attack circling around his guard. He felt the nick of the blade without ever seeing it. A razor line stung across his knuckles. Insubstantial, but infuriating that he'd allowed that much through. He swung the *dao* at her head. She had no choice but to retreat, but in a heartbeat she was back before him.

This was Wudang sword—a form based on circular patterns and the redirection of energy. Her short sword truncated the movements, making the techniques faster, more efficient.

This was the first time they had truly engaged in battle. Li Feng was more artist than killer, but she was presenting a good semblance of the killing part. Her eyes were black and unfathomable as she searched for an opening. A hunting falcon narrowing in on its prey. But there was something beyond strategy in her gaze. He knew that look. He knew the intent.

His blood ran to ice. She had asked too often about Two Dragon Lo, the bandit king who had been determined to die in his own way.

'Li Feng—'

He should have known better than to try to speak. Her sword cut at his throat. He dodged the swipe, only to take a kick to the gut. He fell back, momentarily stunned. A flash of steel caught his eye. The relentless sword was coming for him. Instinct took over and he grabbed at the blade. The sharp edge cut into his palm, but Li Feng was momentarily disabled. Tucking the *dao* back, he swung the back of his hand into her jaw.

The crack of bone made an ugly sound and Li Feng staggered. His gut wrenched at the sight of her on the ground. The flash fire of pain in his hand began to register. He clenched his fingers over the wound to stanch the flow of blood while Li Feng twisted on to her feet. The look she shot him was equal parts loathing and respect. But the light had returned to her eyes. She was aware, finally seeing him instead of the ghosts of the past.

'Run,' he demanded.

Her gaze swept over the rest of the courtyard. The feast was in a shambles, tables upturned, dishes scattered. The warlord's men swarmed over the other would-be assassins. There was more commotion outside the walls. Sounds of fighting.

His palm was torn to shreds. Li Feng's face was swollen, the corner of her mouth bleeding.

'You'll have to kill me,' he warned.

Li Feng hesitated. At least she gave him that much.

'Run,' he muttered again beneath his breath.

She had come here ready to die. Was there enough between them for him to stop her? There was the chase, the many escapes. He'd spared her, she'd saved him. And they had one night. One night in each other's arms.

Their battle had positioned her against the archway leading into the rear section of the garden. The rest of the fight was behind him. She looked quickly to her comrades and stepped backwards through the archway, keeping her eyes on him until she disappeared deeper into the mansion.

This section of the garden was eerily quiet, untouched by the violence just beyond the wall. There was one way out of the mansion and that was through the front gates. No one thought to invade this private sanctum of miniature landscapes and silent stones. The sounds of struggle continued through the archway, but in this secluded area, the fight seemed diminished. She could hear the rippling of water as a carp broke the surface of the pond before disappearing again into the black depths. The serenity was an abomination. It did nothing to calm the thudding of her pulse or the anger that gathered inside her like a coming storm.

Who was Han to try to force her hand? He thought she only had two options, defeat him or retreat. But water and wind flowed around rocks and mountains. She would run up the garden wall and go *over* him to get to Guan He. Han would not confuse her. He would not stop her.

'Daughter?'

The plaintive sound came from the far corner of the garden. A tremulous voice that resounded through her like thunder. She turned her head like a puppet on a string, her mind wholly removed from her body.

A woman in blue appeared beneath the veranda, stepping into the waning light of the day. She was slender, graceful, beautiful in a way no other woman could be in a little girl's eyes. It wasn't like seeing Liu Yuan where her memories came back in pieces through fog and time. She knew at once in every part of her who this was. Li Feng flew over grass and rock to fall into her mother's arms.

*'Xiao Feng.'*

Mother's arms curved around her. Li Feng was childish-small again and blinded by tears. In that moment, the heavens were infinitely kind. She had a mother.

Li Feng clung to her. 'What are you doing here? How are you alive?'

'I prayed.' Her mother's fingers brushed frantically over her hair, her cheek, each touch like the brush of a bird's wings. 'I prayed I would see you again.'

Everything was happening so quickly. The sword was still in her hands. Her pulse was still beating from the fight with Han. She was confused, as if she were dropped suddenly into the middle of a dream where she could no longer follow her own thoughts.

Mother pushed her away suddenly. 'Daughter, you have to go.'

'No.' She tried to grab at her mother's hands with fingers that were trembling and clumsy. 'Come with me.'

'They're coming.' Her mother's voice was choked with fear. Is that how she had lived all these years? As a prisoner in fear?

Heavy footsteps pounded towards them and the memories closed in on her. *Li Feng, don't cry. Don't cry.*

'Go quickly!'

Even now, with so many years gone by, a mother's command was still to be obeyed. There was no time to think or ask questions. Li Feng ran at the outer wall and then up it, hooking on to the top with her fingers. Her mother called for her as she pulled herself on to the edge.

'Xiao Feng.' Mother stretched her hand up, palm flat against the wall.

After so many years, her mother still looked the same. That one memory for her had held true.

Li Feng reached down. The tips of their fingers barely touched. 'I'll come back for you.'

Armed soldiers invaded the garden as she slipped over the side of the wall. It was the rock once again shutting out the light. This time it was her mother who was trapped inside and it was Li Feng who was being dragged away.

# *Chapter Eighteen*

Han made a show of protecting the prefect while at the same time blocking the garden entrance. The courtyard had been razed and transformed into a battlefield. General Wang lay on the ground, bleeding. His soldiers formed a protective barrier while one of the men hovered over him, pressing his hands over the wound. The two assailants in black had been wrestled to the ground.

'Keep them alive for questioning!' Magistrate Tan was pale and shaking. With Wang incapacitated and the prefect in shock, the bureaucrat was taking control admirably.

Inevitably, the question came. 'Where is the sword dancer?' Tan asked.

Han indicated the archway with a jerk of his head and followed the team of guards into the garden with his weapon ready. To his relief, the area was empty. Li Feng was safe—for now.

'It happened so quickly.' Tan was beside him.

'This rabble must have followed General Wang here. Violence breeds violence.'

His disdain for the general was clear. Han didn't point out that Guan He was as much of a target as the general.

With a shaking hand, Tan drew a handkerchief from his sleeve and mopped his forehead. Then he looked down with alarm. 'You're bleeding.'

Han opened his fist and closed it again. He'd almost forgotten about his hand. The wound was a reminder of the woman who had given it to him. Li Feng's eyes had been cold when she'd attacked him. The desolation in her face had cut him much deeper than the sword.

'It's not too bad,' he said.

Han had carried a sword for ten years. The sight of blood, even his own, no longer made his head swim. He stared back at the ruins of the banquet. Tables were strewn throughout the courtyard. The entertainers had all fled. The lion costume lay abandoned before the tattered screen, lifeless and trampled like the corpse of a colourful beast. Wang had been moved inside while his men swept the area for other threats. Prefect Guan had retreated once again, leaving the magistrate to handle the aftermath.

'There were three of them,' Tan said. 'The two captured ones had knives.'

'What a senseless plan.' Anger churned in his

stomach. None of them could have expected to survive this. Had Li Feng become so lost that life and death no longer mattered to her?

Tan regarded him with an earnest expression. 'How did you ever find out about it?'

An expression like that could fool one into thinking the man was simply curious, but Han was the son of a magistrate. Like his father, Magistrate Tan was always looking to separate truth from lies. He was watching Han's every action to the slightest nuance.

'I had no idea about this scheme,' Han replied smoothly. 'I came to look for you.'

The magistrate nodded, making a non-committal sound in the back of his throat. The matter was dropped and somehow not dropped. Magistrate Tan looked to where the attackers were being detained.

'If you could accompany the prisoners to the holding cells. They're a treacherous sort and might try to overpower the guards.' He lowered his voice. 'The warlord's soldiers wanted to take possession of the prisoners, but he has no authority here. And we don't want him to think he can seize control so easily.'

'Of course, sir.'

'I'm grateful.'

Han didn't require any political insight to see how the magistrate was setting Han up as his man. With Li Feng in hiding and her companions in custody, Han might need to exploit his connection to the magistrate to keep her safe. She was wanted for attempted murder now as well as an attack against an appointed official.

Constable Guo arrived to shackle the prisoners at hands and feet. Han recognised one of the two men immediately. He had a scar at the corner of his mouth and a black stare that was unmistakable. Li Feng's brother. The other one was a stranger. His posture remained proud and defiant even in chains. These men had no fear of death. Apparently Li Feng didn't either.

The prison wagon waited in the street and the two men were herded inside the compartment. The constable took one side and Han the other as the wagon rolled through the streets towards the hall of justice.

At the prison house, Han supervised as the men were locked inside individual cells. Liu Yuan looked over the closet-sized area without emotion and Han was reminded of the first time he had encountered Li Feng. She had looked over the prison house with the same calculating manner when Han had attempted to put her in chains.

He wondered whether the bandit shared any of the same skills that made it so hard to keep Li Feng confined. But where Li Feng had escaped from what amounted to a village stable, Minzhou had a sturdy prison secured within the walls of the magistrate's yamen.

Liu Yuan didn't speak until the door thudded shut and the chain was locked. He brought his face to the small opening cut into the door.

'Thief-catcher.'

Han turned to face him, but refused to acknowledge him in any other way. Liu Yuan killed out of a sense of duty towards his family. He might have been driven by filial piety, but he was still an outlaw and a murderer.

'If you harm my sister, I'll hunt you down,' the bandit threatened.

'I'm not the one who has put her in danger,' Han retorted.

Two dark, piercing eyes stared back at him from the holding cell. They were disturbingly similar to the eyes that already haunted his days and nights.

Prefect Guan sent a messenger to Han later that evening. As he left the yamen, the sky was dark around him and the city lanterns had been lit. The number of guards outside the prefect's mansion had doubled and there were sentries standing watch on the street corners.

Inside the walls, the courtyard had been swept and scrubbed clean. There were no signs of the attack that had occurred just hours earlier. Han was lead through the grounds to a room beside the garden. The prefect's study was lavishly decorated with wall scrolls and ostentatiously placed vases and art sculptures. Guan sat behind a fortress of a desk fashioned from rosewood.

'Welcome, Zheng Hao Han.' The prefect stood to greet him. 'Please sit.'

He called for tea, asked if Han wanted anything else, made overly polite overtures.

Han had no choice but to wait for the tea to be brought and poured. He sat across from a man who was lecherous, corrupt, and both a bully and a coward; however Guan He's demeanour showed none of those traits. He had a stately appearance: tall and aristocratic, with a thin face that was approaching gauntness, his features absent of the well-fed fleshiness one would expect from a wealthy official.

Han had expected a fearful, cowering man after the way Guan had hidden for the last weeks, but the man he approached presented himself with a semblance of dignity. The stark shadows beneath his eyes were the only sign that something plagued him beneath the still surface.

'You are to be commended for your service today, Mister Zheng. Your courage was unparalleled,' the prefect said.

Han wondered whether it was study of the classics and poetry that gave such men so many extra words that meant nothing. 'It was my duty.'

'I will ensure that you are duly promoted. There are many posts within our city in need of a worthy individual such as yourself.'

'Thank you, sir, but I cannot accept.'

He would become a beggar before taking orders from such a man, but as soon as he had spoken, Han realised he finally had the opportunity to question the prefect directly.

'Magistrate Tan has already enlisted my services,' he amended. 'As I understand, a man under your employment was murdered a month ago.'

'Hmm? Yes, a tragedy.' The prefect seemed to be occupied with other thoughts.

'I was hired to find the killers. It's likely the very same bandits were responsible for today's incident. Does the prefect know of any reason why he would be targeted?'

'They're outlaws, Mister Zheng.' Guan spoke the words dismissively, but his hand tightened into a fist. He rapped his knuckles over the desk in an agitated gesture. 'They care about nothing. Besides, it appears as if General Wang was the one they meant to attack. He has made many enemies throughout the province.'

Had the official forgotten how Li Feng's blade was aimed at his throat? It occurred to Han at that moment that Prefect Guan hadn't done much to apprehend Liu Yuan and his bandits after the murder. Despite being in a position of power, Guan had chosen to hide. Even if there were a dozen bandits hiding in the hills, he could have organised the city guards and swept through the woods as Han had done.

Instead, Prefect Guan had locked himself away and stationed guards around his home as if he was under siege. He feared a greater enemy, someone he was powerless against. Someone like Wang Shizhen.

Han had assumed that the prefect and the warlord were allied with one another, but what if General Wang hadn't come to the city as an honoured guest? Perhaps he'd forced himself through the gates.

'In any case, now that these scoundrels have been captured, we must resolve this case swiftly and make an example of these outlaws.' The prefect's expression darkened. He turned his tea cup around in a half-circle. 'Has…has the dancer been apprehended?'

Han tensed at the mention of Li Feng. 'Not yet, my lord.'

Though she hadn't succeeded in the assassination, she certainly wasn't free of guilt.

Guan He nodded absently. His gaze had become distant while his hands clenched and unclenched restlessly. Han suspected he knew why. The man had watched Li Feng's mother dance before him fifteen years ago, putting into motion the events that would bring about her death and the death of her husband. Prefect Guan had seen a ghost at the banquet, a ghost intent on killing him. He was feeling the tumult of a guilty soul.

Han decided to press his advantage. 'I found something in the courtyard after the outlaws were subdued. I thought it might belong to you.'

He reached inside his robe to pull out Li Feng's pendant. As Han placed it on the desk, Guan He pressed his palms flat just beneath it, refusing to touch the jade. Weariness flooded over him, dragging his shoulders down like a puppet with his strings cut.

'Have you ever been struck by lightning?' Guan asked.

Han shook his head, not comprehending.

'Have you ever met a woman and knew you had to have her? Knew that fate had destined her for you and it didn't matter that the two of you were from different worlds?'

The prefect's passionate outburst unsettled him. The words, though spoken by such vermin, struck too close to the vein.

'I've never experienced such a thing, sir,' Han replied stiffly.

But the first time he had seen Li Feng with her

sword in hand, the rest of the world had disappeared. Before he knew what was happening, he was chasing her over the rooftops. Han hadn't run after her because he suspected she was a thief. He had gone after her because she had started fleeing and, for reasons he could not understand, he couldn't let her get away.

'When it happens to you, that one moment changes you for ever,' Prefect Guan went on, almost feverishly. 'A long time ago, there was this dancer—' He stopped, embarrassed at having revealed so much.

The man had twisted the destruction of Li Feng's family into a tale of passionate love. In his eyes, he had fallen madly in love with a young, beautiful dancer and had to have her no matter what the consequences. It was a tragic, romantic tale, the sort that poets told. Why, the prefect was as much a victim of fate in this story as the poor dancer.

Han wished he could have let Li Feng have her revenge on this man. But then she and her brother would go to the executioner just as their parents had done. The cycle of heartbreak and loss would be complete. He hardly found such tragedy poetic.

'Sir, what does this have to do with anything?' Han asked.

'Nothing. Nothing at all.' The prefect regained his composure and hastily put the jade away in a drawer. 'Thank you for recovering this. You will be compensated for your services.'

Han started to take his leave, but Guan stopped him at the door.

'If you find the sword dancer...' The prefect struggled for his next words. 'If you could bring her here. To me.'

Han could have strangled the man himself. He forced out a cordial nod and exited the study. The house steward offered him a string of cash as reward for recovering the jade. It would have been too conspicuous to refuse the money. Instead, Han dropped the coins into the first beggar's bowl he encountered as he made his way back to the main street.

He had nothing but contempt for Guan He, yet Han had saved the man's life. He defended a set of laws that dictated the bastard had to be protected due to his rank and status. The social order had to be preserved at all costs. It sickened him.

Back in the market area, the restaurant where Han was staying roared with activity. The two floors were packed with hungry labourers and tradesmen and the kitchen sizzled with the sounds of food cooking. The smell of hot grease and garlic assailed him as he descended the stairs to his room.

As Han pushed back the bamboo screen, he was met by a faint glimmer of light. He had only a moment to consider the oddity of it before the knife was at his throat.

'Bastard,' Li Feng hissed, pressing the blade against the soft tissue at the base of his throat. 'Meddling, no-good bastard.'

Her gaze burned through him. Though her voice trembled with anger, her hand was as steady as the earth beneath his feet.

He had been expecting this. He had even hoped she would be there waiting for him, knife and all.

'Guan He owed me blood,' Li Feng spat out. *'Blood.'*

His eyes never left hers. 'I couldn't let you kill him.'

She had been forced to leave her mother, her brother, Bao Yang, all behind. Everyone she cared for was in enemy hands because of Han. Yet here he was watching her, his face an impenetrable mask, as calm and forbearing as a Buddhist monk. She hated it.

'Everything is so straight and narrow for you. Justice is justice.' Li Feng tightened her grip on the hilt. 'Don't you know? There is no such thing as justice!'

Even with a knife at his throat, he wouldn't fight back. His gaze shifted to her jaw, to the place where he'd struck her.

His expression darkened with regret. 'Forgive me.'

'For this? After everything you've done, *this* is what you apologise for?' She shoved at him and he took a halting step back. 'What is it to you whether a man like Guan He lives or dies? He's nothing to you.'

'I don't care about him,' he said through his teeth. 'I did what I did to protect you.'

'Why?' she demanded hollowly. 'Because you're so taken with me?'

His jaw tensed, hardening his already rough features. She could see the rise and fall of his chest as he considered his answer.

'I am,' he said finally.

There was no charm in his reply. Just a simple admission. Ignoring the knife, he bent and pressed his mouth against hers. She permitted the kiss, confused, not knowing why, or even when, she started kissing him back. She matched his passion with her own, inviting his tongue and the familiar taste of him. Like warmed wine and spices. He broke the kiss abruptly, leaving her breathless and yearning.

'Kill me afterwards,' he muttered, wrapping his hand around her wrist to shove the knife away.

He wasn't teasing. There was no room left for any lightheartedness between them. Everything had become serious, as serious as death and life. She let the weapon fall to the ground and grabbed on to his shoulders with both hands.

Their movements were hurried. Inelegant. Pulling and tearing away clothes. No enjoyment of bared skin or soft touches. They disrobed enough for Han to lift her and enter her. The pain and pleasure of him pushing inside her obliterated everything.

He turned them as one and pressed her back against the wall, surging up and deeper into her. So deep she could feel him throughout her entire body. Li Feng closed her eyes with the torment of it. She had come here looking for *something*. It might as well be this.

He flattened his palm against the wall beside her. His tongue invaded her mouth and she welcomed it. His body angled and strained against her with each thrust. She wrapped her legs around his hips to hold on to him. It seemed like nothing more than mindless desperation. Only in this act were they ever of one mind.

Li Feng looked up into Han's eyes as he possessed her. A frown cut deep into his brow. His skin was damp, his pupils opaque and lost. She needed to be held like this, unable to flee, not wanting to move other than to urge him into her.

Her heart beat faster and she dug her nails into the muscle of his shoulders. If he stopped, she would die. She closed her eyes to concentrate on the feel of him as the pleasure rose, to push herself over the edge. She felt his lips graze her cheek. A single moment of tenderness in this desperate union.

'You love me.' His breath was hot against her ear. 'But you don't want to.'

Sensation crested within her, rising to a point where darkness beckoned. She had no will to protest.

His body sank deep, holding her captive as she shuddered around him. He held on tight through it. He might have spoken her name in a choked whisper, but she could no longer hear. She was in her own world, alone.

As she came back to herself, he thrust once more and held himself deep within her. Every muscle in him tensed as he reached his peak.

Afterward there was nothing but the sound of their breathing, which was without rhythm or harmony. After a pause, Han gathered her into his arms. She wrapped her legs around him as he carried her to the pallet. His hand cradled the back of her head as he lowered her to the mat. Then he balanced on his arms to keep his weight from crushing her. The roughness of their coupling had given away to this sudden attentiveness.

Keeping his gaze on her, he followed the curve of her cheek with his fingertips until he was pressing lightly against her jaw. The area was tender and swollen. An ugly bruise would be forming there.

Why was she here? She hadn't known the answer until that moment, with Han beside her as they stared wordlessly at one another.

She had convinced herself she would be dead by now, but she wasn't. Li Feng took a deep breath, letting it flow through her lungs, her heart, her limbs. She was alive—and she was glad for it.

Han had pulled her back from death. She hated him for interfering, as much as she loved him for it.

Han's gaze narrowed on her before he rolled on to his back to look at the ceiling. All the life seemed drained from him, as if he'd poured his essence into her in their frantic coupling.

They lay side by side without touching, though she could feel the heat of his skin no more than a breath away. A bandage was still wrapped around his left hand. It was the least of the injuries they had inflicted upon one another.

'I've lost you,' he said, his voice resonating so low she felt it sinking beneath her skin, into flesh and bone.

'You never had me.'

'I did.' He turned to look at her. A smile played on his lips, slight and a little sad. 'I did.'

She wished in that moment that he was still holding her, but it would be pointless when they had both all but acknowledged that they could have nothing more than this. The chase was over and Han was letting her go. Because he loved her.

Their clothes were still in disarray and the memory of their lovemaking refused to fade. To smooth out her tunic and tie her sash would mean the final closure and she wasn't yet ready to be at their end.

'I'm going once more back to the prefect's mansion,' she said.

'Li Feng.'

Their heads were turned towards each other. She could see the contours of his neck. A pulse skipped steadily at his throat. There was such a thin barrier separating life and death.

'I won't go after Guan He.' Killing him wouldn't give her peace. She knew that now. 'My mother is alive. I'm going to rescue her.'

Han sat up, his eyes wide with surprise. His robe was open at the front and the intimacy of the moment made her heart ache. She pulled herself up beside him.

'And then I'm going to rescue my brother,' she said. 'Are you going to try to stop me?'

With Han, she could be honest. And she could rely on him for honesty in return. He was an adversary, but at some point he'd also become her friend. Her only friend. The world was full of contradictions and opposing forces.

'I won't stop you,' he said finally. 'I'll help you.'

## Chapter Nineteen

'The magistrate will hold back the trial to wait for the constables to apprehend the third suspect,' Han explained. 'Once they go before the tribunal, sentencing and execution will happen swiftly.'

Li Feng didn't flinch. 'Then we have to rescue them tonight.'

Her expression was determined, absent of any sign of fear, but at least the fire had returned to her eyes. The Li Feng he knew had come back from the edge of death.

'I know the layout of the yamen and where they're being held,' he said. 'I'll go there this morning to learn more about the guard detail.'

'I have something I need to do as well,' she said, refusing to elaborate.

She was still keeping secrets from him. At least Li Feng trusted him enough to accept his help, but she always kept a part of her locked away. He knew

Li Feng would never be his, but still he longed for more of her. As much as she would give.

'Be careful. Everyone in the city is hunting for you.'

She levelled her gaze on him. 'I have some experience evading thief-catchers.'

'The best of them, I hear.' It was too hard to smile given the circumstances.

The constable's men were scouring the city, hoping to make an arrest, but General Wang's soldiers were out for blood. It wasn't the first time Han had worked alongside someone, but it was the first time he cared more about his partner's safety than his own. He had to trust in Li Feng's abilities as they parted to their respective tasks.

The yamen was busy with activity that morning. Han's face was becoming a familiar sight at the compound so he was able to enter without being challenged. He masked his intentions with a visit to the constable.

'No progress on finding the sword dancer.' Guo sighed heavily. 'Searching through all the dancers and acrobats in the city has been a waste of time.'

Han kept his expression controlled. 'The sword dancer is likely gone from Minzhou.'

'I'm of the same mind as you. At least we have the co-conspirators.'

'Did they reveal anything?'

'Nothing yet, but the interrogations will start this morning.'

A brief turn about the prison house revealed two guards on the inside as well as two men stationed outside the doors. An additional sentry had been added to the detail due to the dangerous nature of the prisoners.

He was ready to leave when a summons came from the magistrate. Tan Li Kuo was conversing with his deputy magistrate when Han arrived at the study. The senior official waved his hands dramatically while he spoke while the deputy nodded, a grave expression on the younger man's face.

Once the deputy left, Magistrate Tan turned to Han. He appeared in a huff, his rounded cheeks flushed pink. 'I'm closing the tribunal for the day. Too many things happening all at once.'

Tan gestured for him to sit. The portly magistrate dabbed at his forehead with the edge of his sleeve, looking like he'd already run ten *li* that morning.

'I've been dealing with General Wang's soldiers. They're demanding the prisoners be turned over for punishment. Wolves, all of them, but they have no teeth now that the head of the pack is down.'

'Wang Shizhen survived yesterday's attack?'

'For now, it seems. He was moved to one of the inns and his men are standing guard in case of another attack. But on to other matters—what did Prefect Guan wish to see you about last night?'

Han was surprised at his interest. 'Nothing of consequence. He was grateful for my service.'

'As we all are.' Tan nodded emphatically. 'As we all are. How did he appear to you?'

'He seemed shaken and distracted, though that's to be expected.' Han didn't feel the need to mention the prefect's unusual interest in Li Feng or his passionate outburst about his infatuation with a dancer fifteen years ago.

Even though they were alone, the magistrate beckoned him in closer. 'Between you and me, there's a scandal brewing here. Prefect Guan is trying to keep rumours from spreading. Bad for the city's reputation, he says. He wanted the prisoners sentenced and executed secretly so there was no public unrest. Did you hear me? Secretly! As if we were the criminals. I had to shut the tribunal down until we can get this city under control.' Tan wiped at his face again.

'Is there any chance for leniency in this case?'

The magistrate's eyes widened. 'Leniency? I don't see how that would be possible. This was a very vicious attack.'

'But we are not yet aware of all the circumstances surrounding the crime. The *Book of Rites* states that one cannot co-exist under heaven with the murderer of one's father. That he should strike him down in the street without going home to fetch a weapon.'

'Ah, the scholar in you is showing. Why do you mention filial piety?'

Han had to be careful not to reveal too much. 'One of the prisoners claimed to be avenging his father.'

Magistrate Tan stroked his beard, which appeared pitifully thin in contrast to the roundness of his face. 'When considering wrongful death and revenge, there is an interesting parallel case. Not more than two generations ago, a man sought revenge for his father by posing as a courier in a relay station. His enemy was a senior official and when he came to rest at the station, the man killed the official and then immediately reported himself to the court. The public was moved by his loyalty and cried for leniency, but no one, not even the accused, could deny that he had committed a crime. How could the state let a murder go unpunished?'

'But the state allowed the initial wrong to be committed,' Han countered.

He was reminded of so many conversations with his father. Once Father had retreated from public life, he chose to tutor Han himself, hoping one day that his son would redeem the family name. Unfortunately, Han had been a poor student, always questioning as he was doing now.

'Indeed! The magistrate on the case was caught

in the same dilemma,' Tan concurred. 'The only solution was to execute the man for the killing, but honour him after death for his loyalty to his father. So you can see, a man on the path of revenge might be applauded for killing his enemy, but in the same breath he must willingly accept the consequences of his actions.'

'But this attack wasn't successful,' Han pointed out.

'A pity that,' Tan remarked. 'For the accused.'

The magistrate was no longer fidgeting. His hands were folded neatly in front of him and Han was unable to decipher whether he was speaking in the broader sense of the discussion or not.

'Seeing that no one was killed, perhaps forced labour would be a more appropriate sentence,' Han suggested.

Though the argument was a weak one, Han was determined to see if there was any chance for Li Feng and her brother. The magistrate had allowed Constable Guo a second chance, hadn't he?

'Guan He is an appointed official. An attack against him must be construed as an attack on the state,' Magistrate Tan said sombrely. 'Unfortunately, there is only one decision left to me in this case—whether it should be death by strangulation or death by beheading.'

He didn't fault Magistrate Tan. These were not

easy decisions to make. Han remembered the first and only execution he'd witnessed. As a boy, he had always been curious about his father's profession.

A man had beaten a shopkeeper to death and had been sentenced for execution by strangulation. With the morbid curiosity of a boy of thirteen, Han had gone to the public square expecting to see a vile man, an angry man with violence in his eyes. He saw only a peasant who was as thin as a reed and so very afraid.

He had never seen fear like it. The man was trembling, his knees weak. The city guards had dragged him through the streets and placed him in front of the executioner like a pile of rag-covered bones.

In the years to come, Han would spend time among warriors who would talk about dying a good death. This was not a good death.

The executioner stood behind the accused and looped the garotte around his throat before jerking it cruelly back. After that day, Han's mind had revisited the scene night after night until those few minutes stretched out to an hour, to an eternity. It took a long time before the wretched man stopped moving. Han should have looked away, but he couldn't. He remembered every kick, every struggle. The accused man's body continued to shudder even once he'd stopped fighting, hanging on to life long past the point his mind was already resigned to death.

Han never knew the rest of the story. Was the shopkeeper's death an accident? Was it a crime of rage? He didn't dare ask his father for the details. He wasn't supposed to have witnessed the execution.

The next morning, he woke to find his lessons unfinished. The only characters he could summon were the ones that earned him a beating and then another beating: *'I do not want to be a high-ranking officer.'*

He didn't want to have such power of life or death over strangers. It was a much different thing to face a man on a field of battle, with sword in hand.

'It seems to me,' Han began quietly, 'that with this logic, the only recourse for a man of lower rank is to exact violence and be condemned for it. It's no wonder that men grow angry. They turn to rebellion because they have nothing else to lose.'

Tan held up his hand, hushing him. 'I know of the resentment you speak of and it is unfortunate, but let's not forget that in the most difficult of circumstances, the law becomes even more important. Order must be maintained,' he said solemnly.

'But is order truly justice?' Han questioned.

The magistrate sighed. 'Perhaps not. But without order, there can be no protection for anyone. To sanction revenge as a means for justice would be to admit that the laws can no longer function. Do you believe that, Zheng Hao Han? That the state is broken and that man is free to make his own rules?'

Gone was the fumbling and exuberant personality that Tan Li Kuo often presented. Beneath that mask, the magistrate was observant, thoughtful and his question cut startlingly to the very core of Han's doubts about the law, and about himself. Was Han the same as the bandits he hunted down?

'No,' Han replied, finding the answer deep inside from all of his father's teachings, from all that he'd seen and done.

Despite its flaws and failings, he still believed in the necessity for the rule of law. Without the state, the land would be ruled by bandits and warlords. By men like Two Dragon Lo and Wang Shizhen who devoured the weak. This made what Han planned to do tonight even more difficult. He would have to fight against the very structure of what he believed in, but Li Feng and her family had been wronged and there was no provision within the law to set it right.

Li Feng waited for the customers to leave before stepping inside the herbal shop. Physician Wu Song was at the counter, in the process of wrapping up a parcel of ginseng. He looked up as she came close.

'You recognised me,' she said. 'You knew my face when you approached me in the street.'

His pleasant expression changed, becoming almost grim. He moved to the window to roll down the blinds, shading the interior of the shop.

'Young miss, you very much resemble someone I know.'

'You must know my mother.'

An unreadable look flickered across the physician's face. 'Yes, I suppose I do.'

'You should know that the city guard is searching for me,' she warned. 'Our association might put you in danger.'

'I know that as well,' the physician replied, unperturbed. 'What do you need from me?'

'Can you bring her a message? It's of the utmost importance that you get word to her today, before evening comes.'

They moved to the back room to his writing desk. Her knowledge of characters was limited so she had to dictate the message to the physician. Her mother was being kept as a concubine in the prefect's mansion. She belonged to him, according to the law. What Li Feng was planning was akin to theft and kidnapping, yet the physician's brush moved over the paper without pause.

'This servant has been admitted at certain times to the prefect's mansion in order to see to the health of the household,' Wu said. 'If he will receive me today, I will deliver this message.'

His words had the solemnity of an oath.

Wu Song held the paper up to dry, then folded it once in half and then again with tidy creases before slipping it into the pocket of his sleeve.

'Thank you. My family owes you a debt, honourable sir.'

He pushed up from the desk. 'You should go now,' he said gently.

From the first moment they'd met, Physician Wu had been protective of her, though Li Feng hadn't known why until now. The man cared for her mother. Perhaps it was nothing more than the concern of a physician, but he'd also shown Li Feng a rare and simple kindness.

She had started to believe that such kindness didn't exist in the world, but she was wrong. Wu Song was a good man. Han was a good man as well, too good of a man for her. She had been too blind to realise it until it was too late.

# Chapter Twenty

The space beneath the arch of the bridge was cool and damp. A faint light filtered down from the lanterns on the street above to cast them in a world of shape and shadow. Li Feng closed her eyes and slowed her breath, feeling her mind expand and her muscles loosen with each inhale and exhale.

'What do you think of when you're flying over the eaves?' Han asked.

He was leaning against the wooden frame of the bridge, arms crossed over his chest. She was tucked opposite him as they waited for the night to completely envelop them. They were both in black from head to toe.

'I think of nothing,' she said. 'Nothing but the next step.'

They had set out across the river into the north part of the city before evening came and the streets cleared. Now they had to wait for the right time.

Neither of them had twitched more than an eye in the last hour. It would do no good to pace or fret.

The gentle lap of water from the canal created a soft, lulling rhythm and she had fallen into an almost meditative state. She pretended that she was preparing for a performance, an elaborate dance. In her mind, she rehearsed the steps.

Han had drawn out the map of the magistrate's yamen for her, detailing where the guards were stationed. Not that it mattered too much. She needed to glimpse the terrain for herself before she could know how to traverse through it.

The sky continued to darken as they waited. Han's face began to fade into the night and she could hear the cadence of his breathing deepen across from her.

'Tonight is the last we'll see of each other,' he said.

A lump formed in her throat. After tonight, she and her family would be in hiding and he would no longer seek her out.

She'd known they would have to part. To remain together would be dangerous for both of them. They were standing in the dark and surrounded by the swampy scent of the canal. The hollow beneath the bridge seemed a desolate and lonely place to say their farewells.

'You're risking everything to help me, thief-catcher. I'm grateful.'

She avoided using his name on purpose. She was

already too emotional as it was. Despite the effort, her voice still wavered on the last words.

Han reached out and she lifted a hand to ward him away. Sentiment would cloud her focus during the run. Undaunted, his fingers closed around her wrist and he pulled her towards him, firm but gentle. Wrist to elbow to shoulder, until his arms circled around her.

When his lips found hers, all the fight within her drained away. She had lain naked in his arms, had known the thrust of his body deep inside her, yet this embrace in the gathering darkness was more complete than all of those acts of passion. His kiss was gentle, yet shockingly intimate out here with the great city around them. Such an act was a private thing meant for closed doors and drawn blinds. Yet when Han kissed her now, it was more than a precursor to lovemaking. It was language. His lips caressing softly to find her. She responded in kind, pressing close to him. It was longing and it was farewell.

A gong sounded in the marketplace and was echoed by another, then another. The nightly curfew. A foot patrol marched over the wooden planks above. They both grew still, holding on to each other through the rumbling.

In that pause, she allowed herself to imagine what it would be like to have a man like Han beside her.

Someone who was strong and good-hearted. She would turn one day on her pillow to see that his hair had turned grey. Hers would be grey as well and it would be a gift to have spent all those days together. This night would be done and just one adventure of their wild youth.

'Li Feng.' His voice was close to her ear.

The guards had cleared the bridge and there was silence around them. No sound to disrupt her thoughts. She could feel her eyes stinging, but she blinked the tears back furiously. Tears would blur her vision and she needed to remain sharp.

Han continued quietly. 'Once this is done and you're far away, find a place where you and your family can live without fear. A place where you can be happy.'

She nodded against his shoulder. He was an up-standing man in his blood, in his bones. He still believed in justice above all else. This was Han's dream for her in the spirit of such righteousness, but it wasn't a dream that could ever include himself. He was from the world of courts and laws. She belonged to the rivers and lakes outside the city walls.

'The streets should be clear now,' she said faintly. 'It's time, then.'

She allowed herself to touch her fingertips to his jaw as he let her go. 'Once it starts, remember to keep moving until it's done. We can't hesitate; we can't stop even for a moment.'

His eyes glittered in the darkness. 'I won't stop. Not even for a moment.'

The curfew worked to their advantage. At the evening gong, the ward gates had closed and all inhabitants were to remain inside their respective neighbourhoods. The lanes and alleys emptied out. To Li Feng, the city became an open maze. Han followed closely beside her as they ran through the city on quiet feet, twisting and turning to avoid the guard patrols.

At the magistrate's yamen, they flattened themselves against the wall in a side alley. Li Feng inspected the brick wall that surrounded the compound.

'A bit high,' she admitted.

'Can you make it?'

She wouldn't know until she tried. She scanned the wall, looking for hand holds, foot holds, a path that was invisible to all but her.

'Be ready.' Her heart was already pumping faster in anticipation.

'There's a patrol outside the walls as well as sentry inside. There can be anywhere between six to ten men,' Han reminded her.

'I'm more worried about the archers.'

Foot soldiers couldn't catch her while she was high above them, but an arrow could pluck her out of the sky. She couldn't worry too much. Yet. Han left her and she started counting silently to give him enough time to get into position. She reached one hundred and kept on going. At two hundred, she took a deep breath and started towards the wall.

It wasn't so much speed as it was balance, pressure, and placement. She pushed into the wall with her lead foot. One step up, then two. A final nudge against the indentation of the bricks and her hand was at the top. She found a grip against the crenellations to pull herself up.

It had taken no more than a few heartbeats and her blood was soaring. Crouching at the top, she peered down into the interior of the yamen. The courtyard was surrounded by buildings. She mapped out the landscape with all of its structures and obstacles. Columns, steps, eaves, railings. Then she began her run.

She stayed low on the wall, running over the rise of the crenels with the grace of a cat. An alarm sounded. The foot patrol had spotted her.

Li Feng reached the main judicial hall. She hooked her hands into the ornamental carvings that looped around the eaves and used them to hoist herself on to the rooftop. The moon was above her, the lanterns below. From here she was an easy target. There were shouts from within the yamen and more cries from outside the surrounding wall. She caught her first glimpse of archers assembling.

*Keep moving.*

She did just that, rolling over the slate tiles and ducking behind the roof ornaments as the first arrows sang past her. She had to think moment by moment, stringing each movement together, planning the next step by feel and sight.

She dropped to the stone floor. The foot patrol gave chase, but they were armoured and slow. She wove behind the columns, drawing out more guards. Vaulted over a railing to gain a few steps ahead of the mob. The yamen was a compound with its own winding alleyways. She ran down one narrow lane and used the two surfaces on either side to climb up like a spider, hands and feet flat against two walls.

It was exhausting work, but she was back on the rooftops. It wasn't long before a new cry sounded. They'd found her again.

She ran to gather momentum and attempted to leap clear of the yamen to an adjacent rooftop. For the space of a heartbeat, there was freedom as she flew through the air. Then she landed. Short.

Her fingers jammed painfully against the edge of the roof and her nails clawed uselessly over wood and tile before she plummeted downwards.

The fall seemed endless as the breath rushed out

of her and her heart seized. She collided with the ground, feet first. She tumbled backwards out of reflex, and then lay stunned, unable to move. The impact had jarred her to the bone and she feared she'd broken her legs.

*Breathe.* The tightness in her chest was just her lungs clutching on to that last breath. It seemed a long time passed before her vision cleared. She saw the sky, heard the footsteps. Dimly, she remembered she had to keep moving.

Li Feng dragged herself up, found that everything was still working and staggered off. She was disoriented from the fall and realised too late she'd made a wrong turn. The mob behind her was closing in. Her left wrist throbbed painfully. The hand was stiff and nearly useless. The death of her.

Her legs regained their strength the more she moved, and soon she was running at full speed again, winding through the streets. She had to find her way back to the water. Keep corners and buildings between her so the archers wouldn't have a clear shot. She could outrun soldiers wearing armour and carrying heavy swords, but one sharpshooter could end it all.

The bridge came into view ahead of her. It was the highest bridge in the city, spanning the Min River below. Gasping for breath, she climbed to the top of the rail, her wrist protesting against the strain. Only then did she glance back once over her shoulder. A good-sized patrol chased after her. She'd done her part. For the rest, she would have to trust Han.

Her muscles were burning, but she couldn't stop yet. She filled her lungs with what very well might be her last breath and dived into the black water.

There were shouts from within the walls and the sounds of pursuit. Li Feng had breached the yamen and was facing off against a horde of armed guards. Han fought the urge to go to her aid. He had to trust her to do her part, just as she trusted him to do his.

Han tied a scarf around the lower part of his face and prepared to play the part of an outlaw. When it came to justice, an individual could question right and wrong. A man could waver and sympathise and have doubt, but a state had to be exacting and act without hesitation. Han wasn't nearly as unbending as his father. He couldn't stand down. He still believed in the rule of law, but he no longer believed that justice was justice. Justice wasn't the same for everyone. It wasn't a sacred, immutable force.

He unravelled a length of rope with a hook attached, which he used to catch the top of the wall. After a quick climb, he dropped down into the rear of the compound. A lantern glowed above the front door of the prison house. As expected, there were two men stationed there. Their swords were drawn, but they were distracted, anxious. There was an intruder somewhere on the grounds.

Detaching a wooden staff strapped to his back, Han disarmed the first guard with a strike to the wrist. He caught the second guard in the face with the upswing, a blow that likely broke his nose. The staff wasn't Han's strongest weapon, but he was proficient at it.

The first guard disappeared to call for reinforcements. Every moment was critical now. Li Feng had the night patrol engaged inside the main gate. The confusion created a small opening for him.

The second guard stood his ground. He held on to his sword while blood streamed from his nose. He had a fighter's spirit…curse him for it. Han jabbed forwards. The guard attempted to block and all it took was a quick twist of the staff for Han to lock on to the sword and jerk it out of the guard's grip, a technique he'd learned from a fighting monk. Han disarmed the guard and moved in with a blow to the knee, to the shoulder. As the man staggered, Han swung his hook. The weight acted as a lead, entangling the rope about the guard's arms. From there, Han wrestled him to the ground and tied the knot.

The shouts from the courtyard grew louder. Li Feng still giving them a good chase. Han kicked the prison door open, prepared for another fight. To his surprise, the prison house was empty save for the two prisoners staring at him from their holding cells.

Han pulled down the scarf covering his face. 'Quickly. There's not much time.'

The one that Li Feng called Bao Yang was the first to speak. 'He sent *you*?' he asked in surprise.

Han didn't have time to ponder that statement or the lack of additional guards. Using the constable's key, he unlocked the cell doors. He went to remove the chains around Liu Yuan's wrists only to watch him struggle free of them on his own.

Han should have known. This was Li Feng's brother.

'Release him and be ready.'

Han gave Liu Yuan the key and put his mask back in place before going outside to grab the incapacitated guard. The sounds of the chase had subsided and there were footsteps approaching. Returning inside, he shoved the guard into a now-empty cell. He threw his staff to Bao Yang who caught it with one hand. Another staff was strapped to his back. That one he tossed to Liu Yuan.

'We'll need to fight our way out,' Han said.

'With sticks?' Liu Yuan said in disbelief.

Bao Yang merely laughed. He gave the staff a twirl, before adjusting his grip. Han unsheathed his sword, disturbingly aware that he was now fighting alongside outlaws against law-abiding citizens.

'The sun sets in the east.' Bao Yang smirked, reading his hesitation. 'And all for a woman.'

There was something sharp and laced with poison hidden in the remark. This was not a man Han wanted at his back in a fight.

'Not a woman,' Han replied curtly.

Liu Yuan flanked him, staff ready. This was for Li Feng and her brother and the injustice they had suffered, but it was also for an inequity in the law that Han had finally acknowledged. He felt no need to explain such motivations to rebel-bandits.

'Guards will be coming,' Han warned as he pushed the door open.

Guards were already there. A patrol ran towards them, torchlight flickering over drawn blades. They were outnumbered and trying to fight their way to the heavily guarded front gate would be suicide. The best chance of escape was the same way he'd come in.

'To the wall.' Han raised his sword to prepare for the first attack. 'Follow me.'

The guards were upon them. They had to fight their way through the patrol, moving steadily towards the perimeter. Bao Yang and Liu Yuan took positions at his back, shifting as the fight shifted. Out of the corner of his eye, he saw a staff striking someone's head here, a blow to the knee there.

'Killing them would be easier,' Bao Yang muttered.

They were shoulder to shoulder as the guards attempted to regroup.

'Killing is *never* easier,' Han growled. *Bandit-scum.* He refrained from adding that last part.

He ran for the wall with the two men close behind. The guards followed them, staggering, but not debilitated. Soon the brick face loomed before them, rising over twice a man's height. How did Li Feng manage to scale over such heights so quickly? This was where her lightness was highly desirable. It would take them time to make the climb. Han unwound a second hook from his belt and threw it to Liu Yuan.

'You go on. I'll hold them back,' Han said with grim resolve.

'No need. I'll help you.'

Liu Yuan laced his hands to form a sling. Bao Yang placed his foot into them and jumped upwards while Liu Yang provided additional lift. This raised the other man high enough grab the top of the wall.

'Acrobatic trick.' Liu Yuan grinned. 'You next, thief-catcher.'

'I'm too heavy.' He was larger than the other two men, but more important, he'd come here with the specific purpose of rescuing Li Feng's brother. There was nothing to be gained from his own escape if Han left him behind. 'I'll lift you.'

Liu Yuan was light-footed enough to climb on to his knee, then up to his shoulder as if scaling a tree. All Han had to do was straighten his back and Liu Yuan had enough lift to jump to the top of the wall. It was all accomplished in one smooth pass, as easy as walking.

Han was left alone to face what remained of the patrol. Even at his best, he couldn't defeat four men and he was already breathing hard. At least he had succeeded in his goal. There was dubious honour in that.

'Thief-catcher.'

A length of rope slid down the wall, ending just beside his ear. Han sheathed his weapon and grabbed for the rope, wrapping the length around his wrist. A sharp tug came from above. Han planted his foot against the wall and began to climb steadily, aided by his now co-conspirators. He rose above the reach of the guards, but froze as an arrow struck the wall to the right of him. Heart pumping, he pushed himself to climb faster.

Near the top, something punched hard into the back of his shoulder and a searing pain radiated through his entire body. He grabbed on to the rope and held on with a white-knuckled grip.

From inside his skull, a voice shouted at him to

move, but he was paralysed by the pain. The best he could do was hold on tight as arrows struck on either side of him. His vision wavered before him.

This was something that needed to be done; he had no doubt of that. But Han had also known from the beginning that if he was caught, the punishment was well deserved and he had no choice but to face the consequences.

# Chapter Twenty-One

Li Feng broke the surface of the water and gasped for air. Her lungs were burning and her pulse throbbed with the alarm of a body being pushed past endurance. Swimming in darkness was disconcerting, but the current wasn't strong in this part of the river. She'd allowed it to pull her downstream, away from the city proper.

She took a deep, rejuvenating breath, treading her arms and legs to stay afloat. The arch of the next bridge lay ahead. Lanterns dotted the span of it, the lights bobbing in the breeze. She had hidden a dry change of clothing beneath it. Water weighed her down and she needed to be able to move. To keep moving.

She lowered herself back under the water, kicking hard to slide along the current like a black eel through the river. It was the easiest way to avoid the city watchtowers, but soon news of the escape would spread. The constable and magistrate would be roused and lookouts would be posted at the bridges. She needed to be well on her way to the prefect's mansion by that time.

By now Han would be inside the yamen. Her brother and Bao Yang would be free or they would all be dead. There was a saying that brothers and sisters are like hands and feet, but Li Feng could only ever have one father and one mother. That was why she had chosen to do this part of the plan. Bao Yang and her brother could protect themselves while her mother was defenceless.

She dragged herself on to the bank. Dripping and shivering from the chill of the night air, she struggled into a dry tunic and leggings and climbed back up the slope to the streets. She flexed her fingers. The joints were stiff and swollen, but the injury was nothing serious.

She was met with eerie and empty streets in the residential part of the city. The message Li Feng had sent with the physician had indicated that she would be coming that night. Mother needed to be ready to leave.

Despite the bodyguards at the front gate, the prefect's mansion was not as secure as the magistrate's yamen. Li Feng climbed the wall and then leapt on to the roof. Moving from rooftop to rooftop, she found her way to the private inner garden where she'd first been reunited with her mother. Dropping silently into the courtyard, she entered the corridors of the mansion.

The house was asleep. Li Feng stepped silently over wooden floors sanded smooth. After a lifetime of living in hovels and wayside inns, the prefect's mansion was a palace. It made what she was there to do seem even darker.

The bedchambers would be at the rear of the mansion, in the most private of spaces. The prefect would be there, asleep in his bed and helpless. She hadn't been entirely truthful when she told Han she wouldn't seek Guan He's death. The bastard was obsessed with her mother. Li Feng imagined him sending his henchmen after them, just as he'd done fifteen years ago.

Li Feng reached beneath her sleeve and slid the sword from its sheath. This act would severe any tie she could possibly have to Zheng Hao Han. In his heart, he still believed in justice and order. If government officials could be killed in the darkness of the night, then no one was safe. There was no law.

Mother appeared soundlessly at the end of the corridor. She was wearing a light spring robe with a travelling cloak draped over her shoulders.

'Li Feng, be careful with that sword!' She gasped, her hand rising to her throat. 'What were you planning to do with it?'

Seeing her mother before her was still a dream,

but with each passing moment the truth of it became more real.

'It's for protection,' she lied. 'Will that scoundrel come after you?'

This time Li Feng was no longer a helpless child. She was ready to end the threat now if that was what was necessary. Their family deserved their freedom.

'That man has no say in what happens to me,' Mother said, straightening her shoulders. 'Not any longer.'

Li Feng glimpsed the majestic figure of her memories. The goddess that the world had revolved around. Her mother. The woman who had desperately tried to protect her, who now seemed afraid to approach her.

Suddenly there was shame in her heart. Li Feng didn't want to be an assassin. She didn't want to be someone cold and hardened and vengeful. She wanted to be her mother's daughter. She tucked the blade away.

'Let us go now.' Mother went to her, taking hold of her arm.

Mother glanced back once towards the chambers at the back of the house before they left the opulent prison behind.

There was a boat waiting at the dock. Liu Yuan inhabited the boat when he was in the city and it was where Li Feng had stayed hidden with him for the last few days. A single lantern hung from the cabin, casting light on two figures at the bow. Mother stopped short. Then, with a sob, she rushed forwards. Liu Yuan leapt on to the dock to catch her in his arms.

Li Feng watched them, emotion swelling within her. The three of them had found one another through time and distance and so much turmoil. In that moment, the isolation of the mountains and the loneliness of the cities swept away. Father's spirit would be watching from above. They were together at last.

But only her brother and Bao Yang were on the dock.

'Han.' She spoke his name fearfully.

'I'm here.'

She spun around and his presence surrounded her. He wouldn't embrace her, not with so many people watching them, but it was enough that he was standing before her.

'You succeeded.'

His smile was forced. 'Did you have any doubt?'

His posture was rigid and there was tension about his jaw. Something was wrong. 'You're injured.'

'Archers.'

She started to reach for him, to enquire about how

badly he was hurt, but he stopped her. 'We cannot stop yet,' he reminded her quietly.

They had to keep moving. The news would spread that the would-be assassins had escaped and there would be sentries swarming the bridges. She would go and he would stay. It had to be that way.

Li Feng struggled to find some way to express the flood of emotions within her. The most difficult feeling to sort out was how she felt about him. Maybe it could never be fully understood. It was what the Taoists called knowing without knowing.

'If anyone sees that you're wounded, they'll know you were involved,' she said.

He shrugged. 'It's not so bad.'

They didn't have long. Only these few short words and she was wasting them. *Wasting them.* Inside, her heart cried with despair at her useless tongue.

'You can tell them you tried to stop us and we overpowered you,' she said.

'I have a reputation to uphold, sword dancer,' Han scoffed, but his eyes held a deep, growing sadness.

Her throat tightened and the next words came with great difficulty. 'If we had met in different circumstances, in another life—'

He hushed her, touching a hand gently to her face. His thumb rested at the corner of her mouth. Then he did nothing but look. She did the same until it became too difficult. Each moment she was there beside him made her want to stay.

She turned towards the boat without saying anything more. Liu Yuan was helping Mother into the boat while Bao Yang untied the knots that kept them anchored. Han followed behind her, the wooden dock creaking beneath his footsteps. He would stay with her as long as he could.

'We're even now, thief-catcher,' her brother said as they approached. 'No one owes the other anything.'

'How do you figure that?' Han demanded.

'I could have left you on that wall to be shot full of holes. Instead we dragged you through the city.'

Han shook his head. 'With that logic, the two of you are certainly family.'

Mother's gaze flickered to Li Feng, then back to Han with so many questions in her eyes. Yet somehow she understood enough.

'Thank you for all you've done for my family,' Mother told him humbly.

Han nodded, and then turned to help Li Feng on to the boat. His hand paused at the small of her back to steady her. With her sense of balance, the touch was unnecessary, but she savoured the contact. Their time together was altogether too brief and she'd spent most of it escaping from him.

'Now I must go and help hunt down some dangerous fugitives,' Han told them. 'I hear they've escaped into the woods to the south of the city.'

Liu Yuan extinguished the lantern and they pulled the boat away from the dock. Li Feng raised her hand in farewell, but it was too dark to see if Han returned the gesture. The night had swallowed them all and she imagined the dark and solid shape standing at the edge of the river as she floated away.

## Chapter Twenty-Two

Han was discussing the night's arrests with Constable Guo when the summons came the next morning. There had been no sleep for anyone. The prison had been filled with suspects from last night's search, but they turned out to be mostly vagrants with no homes to go to, curfew or not.

'Magistrate Tan needs to see both of you at Prefect Guan's mansion,' the messenger relayed.

Han's shoulder had been bandaged tightly with several layers of cloth to stanch the flow of blood. The arrowhead had pierced muscle before being stopped by the bone at his shoulder. His silk undershirt had kept the tip from lodging, but though the arrow was removed, the pain was very much still with him.

His mind had dulled the sharpness of it into a throbbing ache as the night wore on. He'd managed to procure a dose of opium tea from an herbal shop in the early hours of the morning, but the effect of the medicine was wearing thin. He tried very hard to move his arm as little as possible and put on a straight face as he entered the front gate of the prefect's residence.

Magistrate Tan was in the study. The prefect was with him; or rather Guan He's body was present. He was sitting rigidly in his chair, head back, eyes closed. A grey pallor had set into his skin.

'Not a good night at all,' Tan muttered, shaking his head.

'Was it the fugitives?' Han asked, playing his part. He knew that would be seen as an easy, but unlikely conclusion.

'Those rebels employed swords and long knives,' Tan said accordingly. 'This was clearly poison.'

The magistrate indicated the cup of tea set before the prefect. Han took the liberty of lifting the lid to see the dregs of it that remained.

'What's wrong? You seem a bit stiff,' Magistrate Tan commented as Han straightened.

'Old battle injury,' Han replied without blinking.

'The guards reported no intruders and Prefect Guan appears rather comfortable...other than being dead. The only person missing from the household is one of Prefect Guan's concubines; disappeared in the middle of the night.'

Han's stomach knotted. 'The concubine betrayed him for a lover, perhaps?'

He provided the most banal of conclusions, without any cleverness behind it. Magistrate Tan was not so easily deflected. The magistrate directed Constable Guo to secure the household and waited for him to depart before continuing.

'It seems we have an interesting connection here. The concubine was the wife of a man who had been executed for attacking the prefect so many years ago. She had been sentenced to commit suicide, but the attending magistrate had petitioned Guan He for leniency.'

Han nodded. 'Guan He's concubine killed him for revenge, then.'

'Perhaps.' Tan stroked his beard thoughtfully. 'This was before my appointment to Minzhou, but I realised the magistrate at the time might have exercised some, shall we say, restraint when reporting on his superior. The report didn't mention that the woman had been spared or that Guan took her in. She has been living in seclusion in his home all these years. Imagine a woman forced to share a bed with a man responsible for destroying her family. There's nothing more fearsome than a tigress protecting her cubs.'

Han thought of the woman standing in the boat. She'd had Li Feng's graceful figure, slight at the waist and long-limbed. Her face was strikingly similar to her daughter's, with a few creases as a sacrifice to time. Her eyes had been full of tears at the joy of seeing her children again. There was gentleness and elegance about her, a spirit that Li Feng might have embodied if not for the tragedies of the past. Yet Li Feng's fire came from somewhere.

'Still, I don't believe this is the answer to our riddle,' the magistrate declared.

'No?' Han had nearly convinced himself. He was getting caught up in the investigation.

Tan circled the desk, keeping his eyes on Prefect Guan the entire time. 'The last time the servants saw him was late in the evening. He's rather well-dressed for that time, wouldn't you say? And his robe is heavy for the season. Quite opulent.'

Han had an idea where the magistrate was going. 'You think he was prepared to die.'

'Dressed in his best. Here he is, in his private study so he can be found in death looking as he wanted to be remembered, an esteemed official.'

Magistrate Tan was deflecting suspicion away from Li Feng and her entire family all on his own.

'I can't imagine a powerful man like the prefect taking his own life because his favourite concubine left him,' Han said.

Tan shot him a sly look. 'For a man of the sword, you have a scholar's weakness for sentimentality. Guan He didn't kill himself for a woman. He committed suicide to avoid the shame of having his crimes discovered. Our new Emperor has taken it upon himself to rid the government of corruption, even going so far as to review the actions of appointed officials down to the prefecture level. Prefect Guan must have been very concerned.'

'Now I'm intrigued. You have some conspiracy in mind.'

'It all hinges on one theory we have not yet considered: it was Prefect Guan who hired the assassins.' Magistrate Tan paused, obviously enjoying himself.

'The prefect hired the assassins to attack Wang Shizhen?' Han recounted slowly.

'Because the general had discovered his illegal activities. When you suspected that Prefect Guan was involved in corruption, I looked further into his operations. Guan He was skimming from the prefecture's salt production and selling it himself to keep the profits. However, given the wide-reaching nature of salt-smuggling operations, I'd wager that he encroached into Wang Shizhen's territory and the warlord eventually discovered who was responsible.'

'The shipment of jade and gold would have been a bribe, then,' Han suggested. 'To appease the warlord.'

'But once General Wang knew a prefect was involved, he became greedy and ambitious, demanding more. He wanted a hand in things, to wrest more control. Rumour has it that Wang is building his army with aspirations of becoming military governor of the entire province.'

Magistrate Tan shook his head, his frown deepening enough to be called a scowl. Ever since the Anshi Rebellion, the Imperial court sought to control the rise of powerful warlords in the provinces.

'Prefect Guan had insinuated that the murder of his steward wasn't the work of bandits, but rather an attempt by the warlord to intimidate him,' Han offered.

Now they fed off of one another, co-conspirators hand-in-hand.

'So he invites Wang to his home and stages an assassination attempt on himself,' Tan began.

'But the real target is the warlord.'

'Yes! Wang was the one the assassins attacked,' the magistrate pointed out eagerly.

The prefect had only been spared because Han had intervened, but he kept quiet on that. 'To the prefect's dismay, General Wang survives his wounds,' Han said.

The general was still fighting death, but it was believed that, as strong as he was, he might recover.

'And the assassins escaped last night,' Magistrate Tan added. 'Guan He planned for his hirelings to be executed quickly to preserve their silence. He must have seen that everything was unravelling. Either his corrupt activities would be exposed to the Imperial Censorate or the bloodthirsty General Wang would recover and exact revenge. Poison was the coward's way out.'

The magistrate was completely wrong, at least about who had planned the assassination, but Tan's theory could explain everything. He had outlined the intrigue so plausibly. There was likely truth to some of it: the bribe to Wang, the smuggling, perhaps even some intimidation and Wang's plan to wrest control of the salt trade and the province. Li Feng and Liu Yuan were left completely out of it. They were commoners, of little significance in this power struggle between a scheming government official and a fearsome warlord.

'It seems like justice prevails,' Han said carefully. 'The province is rid of one corrupt bureaucrat and Wang Shizhen's attempt to take control was thwarted.'

'Our job is not yet finished,' Tan said.

Han didn't overlook how the magistrate casually included him in the statement.

'We must be very quiet about this. The Salt Commissioner is likely involved as well as many others. I don't want anyone to suspect we know anything before I can bring evidence against all of them at once. Then there's the matter of the two fugitives and the sword dancer as well.'

Han felt the wind rush out of him. He was starting to celebrate before the battle was won.

'Constable Guo and his men have had no success finding the sword dancer. You were the only one who truly got a good look at her.'

The magistrate's tone had shifted. He met Han's gaze squarely and there was something unspoken beneath everything he said. Han recalled the lack of guards in the prison house last night as well as Bao Yang's cryptic statement: *He sent you?*

'At him,' Han said his heart pounding.

'Pardon?'

'I was the only one who truly got a good look at *him.*'

He was taking a gamble. In the next moments what Tan said or didn't say would tell him everything. They were no longer speaking with words, at least not the plain sort that could be heard by the ear. They were speaking the language of meanings within meanings.

Magistrate Tan said nothing. He waited, blinking curiously.

'There was something unusual about the dancer that I didn't realise until now,' Han continued. 'My mind was focused on the fight at the time, but the more I think about it, the more I'm convinced that was no woman who battled with me. He was too strong and no woman could be that skilled with the sword.'

Tan looked surprised, then pleased. 'No wonder we have been confounded in this search! And the reports of the prison break last night did speak of three men. I will inform Constable Guo immediately. Will you go after them as well?'

A pause there. A meaningful one that was full of anticipation.

'I was hoping to continue my humble work here,' Han replied, full of formality. 'If you'll have me, sir.'

'Ah, well said, well said!' The magistrate reached for Han's bad shoulder to clasp it in a brotherly fashion, but he stopped himself. Tan's hand retreated beneath his sleeve. 'I'm glad to hear it. Let the other thief-catchers chase after the rabble.'

With a satisfied nod, Tan started towards the door. 'There's an interesting saying about poison, you know. Use poison to fight poison.'

The same way it took one scheming and clever bureaucrat to combat another. Han glanced one final time at the prefect as he passed by the desk. Guan He's arm had fallen to his side. His hand was clenched around the jade pendant. The tassel that dangled from it was blood red against the grey, lifeless skin.

# Chapter Twenty-Three

In Buddhist thought, small actions had far-reaching consequences across distance, across time. Han hadn't spent much time pondering on such implications in the spiritual realm, but as a thief-catcher he knew that every action left a mark. No matter how faint the trace was, it could be sought out and mark upon mark would link together to create a trail.

In the weeks that followed, Han discovered such seemingly insignificant details. There had been a simultaneous disturbance outside of the prefect's mansion right before the attack, but the perpetrators appeared to be nothing more than a street gang, throwing rocks and insults before being chased away. In the light of the more serious crime, the incident was overlooked.

A group of wine merchants from out of town left unannounced from their rooms at the inn. A well-respected physician quietly closed his shop and left Minzhou, taking his vast store of herbal remedies, as well as his knowledge of perhaps a few poisons, with him.

Han chose not to pursue these leads. There were more urgent matters that required his attention. An investigation into the prefect's death had, as Magistrate Tan predicted, uncovered a trail of smuggling, bribery and corruption. Records at various salt wells had been falsified to report lower production and salt agents were paid off to turn a blind eye. There were arrests, interrogations, trials. As for the warlord, Wang Shizhen retreated west to recover from his wounds.

The crafty Magistrate Tan, whose methods were often unconventional, proved to be at heart an upstanding bureaucrat.

'When I first came to this position five years ago, Guan He was on his best behaviour,' the magistrate recounted. 'The records from the salt works show the prefect must have attempted to pull back on his activities, but after a few years he became confident enough to continue his smuggling activity. Now our land is free of one more corrupt official. Minzhou must prepare itself for the newly appointed prefect, approved by the Emperor himself.'

'I'm surprised that you weren't promoted, given your effort to expose corruption within the prefecture,' Han replied.

'No, no!' Magistrate Tan waved away that notion

with good cheer. 'One needs to bring in officials from outside to ensure honesty. One without any local connections. I've made myself too much at home here.'

From what Han could see, Tan Li Kuo was caught up in the spirit of reform that had been stirred up by Emperor Xuanzhong.

At the end of the third week, two familiar faces appeared at the magistrate's yamen. Father had brought Chen-Yi to begin his studies in Minzhou. His younger brother was taller than Han remembered, no longer a boy, but not quite yet a man. His expression had grown more serious with age.

Father appeared thinner than Han remembered. His cheekbones were more pronounced, giving him an even more imposing look. His black hair showed hints of silver and his beard was neatly trimmed. Even dressed in the plain grey robe of a peasant, the man commanded respect.

As they met in the centre of the courtyard, Han was stricken by the similarities between the three of them. In Chen-Yi, he could see himself in the past, in Father, his future. He was caught in a feeling of inclusion and closeness that he had sorely missed being away from them so long.

Han bowed his head as a sign of respect. 'Father.'

'Hao Han.'

They stood side by side as Chen-Yi went to speak to Magistrate Tan.

'Your mother sends her regards,' Father said.

'How is Mother?'

'Well.'

Outside of passionate discussions about the law and the classics, Father always used words sparingly.

'She will be happy to see you settled,' Father said. 'This appears to be a good position for you.'

'Magistrate Tan is an admirable official.'

There was a pause as they stared at the door to the magistrate's office. Then Father cleared his throat loudly. 'Your mother is eager to know when you'll start a family.'

A weight lifted from Han's chest. The conversation didn't seem like much, but given that Father had come in person and was speaking as if they had never parted, this was acceptance.

'I can't say for certain,' Han replied. When he thought of his future, there was only one person he could imagine beside him. He didn't know where Li Feng had gone to or how she would react if he was able to find her. 'But perhaps there will be news soon.'

One month went by and then another, through the plum rain season and the swelter of the summer. With the passage of time, Han's ability to track Li

Feng decreased, but so it would be for anyone else who had an interest in hunting down the mysterious sword dancer and the fugitive assassins. Neither Li Feng nor her brother, nor her mother were free of suspicion.

Though Han and Magistrate Tan were often of similar mind, they were not completely in each other's confidences. The events of the prison break remained an unspoken topic between them. In retrospect, Han and Li Feng had been successful because someone had reduced the guard patrols at the prison house. Similarly, the watchmen at key points along the river happened to be called away from their stations to receive detailed instructions about the escaped fugitives, at the very same moment those very fugitives floated by on a black painted boat.

Han suspected the involvement of someone with influence, but he let Magistrate Tan keep his secrets. Han had plenty of secrets of his own.

After three months, Han set out. The markers were still there, if one chose to look. There was a ferryman who recalled a widow travelling with her son and daughter across the flooded river. A brother and sister performed a remarkable acrobatic routine to earn some money during the dragonboat festival in another town. In a mountainside village, a young woman lowered herself over a cliff to rescue a child who had fallen. The child was huddling on a ledge and it was said the woman stepped over rocks and tree branches with the lightness of a bird.

Han set foot in the village just before nightfall. It was a small, remote location in the shadow of the mountain, the sort of place where everyone knew everyone and there were no walls surrounding or separating the houses. The villagers prospered from the harvesting and processing of tea as the dampness of the mountain air was perfectly suited for tea plantations.

The river ran through the centre of the village with shops and houses situated on either side of the water. Several bridges connected the two sides. Han stabled his horse and headed for the local tavern to seek the usual information, but he found that this time his interrogation techniques weren't necessary.

The proprietor of the herbal shop was closing his doors for the day just as Han passed by. A woman stood beside him, her hand on his arm. Han presumed her to be the man's wife, yet there was something about the way she held herself, the graceful turn of her wrist, the tilt of her jaw and the arch of her back.

Han's heart slammed into his ribs. Li Feng had married a country doctor. She'd found happiness elsewhere just as he'd told her to in his stupidity.

But the woman turned around and Han saw that

she wasn't Li Feng. She was Li Feng's reflection. Her mother.

A figure darted across a nearby footbridge, moving with the lightness of the breeze. By the time he'd reached the end of the row, Li Feng was already up on the roof. He searched left and right for possible footholds, confounded. How did she always manage to climb so quickly?

'Li Feng!' Han watched from the street as she leapt from shop to shop. 'I'm not here to arrest you.'

Perhaps that wasn't the most reassuring thing to hear from a thief-catcher. The sound of her laughter trailed down to him as she climbed on to the second storey of the tea house. He had no choice but to chase after her, going into the tea house and up the stairs.

He made it on to the roof and took a few tentative steps, finding his footing on the uneven tiles.

Li Feng was sitting near the apex of the rooftop. Her posture was relaxed, feet planted against the downward slope, arms resting casually about her knees. She laid her head down on them, looking at him sideways.

'You found me,' she said.

'I'll always find you.'

Her eyes were bright as he came and lowered himself down beside her. From there, they could see across the river to the shops on the other side. He let himself breathe in the mountain air and absorb Li Feng's presence next to him. He had been determined to journey all the way to Mount Wudang if that's where she had gone. There were times when he'd doubted his abilities. Or he'd feared that when he found her, Li Feng would disappear again and it would be the final sign that she didn't want him after all.

He took this moment now to fill in the emptiness of the last few months, letting his eyes take in the sight of her.

'I thought of you,' Li Feng said finally. She wriggled her toes within her slippers, the only girlish gesture he'd ever recalled from her.

'I thought of you as well,' he said, feeling like a pale-faced scholar.

The emotions that rushed into him upon finally seeing her overwhelmed him. They were like new lovers too afraid to look directly at one another.

'I always knew you would find me,' she said. 'But why did it take you so long?'

His heart warmed. He had missed those expressive eyes and the playful way her lips twisted. With her admonishment, it was like old times again.

'I had to recover from being shot in the back. For you,' he reminded her. The shoulder still ached sometimes when he moved that arm.

'Let me see.'

'See?'

Han angled his shoulder towards her and her hands slid beneath his robe to pull back the cloth. He'd forgotten how uninhibited she could be. Li Feng's fingers brushed carefully over the spot where the arrow had pierced him. Her touch was cool against warm flesh.

It had been a long time since he'd held her. Too long since they'd touched, yet while he was being practically disrobed on a rooftop by the object of his daytime thoughts and his night-time dreams, it wasn't desire that consumed him.

He watched her face, that curious expression he'd missed so much, and took in a breath to fortify himself.

'Marry me,' he said quietly.

Her hands stilled on him. Han's body tensed as he waited for her answer, but her lips couldn't seem to form the words that her heart wanted to shout.

Li Feng traced the raised edge of the scar on his back, partly to bide some time, but also because it felt so good to touch him after so long. Her brother had told her how Han nearly passed out when they'd removed the arrow, but he'd forced himself to remain conscious and to continue. The escape wasn't yet successful and Thief-catcher Han was relentless when there was a task at hand.

'You want me to be your wife?' she asked incredulously.

'I want you to be my everything.'

Her chest squeezed tight. 'How can I?' she asked. Which wasn't at all what her heart wanted to say.

When he faced her, his look was playful, though apprehension gripped him. 'Well, you've stopped running at least.'

'But what will you do? Will you hide here with me, away from the world?'

'We'll live in Minzhou,' he said matter of factly, as if there were no difficulty. As if she were a country girl who had caught his eye and all they needed to wed would be permission from their respective families. 'I have a position there working for the magistrate's office. A steady income, enough to start a family.'

She wanted to laugh. When they'd first met, he'd hunted her down across the province and vowed to arrest her. Now he came here as if he were a lovestruck youth.

'Han, I'm wanted for attempted *murder* in Minzhou,' she reminded him.

The fact didn't deter him. 'Prefect Guan is dead.'

'Dead?'

They had purposefully travelled far into the mountains, to a village that was quartered off from news from Minzhou. Li Feng was surprised to hear of it, but didn't grieve for him. The prefect had determined his own fate.

'Hopefully this will bring Liu Yuan some peace,' she said.

'Where is your brother?' Han asked.

She cast him a wary glance.

'I'm not here to arrest him either,' Han insisted. 'I'm enquiring out of courtesy. And since he is the head of the family, perhaps I should ask him for permission to marry you.'

Han was certainly persistent. Li Feng hid her smile as she replied. 'Liu Yuan left shortly after we settled here. He'll be back one day, once he finds his own sense of peace.'

They had learned of her mother's life as the prefect's concubine. The very man who had brought about her father's death had intervened to set aside her sentence and proclaimed his love for her. It was too much to bear and Mother had at first begged for Wu Song to give her poison to end her suffering. The kind-hearted physician had refused and he'd become her confidant and friend. When Wu had come to find them in this remote village, he finally revealed the secret feelings he'd harboured for so long.

Her mother's newfound love freed Li Feng to find her own happiness, but also saddened her. She'd given up her heart to a man of honour and principle, who could never be with an outlaw like her.

Yet there were nights when Li Feng hoped that her past crimes, if nothing else, would bring Han to her. Theirs was always the oddest of romances.

'Even though the prefect is dead, that doesn't negate the crime,' she pointed out, echoing his own words back at him. 'I'll be recognised for certain.'

'Only the prefect's household knew of your mother and anyone associated with Guan He has left the city in disgrace,' Han told her. 'As to the incident at the banquet, the official warrant is for a man who was wearing a woman's costume.'

'How—?'

'Because no woman could possess such sword skill,' he finished blandly.

She seethed. 'Of all the ignorance! The sword is a soft weapon, suited for speed and precision rather than brute strength—'

'Li Feng.' He had to say her name twice before she would listen. 'Li Feng, you haven't given me an answer. I would like very much for you to be my wife.'

He looked so serious, more determined than she'd ever seen him.

She didn't need to be reminded. His question had echoed within her mind repeatedly since he'd asked it. Instead of replying, she pressed closer to him, her fingers twining into the front of his robe, and kissed him. His arms closed around her, warmer and stronger than she remembered.

'I will marry you,' she whispered, finally allowing her heart to speak. He kissed her again, deeply, with his hands framed about her face. Thief-catcher Han, the man who would not let her get away.

Their hands remained linked as they sat on the roof, side by side, to stare at the sky above. The first stars were out and a stream of lights formed overhead as the night descended.

'I'm dreaming,' she said to the heavens.

'So am I,' Han said warmly.

'I hope I'll make a good wife.' She didn't know much about being one.

'You will,' Han promised. 'I hope we can both be content remaining in one place.'

'Let's try it. Starting now.'

Han put his arm around her and she nestled close into that perfect spot on his shoulder. For a long, long time they remained there, watching the rise of the moon and counting the stars. Sitting still. Together.

\* \* \* \* \*

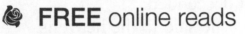